Ann Quinton is married and lives with her husband and collection of Siamese cats in a small Suffolk village near the coast. She has three children, two sons and a daughter. Before leaving to start her family, she worked in the library service, both in a county library and in a scientific research station, where she met her husband.

As well as being a writer Ann is also a well-known local artist, working mainly in pastels, exhibiting regularly. She is also very interested in music, both as a listener and performer, and has worked professionally as a pianist and accompanist.

THIS MORTAL COIL

'PETS. Exits arranged. Professionally. Effectively. Terminally. Apply: The Coil Shuffler.' Thus reads the business card of a professional assassin. When physiotherapist and lay reader Rachel Morland stumbles across one of these cards on the body of a frail parishioner, her suspicions are at once aroused, not least because she has seen it before — when her beloved husband apparently committed suicide. Policeman Mike Croft, a friend of Rachel's, also realises the significance of the calling-card and, together with his former boss, Nick Holroyd, sets out to track down the killer . . .

Books by Ann Quinton
Published by The House of Ulverscroft:

THE RAGUSA THEME
TO MOURN A MISCHIEF
DEATH OF A DEAR FRIEND

ANN QUINTON

THIS MORTAL COIL

Complete and Unabridged

ULVERSCROFT
Leicester

First published in Great Britain in 1998 by
Severn House Publishers Limited
Surrey

First Large Print Edition
published 1999
by arrangement with
Severn House Publishers Limited
Surrey

The right of Ann Quinton to be identified
as the author of this work has been asserted
by her in accordance with the
Copyright, Designs and Patents Act, 1988

British Library CIP Data

Quinton, Ann
   This mortal coil.—Large print ed.—
   Ulverscroft large print series: mystery
   1. Detective and mystery stories
   2. Large type books
   I. Title
   813.5′4 [F]

   ISBN 0–7089–4040–4

Published by
F. A. Thorpe (Publishing) Ltd.
Anstey, Leicestershire

Set by Words & Graphics Ltd.
Anstey, Leicestershire
Printed and bound in Great Britain by
T. J. International Ltd., Padstow, Cornwall

This book is printed on acid-free paper

For Anne and Henry with my love.

Acknowledgements

I should like to thank the many people who helped me with the research for this book, in particular Lynn Abbott, Charles Burnham-Slipper, Judy Ayre, Simon Grew, Stephen Harvey and Jeremy Trowell.

To die, to sleep;
To sleep: perchance to dream: ay, there's
the rub;
For in that sleep of death what dreams
may come
When we have shuffled off this mortal
coil . . .

Hamlet, Act III Scene I

Prologue

'That advert is in again, Dennis.' The woman tapped the newspaper she was holding. 'Listen . . . ' She read out to her husband. ' 'PETS. Exits arranged — Painlessly, Efficiently, Tastefully. Apply: The Coil Shuffler. Box AJ 6108.' What do you think it means?'

'It's a funeral director's advert.'

'It's not under that section, it's in the personal column.'

'Well, maybe it's something to do with the Euthanasia Society.'

'They're not allowed to advertise, surely? It's still illegal in this country.'

'Well, I don't know, woman. What are you on about?'

Dennis Porter was a retired insurance clerk in his early sixties. He was a quiet, unassuming man, very different from his wife, Madge, two years his junior and far more bombastic in manner. He eyed her warily and both started as there was a thud on the floor of the room above them, followed by the rattle of a cane against a wooden surface.

1

'*That*'s what I'm on about!' Madge hissed at her husband and she raised her eyes to the ceiling.

'Madge? I want my tea . . . ' The voice floated down the stair-well and into the room, querulous and weak and yet somehow penetrating.

'It's not time yet, Uncle.'

'It's half-past five.'

'No, it isn't. I'll bring your tea up soon.'

'I want to go to the toilet!'

'I'll be up in a minute, just hang on a little longer.'

There was further noise of movement from upstairs and then the elderly voice announced with satisfaction: 'It's too late!'

'The old bugger — he does it on purpose!' Madge Porter thrust the newspaper into her husband's hands and made for the stairs. 'If we don't do something soon I shall be admitted to the asylum and *then* who will look after him?'

Dennis Porter shook his head, but as his wife clattered up the stairs he adjusted his glasses and carefully read the advertisement through.

1

The Golden Rooster Club, situated in the original medieval centre of the city, not far from the cathedral, occupied an ambiguous position in the entertainment business. Officially it consisted of a respectable restaurant, two bars and a night-club, but it had long been a thorn in the flesh of the local constabulary, who referred to it as the Yellow Cock. It had been raided several times, but apart from minor irregularities the police had never been able to gather enough evidence to close it down or bring a successful case against the owner, Edwin Briers, although it was known that he was involved in drugs, prostitution and protection rackets.

Edwin Briers himself was a tall, solidly built man in early middle age. The dark, discreet business suits which he affected when he graced the premises didn't quite contain the unwieldy flesh that strained at the buttons and threatened to overspill the waistband. He looked like a prosperous bookmaker and his affable, hearty manner had taken in many a hapless punter who had failed to see beyond his surface jocularity to the

3

hard, ruthless nature underneath. You didn't mess with Edwin Briers; not if you wished to remain healthy and in one piece.

That evening he had been mostly closeted in his office, only emerging at brief intervals to show himself in restaurant and night-club where a risqué floor show was entertaining his customers. At half-past midnight he decided to call it a day and gathered up the papers he had been working on before summoning his assistant, who lounged in the next room. Assistant by name but minder by any definition, Cameron Rowe swung to his feet and went in to his boss. Tall and muscular, his black, crimped hair worn in a pony-tail and fleshy lips admitted to his mixed blood. He waited stoically as Edwin Briers locked his filing cabinet and pocketed the keys.

'I'm finished here. Drive me to Burstan Grove.'

Only by the flaring of his nostrils did Cameron Rowe betray his annoyance. It meant either a long wait in a cold car whilst Briers enjoyed the services of his mistress or a long walk home. He zipped up his jacket and went down the back stairs to the yard where the dark red BMW 328i coupé was parked. He manoeuvred it through the narrow gateway and drove round to the

4

front of the building and Briers stepped out of the door and slid into the front passenger seat. Neither of them noticed the person hovering in a doorway a little further down the street.

The watcher, who had been there several hours, gave a grunt of satisfaction as the BMW moved off and quickly got into the van that was parked round the corner. After following for a short distance it exited left at the next junction and took a parallel road. There was no need to sit on the tail of the BMW, the watcher knew where it was going, had monitored its route on many occasions. By taking a short cut through the back streets the van would arrive at the destination first, ready for another bout of surveillance.

The BMW swung round the corner into Burstan Grove and drew up outside a row of terrace houses. There were lights showing in the upstairs windows of the middle one. Edwin Briers glanced upwards and then reached over and removed the keys from the ignition.

'Off you go, Cam. I'll drive myself home from here.'

'There's no point in hiring me to protect you if you keep swanning off on your own.'

'The sort of protection I need from this lady you can't give me! Now, get your ass

5

out of here and report in at ten o'clock; I've got a tricky meeting scheduled.'

Edwin Briers waited for a few minutes after Rowe had loped down the street and then let himself out of the car, locked it and climbed the short flight of steps leading to the front door. He pressed a button and spoke into the intercom. Almost immediately a light came on in the hall, glowing redly through the stained-glass panels, and then the door opened and he went inside. The watcher had a quick impression of a scantily dressed woman drawing Briers into an embrace and then the door was shut and shortly afterwards the hall light was extinguished. After waiting a little longer to make sure Briers was not going to re-emerge for something left behind in the car, the watcher picked up the brick lying on the back seat and cautiously approached the BMW, jamming it under the nearside front wheel, then retired to the van prepared for a long wait, alleviated by sandwiches and a flask of coffee.

★ ★ ★

It was five o'clock before Edwin Briers emerged from the house. He was humming softly under his breath as he let himself into the car and fastened his seat-belt. He looked back at the house, now shrouded in darkness, and grinned. Fran was out to the world, let her sleep. She certainly knew how to administer to a man's needs. And she made no unreasonable demands on him; no nonsense about divorce and becoming the second Mrs Briers. He fired the engine and tried to move off. There was a crunching sound and the car shuddered and stopped. He swore and switched off the engine and got out to investigate. The smashed brick was still partially wedged under the kerbside front wheel and as he kicked it away he wondered how Cameron Rowe had managed to park the car right on top of it.

Bent over the car, he didn't notice the dark-clad figure dart out from behind the hedge and slip into the back of the car, crouching on the floor behind the driver's seat. The first he knew of his hidden passenger was a movement behind him as he pulled out away from the kerb. Before it could really register a hand grasped his shoulder and he felt something cold and sharp against the back of his neck.

'Keep driving and *don't* try that . . . ' a voice snarled in his ear as his hand automatically moved towards the horn. 'We're going for a little ride.'

'Who are you? What do you want?'

'Concentrate on your driving and don't try anything. Take the Heston road when you reach the roundabout.'

It was still dark when they reached their destination — the disused warehouse complex by the old canal cut — but it had started to rain. The rutted ground gleamed blackly in the car headlights and water trickled down the windscreen. Briers made to switch on the wipers but the voice behind him spoke.

'Don't bother, we're here.'

During the brief journey Briers' emotions had run the full gamut from outrage through fear to speculation. From his glances in the mirror all he could see was a shadowy figure wearing a Balaclava mask. Like something out of a Belfast ghetto, he thought, but he had never tangled with the Micks. He had no idea how big his assailant was, how old or from where he had originated. The voice was anonymous; no accent but strained as if its owner was deliberately pitching it lower than its normal range. He was very aware of the knife pricking the back of his neck and the sweat prickling his shoulder-blades but he wasn't as scared as he had been initially. He hadn't been killed, which surely meant that he was being kidnapped. If the Wingate lot were behind this they might get a nasty shock.

'Pull over on to the bank and switch off.'

He obeyed the command and brought the car to a halt a couple of yards from the canal's edge. The surface was pocked by the driving rain which slanted across the black oily water in silver needles. It was the last thing he saw. A hand grasped his hair and forced his head back against the headrest and the knife slashed across his throat from ear to ear.

As his life-blood gushed out, his head and shoulders were gently eased forward until he was slumped over the wheel. The murderer pulled a handkerchief out of a pocket and wiped the knife on it, which was then pocketed, and spread the handkerchief over the front passenger seat. From another pocket a small square of printed cardboard was produced and laid face upwards in the middle. This done the killer slipped quietly out of the car and disappeared.

★ ★ ★

The body was discovered a couple of hours later by a patrolling panda car and a full-scale murder investigation was set up. DI Trevor Dickins was the duty CID inspector that morning at Brent Hill Station and was quickly on the scene. The rain had subsided to a fitful drizzle and the scene was bathed in a grey, pearly light.

'Do we know who he is?' Trevor Dickins shouldered his way through the knot of uniformed police. He was shorter than most of his colleagues, barely regulation height, but he made up for his lack of inches by a forceful manner and a tough, compact body tuned to a peak of muscular perfection by a strict regime of working out and jogging. He had close-cropped ginger hair and the pale green eyes that went with it.

'He hasn't been moved, sir.' The police constable pointed to the victim. Only the back of his head and shoulders could be seen and the edge of the gaping wound beneath his left ear. 'The car is registered to an Edwin Briers.'

'Eddie Briers?' Trevor Dickins gave a whistle. 'Someone's done us a good turn, rid society of a menace. With him gone our work load will halve. Hasn't the police surgeon turned up yet?'

'He's been sent for, sir.'

'Then why the hell isn't he here! You and I know that laddie here is not going to get up and walk again but until he's pronounced dead I can't get on with *my* job.'

Whilst he waited for the police surgeon and the Scene of Crime Officers to arrive, Trevor

Dickins contented himself with a visual appraisal of the scene. Squinting through the window he noted the handkerchief on the front passenger seat, smeared with bloodstains, and the card lying like an island in the middle.

'Nothing's been touched, I hope — that was there when you arrived?'

'Yes, sir. Looks like some sort of business card, doesn't it?'

'When I want your opinion, sonny, I'll ask for it.'

The young constable exchanged glances with a colleague. Dickins was known throughout the station as a mean, hard bastard; too ambitious for his own good. Nobody liked being in his team but he got results. The DI pulled out his handkerchief, wrapped it round his hand and carefully opened the passenger door and bent closer to get a better look.

'I've seen something like this before somewhere. As soon as the photographer has done his stuff get it bagged up and sent to Forensics.' He straightened up. 'What I want to know is where's his minder.'

'Sir?'

'Eddie Briers had a lot of enemies. He wouldn't crap without his minder being there

11

to hand him the bog roll. Tall chap with a pony-tail, half nigger.' He snorted as he saw the other man's expression. 'Not being politically correct, am I, Constable? What was known in the good old days as a touch of the tar brush.'

'You think we should be looking for another body?'

'Cameron Rowe — that's his name — could be floating in that canal, could have scarpered or maybe he was bought and did for his boss himself.'

Further speculation was interrupted by the arrival of the SOCOs and after a few terse instructions Trevor Dickins left them to get on with their job and went back to the station to report to his superintendent.

★ ★ ★

The physiotherapy department of St Crispian's was in the newly modernised wing of the hospital. The gym boasted state-of-the-art equipment and although it had been open for over six months a faint smell of fresh paint still lingered in the rooms and cubicles and the gleaming surfaces and highly polished floors were almost an assault on the senses.

Michael Croft leaned back against the wall and cautiously stretched his aching legs. The left one felt like a bruised jelly and he was dismayed by his general feeling of weakness and only too thankful to have a break whilst his physio answered an urgent telephone query. Rachel Morland was a slave-driver but she seemed more optimistic about his chances of recovery than he was himself. At least he'd come a long way from that terrible period when he'd thought that he was paralysed for life and would spend the rest of his days in a wheelchair. He watched her through the glass partition. She was an attractive woman whom he reckoned to be in her early thirties and she presented a trim figure in her navy trousers and white jacket. Her hair was dark and cut short, curling in wisps over her forehead and ears, and she had what he thought of as pansy eyes; dark brown with a purple tinge.

She put down the receiver and came back into the room.

'Sorry about that. I'll just do some icing and brushing now to loosen up your anterial tibial muscles and that will be enough for today, I think. You're making good progress and we'll soon get you back to rights.'

'Look, Rachel, let's be honest with ourselves. You say you're going to get this blasted leg working properly again and I have faith in you but I'm never going to be a hundred per cent. My career as an active policeman is over; I can't even drive. I'm strictly grounded to the office these days; computer fodder.'

'You will be able to soon, I can promise you that.' She smiled at him sympathetically. 'You're getting stronger each day.'

Later, whilst he was changing, she reflected on what she knew about him. According to her notes he was thirty-five years old, six foot tall and carrying 76.80 kg in weight. He had been injured in a shooting accident whilst on active duty; a bullet wound in the lower back that had damaged vertebrae and caused severe trauma in the nearby tissue. This had resulted in temporary paralysis of the lower limbs and he had spent some time at Flint House, the police convalescent home at Goring-on-Thames. He didn't like talking about the incident and had turned aside her probing questions with barely concealed annoyance. All told, he was a very reticent character, being equally uncommunicative about his home life. When he had first become her patient she had tried to put him at his ease by chatting about his family, but although he had admitted to a wife and son somewhere in his past he had refused to be drawn into any further revelations and she reckoned that he must be divorced. From things he had let drop she thought that he lived on his own.

She watched him leave his cubicle and cross to the waiting room, dragging his left leg like a flipper, and made up her mind to give him further intensive hydrotherapy treatment at his next appointment to help with the dropped foot. He lurched back and poked his head round the door.

'My lift hasn't turned up — probably something's come up at the Station. May I use your phone to ring for a taxi?'

'Whereabouts do you live?'

'In Westgate — Belvoir Road.'

'I'll run you home. You're my last patient so I've finished for the day.'

'I can't put you to that trouble.'

'It's no trouble. I'm supposed to be visiting a friend in Bacton Road this evening — that's nearby, isn't it?'

'Yes, a couple of streets away. But I really can't . . . '

'It's no bother. I can drop you off on my way. Just give me a couple of minutes to clear up here.'

A short while later Michael Croft limped beside the physiotherapist out of the building.

'I'm parked in the staff carpark over there. The red Fiesta is mine.'

When they reached the car she stowed her bag in the back and waited whilst he folded himself into the passenger seat.

'I hope you're not one of those men who get uptight about women drivers.'

'I presume with a policeman in the car you'll stick to the speed limit and not jump any lights!'

She smiled. 'I promise not to embarrass you in any way. Which end of Belvoir Road do you live?'

'Number 39 — in the middle.'

It was the evening rush hour. They got snarled up in the traffic and the journey took longer than it should have done. When the car drew up in front of his house he released his seat belt and turned to her.

'What time is your friend expecting you?'

'Around sevenish.'

'Then you'll be too early. Come in and I'll make a pot of coffee.'

'Oh, I don't think so . . . '

Belatedly he remembered that she wore a wedding ring.

'Look, I'm not making a pass at you. You've got some time to kill and I'm dying for a coffee, but if your husband will object?'

'I'm a widow.'

16

'I'm very sorry. You're young to be a widow . . . ?'

She ignored the query in his voice but switched off the engine.

'As you say, I've got time to kill. I'd love a coffee.'

2

The call came through to Brent Hill Station as Nick Holroyd was preparing to hand over to the next shift. It was logged as a suspected break-in at the Riverside Sports Centre, reported by a passer-by, and as sergeant in charge of panda cars he elected to visit the scene himself as well as diverting one of the patrol cars to the area. It was probably nothing serious, he thought as he cleared his desk, just one of the unemployed yobs who hung around the place trying his luck with a vending machine. It shouldn't take long to sort out and then he could carry on and pick up Mike on his way home.

When they arrived at the sports centre they discovered a door swinging open at the far end of the building and ran towards it. A pane of glass had been neatly cut out just above the handle.

'Looks like a professional operation,' said Nick Holroyd, mentally revising his ideas about an opportunist job. 'It's too much to hope he's still on the premises. Better see what damage he's done.'

They went through the door carefully,

avoiding contact, and found themselves in a storeroom. Next door was a kitchen and off this was a series of rooms used as offices. In the first one a wall safe flanked by cupboards drew his attention. He went over to examine it whilst his constable explored the other rooms. The safe showed signs of interference. The surface around the handle and lock was scratched and dented but it appeared to be intact. Whoever had broken in had been unsuccessful in opening it.

'Here, sir . . . ' His colleague called from further down the corridor and he hurried to join him. The sergeant was bent over a body that lay sprawled on the floor of the office, jammed between a desk and a filing cabinet.

'Looks in a bad way, sir. I reckon it's the caretaker — must have disturbed him at it.'

The prone figure was that of an elderly man dressed in overalls. He was laying on his front and the wispy grey hair on the back of his scalp surrounded a nasty contusion.

'He's still breathing. Ring for an ambulance and reinforcements. This is GBH, Constable, I wonder how long he's been lying here?'

Whilst he waited for the medics and police team to arrive, Nick glanced at his watch. Hell, he was going to be late for Mike, who should have finished his physiotherapy session by now.

The ambulance arrived and whilst the attendants were ferrying the injured man into the back a couple of cars drew up with screaming brakes and DI Trevor Dickins jumped out of the first one. He took in the scene with his protruding gooseberry eyes and grinned nastily when he saw Nick Holroyd.

'Hello, hello, hello — what have we here? Need my help, do you, *Sergeant*?'

'I thought you'd be busy on your murder case,' replied Holroyd shortly.

'Won't need to waste much sleep over that. When one gang boss arranges the carve-up of a rival I reckon he's done me a favour. It's as good as in the can already. What's going on here?'

Holroyd explained the situation briefly as the ambulance negotiated the gateway and roared off down the road, its siren wailing.

'Is he going to croak?'

'Doesn't look too good. He's getting on.'

'They didn't even wait till it was dark. Must have known the caretaker was an old man who should have been pensioned off years ago. Probably expected him to be sitting in his cubby-hole with a cuppa. Anything been taken?'

'It looks as if they had a go at the safe but apart from that they concentrated on computer equipment. There should be a manager around, if we can contact him he'll be able to tell us what's missing and where the old boy lives — his family must be told.'

'*We*, Sergeant? I don't need to be told my business by a woodentop.'

Nick Holroyd controlled himself with effort and said in a toneless voice: 'Well, I'll leave it in your capable hands. I'm off duty now anyway.' As he walked over to his car he got in a parting shot. 'How is Louise? I haven't seen her lately. Give her my regards.'

It was the other man's turn to stiffen and he glared after the car as the sergeant got in and drove off.

★ ★ ★

Although he was sure he was too late, Nick Holroyd called first at the hospital physiotherapy department. As expected he found it closed and continued on to Belvoir Road. He was surprised to see the Fiesta parked in Michael Croft's drive and he swung in behind it to get off the busy road. It looked as if Mike had got himself home and had visitors. He'd just apologise and check he was okay and get on his way. Mike was a long while answering the doorbell and Holroyd listened to his uneven gait lurching down the hall with his usual mixture of exasperation and guilt.

'Sorry I didn't make it, I was held up,' he said when the door opened.

'I guessed something had come up.'

'A break-in down at the sports centre. I thought it would just be routine but the caretaker was attacked and badly injured. I just called to make sure you'd got home.'

'I got a lift — come in and meet her.'

'No, I won't come in if you've got company.'

'Don't be daft. It's Rachel Morland, my physiotherapist. I've just made some coffee — come and join us.'

Nick Holroyd allowed himself to be persuaded and followed the other man into the living-room where he was introduced to the woman sitting on the sofa. He recognised her from previous visits to the hospital whilst acting as Mike's chauffeur. She looked younger and less authorative minus her starched jacket and removed from her usual background. The recognition was mutual and she acknowledged it as they exchanged greetings.

'I've seen you before at the hospital waiting for Michael, haven't I? You're a policeman too.'

Brilliant deduction, thought Holroyd sarcastically. 'Got it in one. This uniform is for real.'

A light flush stained her cheeks but she stared him down as she got to her feet.

'Well, I'll be on my way, Michael. Thanks for the coffee.'

'Sorry, that was very boorish of me,' admitted Nick Holroyd. 'Put it down to a bad day. Don't go because of me.'

'No, stay a little longer,' said Michael Croft. 'Your friend won't be home yet. I'll go and refill the pot and get another beaker.'

He limped out of the room and left the two of them eyeing each other warily.

'Michael's lucky to have such a solicitous friend,' she ventured. 'It must help him to have your support.'

'I'm responsible for his condition.'

'Responsible?'

'Hasn't he told you about his accident?'

'Well, of course. He was injured in a police operation, was shot in the back.'

'It was my fault.'

'I don't understand . . . ?'

'Has he really not told you? He was

23

my sergeant and I deliberately led him into danger. We were working on a tricky undercover case and it went horribly wrong and he got shot. It should have been me.'

'So you've got a guilt complex and that's why you're acting as nursemaid?'

'Hell, no, he's my *friend*. I do feel responsible but I'm not just trying to appease my conscience.'

'He's going to recover, you know. He's getting stronger each day. It could be much worse.'

'Oh, I know. He could be a permanent paraplegic. But this is a double whammy for him.'

As she looked puzzled he jerked his head towards the photo that stood on top of the bureau. 'Do you see that?'

She had been trying not to look at it ever since she had entered the room. It showed a young woman, laughing into the camera, her arms around a little boy of about three years of age.

'Are they his wife and son? Are they separated?'

'They *were* his wife and kid. They're dead.'

'Dead? But how dreadful! How . . . . ?'

'They were killed in a road accident about two and a half years ago. A hit and run driver. They were walking along the pavement and this car mounted the kerb and mowed them down. He was just coming to terms with that when this happened.'

'Poor Michael, I had no idea . . . Did they never find the driver?'

'He smashed himself up later that same day; pissed as a newt at four in the afternoon. At least Mike was saved the ordeal of a trial.'

At that point Michael Croft limped back into the room and waved the coffee-pot at them.

'I've made a fresh brew. Grab this beaker, Nick, and fish the sugar bowl out of the cupboard. I always forget your sweet tooth. I'm the one who should be boosting my sugar intake.'

'You're nearly back to your normal weight, aren't you?' asked Rachel, sipping her coffee.

'Yes. I shall be putting on the pounds if I don't get more exercise.'

'If you keep to the regime I've worked out for you you'll be okay. He needs to work those leg muscles as much as possible,' she said to Holroyd. 'The more he uses them the stronger he'll get.'

'And there was I thinking he needed to take it easy. Perhaps I should let you walk home from the hospital.'

'Don't you start. She bullies me enough already. I don't know what happened to the old TLC.'

'Well, you know what they say,' she smiled at him, 'you have to be cruel to be kind. I really must be going.' She put her mug down on the table and got to her feet.

'Same time tomorrow?'

'Yes, but next week my colleague will be working with you for three days instead of me.'

'Having a holiday?'

'I'm going for an interview.'

'Lasting three days!' said Holroyd. 'Whatever sort of job are you applying for — hospital manager?'

'You mean you're leaving?' asked Mike Croft.

'Not immediately, but I hope to start training for my real work soon.'

'You're not saying this physio job is just a hobby?'

'Of course not. I'm a trained physiotherapist and that's what I did before I married, but I've been . . . called to other work.'

She looked at the two men and wondered how they'd react to what she was going to say; Michael Croft, dark and brooding, and his friend so different in looks, with fair, strawlike hair and light eyes. Michael would probably be sympathetic but Nick Holroyd was a different matter. She knew the police force had a reputation for being sexist and she could see that he would be typical of this attitude. From the little she knew of him he appeared to have a chip on his shoulder and was sarcastic and brusque.

'I'm a Reader.'

The two men looked blank.

'So am I, when I have time,' ventured Holroyd.

'No, you don't understand. It's . . . it's like being a deacon . . . in the Church of England.'

'You mean you're a woman *priest?*'

It was all there in his voice, just as she had expected. The wariness, the derision, the complete absence of any spiritual knowledge.

'Not yet, but I hope to be one day.'

The two men were staring at her and she returned their gaze levelly. 'Is this a problem? You don't agree with female clergy?'

'I know nothing about it. I'll pass on this one,' said Holroyd hurriedly.

'How did you come to get involved in religion?' asked Michael Croft.

'My husband was a priest. He was vicar of St Bartholomew's.'

'What happened? Has he opted out and

you're trying to take his place?'

Michael Croft threw his friend a warning look. 'Rachel's a widow.'

'Actually you're right in a way,' she said lightly. 'Since Christopher died I've become more and more convinced that my real work is with the Church.'

'I'm sorry. About your husband, I mean. When did he die?'

'Two years ago. He had cancer . . . Anyway, I now help out in St Luke's parish. I've got this interview with the ABCM — that's the Advisory Board of Church Ministry — and if they decide I'm suitable material I hope to go on and train, probably at Westcoll House in Cambridge.'

'So you'll give up your physiotherapy work?'

'Not necessarily. I could become a non-stipendary priest. They are becoming more common these days.'

'You mean you'll keep on your day job and do your religious stuff in your spare time? That would be a heavy workload.'

'That's my problem.' For the second time she got to her feet.

'Don't police personnel also work long, unsociable hours?'

★ ★ ★

'They were absolutely dumbfounded. I could have been talking about yogic flying or the Moonies instead of the C. of E. To them Christianity is on a par with all the fringe religions — a weird, suspect sect.'

It was a little later that same evening and Rachel Morland was relaxing in the sitting-room of her friend's bungalow discussing her earlier detour. Pat Fenton was ten years older than Rachel. She was a district nurse and they had originally met at a local medical conference many years previously. She was short and dumpy with plain features but her warm, sympathetic character overcame these deficiencies. Her patients remembered her compassion and understanding, not her moonlike face and thick ankles. She exuded an air of quiet competence and restored confidence and hope in the ill and elderly.

'Well, they're in good company. Christianity is pretty irrelevant to most people these days.'

'I might have known I wouldn't get any sympathy from an old cynic like you.'

'I see enough of the dead and the dying to be realistic. You may be concerned with the afterlife, I have enough to do easing the burden of the living.'

Rachel sighed. Pat attended church on high days and holidays just to please her but it had no real meaning for her friend.

'If I can't convert you I wonder if I'm doing the right thing. I have these awful doubts. About whether I've got a true vocation or I'm just going in for it because of Christopher.'

'You want to carry on Christopher's work. What's wrong with that?'

'Yes, I suppose you're right.' Rachel put down her sherry glass and looked affectionately at her friend. 'You're good for me, you know. You make everything seem so simple, so down to earth. Anyway, what sort of week have you had?'

'Busy. I've got a heavy workload at the moment, mostly geriatrics. You deal with people disabled by accidents, I cope with people disabled by old age.'

'I have quite a few elderly patients too. People recovering from broken bones due to osteoporosis and hip replacements.'

'Yes, I know. Old age is a terrible thing and we've all got to face it.'

'Now, don't go all morbid on me. At least you're cushioned financially. You'll retire in comfort.'

Rachel glanced round at the room as she spoke. All the furniture and fittings were new and expensive and every room in the bungalow was the same. Pat had come into money a few years back. An elderly uncle,

30

whom she had hardly known, had died and left her a fortune. And she deserved it, thought Rachel, thinking back to when she had first known Pat, who had been living on a miserable pittance of a salary, struggling to support and look after her elderly parents. She could have given up her career when she became rich, but she was a dedicated nurse and although she had moved to this super-modern bungalow, ran a Rover 620 and indulged in several exotic holidays each year, she carried on with her profession.

'Why don't you move in with me?' Pat Fenton brought up the subject she had broached many times before. 'This place is really too big for me and you could have your own suite. Leave that pokey little flat; it must be stifling after living in a Victorian rectory.'

'It suits me fine at the moment, especially as I'm not sure what my movements are going to be in the near future.'

'You're a stubborn woman, Rachel Morland, but I've had another idea. I'm thinking of going on a cruise in the Caribbean in a few months' time. Why don't you come with me? As my guest, of course.'

'Uncle Fred is still coming up trumps, is he?' said the other woman lightly.

'Yes. Not only did I inherit the whole

31

caboodle but he left all these stocks and shares which are still paying out fantastic dividends. He was a canny old man and knew just what to invest in, God bless him. How about it?'

'You know I couldn't possibly get away at the moment but thanks for the offer.'

'Don't dismiss it out of hand, think about it. Well, I think the meal is almost ready, I'll just go and check. It's *boeuf provençal* — can you smell it?'

'Yes, I noticed it as soon as I came in.'

Whilst Pat Fenton disappeared into the kitchen Rachel prepared to eat an over-seasoned concoction and tell white lies about it. Pat would never be the world's best cook and a few Continental holidays had fuelled her enthusiasm for adventurous cooking. The trouble was, her idea of Mediterranean cuisine was to overdo the herbs and seasoning. Large quantities of garlic and spices thrown in with a tin of tomatoes and stewing beef did not, in Rachel's opinion, constitute the real thing. Sun-dried tomatoes, pesto and Delia Smith had passed her by and she didn't even chop up her herbs properly. One got these disgusting pieces of green stuck in one's teeth. Rachel chided herself for these uncharitable thoughts and wandered into the kitchen to see if she could help.

Later, whilst she was sipping coffee and hoping she had a supply of indigestion tablets back in her flat, Rachel brought up the subject of the two policemen again.

'I learnt something very distressing today. Michael Croft's wife and child were killed in a car accident. Poor man, to lose your family and then suffer a crippling accident. Some people seem to suffer more than their fair share of misfortune.'

'You seem very interested in him, Rachel.'

'Of course I'm interested in him. He's one of my patients. I hope I'm just as concerned over all my patients.'

'I think you're attracted to him.'

'Don't be ridiculous! We operate strictly on a patient — medic basis. I admit he's a very attractive man, but he's very self-contained. He certainly doesn't court sympathy. His friend's something else altogether.'

'How do you mean?'

Rachel pondered. 'Very prickly and quick to take offence. Now, he's a man not at peace with himself. You'd think he was the one who had suffered adversity.'

'Perhaps he has a wife who doesn't understand him.'

'Perhaps he has,' said her friend with a

33

grin. 'They reckon the police force is one of the careers that put the greatest strain on marriages. But enough of them, I want your help. I want to talk through some of the scenarios the Advisory Board are likely to face me with. There's sure to be something about AIDS.'

* * *

'He knew what he was doing. A beautifully clean job.' Quentin Stock, the pathologist, had just finished the autopsy on Edwin Briers when DI Trevor Dickins arrived at the mortuary, not too unhappy that he had missed the proceedings.

'We think it was a contract killing.'

'You're talking a professional assassin? That figures. He got him from behind — not such an easy task when you think that the headrest was in the way — and slashed him from left to right. Sliced through the carotid arteries and trachea and damn near took his head off. And working from that angle he avoided getting drenched in blood. Yes, a very professional job.'

Quentin Stock seemed almost overcome with admiration and compounded this impropriety by insisting that Dickins inspect the drained and gutted cadaver lying on the stainless-steel table.

'You realise who he was?' asked the detective.

'I try not to recognise my customers but I couldn't help knowing this one. His photo is splashed all over the local rags too often not to.'

'He'll get a Mafia-like send-off but there'll be a lot of people who'll sleep easier in their beds now he's been wasted.'

The pathologist nodded to his two assistants, who had been hovering in the background.

'He's all yours. Pretty him up for his missus.'

He stripped off his rubber apron and ushered Dickins into his office next door.

'I know you're in it for the money but what the fuck makes *them* do this kind of work?' The DI paused in the doorway and jerked his head at the two mortuary attendants who were homing in on the late Edwin Briers.

'Freddie Bains is a natural necrophiliac. Spent his lifetime with the dear departed. He's coming up to retirement age now but he's happy in his work. Started off as a stretcher-bearer in the Korean War, then worked for an undertaker and gravitated here in the seventies. Damien Winter — well, I reckon he's a surgeon manqué. Hasn't got the nous to get through medical college so he settles for this. Works on the dead rather than the living.'

'Rather them than me.' Trevor Dickins hitched himself on to the edge of the table and listened whilst the pathologist played through the running commentary he had recorded whilst carrying out the autopsy. When it had finished Quentin Stock snapped it off.

'There you have it. Perfectly straightforward. He was a healthy specimen apart from carrying too much weight. Could have gone another twenty or thirty years if he'd been left to run his natural span.'

'The killer must have got *some* blood on him.'

'On his hands and wrists. Most of it would have gushed forward over the steering-wheel and controls. What's the car like?'

'A blood-bath,' said Dickins gloomily.

He was glad to get outside the mortuary building and drew in deep lungfuls of fresh air whilst his eyes adjusted to the watery sunshine. He himself could cope with violence in the streets. Hell, it was his job. The butchered and the dying *in situ* were something he had learnt to deal with over the years. He could almost admit to getting a buzz when confronted with a victim and a new case, the adrenalin certainly flowed; but the cold, clinical side of death involving the mortuary slab and dissection was another thing altogether. He knew his colleagues felt the same, all of them that is except Nick Holroyd, who had always shown an unnatural interest in what went on inside the mortuary to the extent of insisting that no autopsy took place on any of his bodies unless he was there, soaking up all the minute details which most officers were only to happy to leave to the pathologist. Ex-Detective Inspector Nick Holroyd was a queer fish. Ex-Detective Inspector . . . He rolled the title round in his mind, savouring the ex . . . Ex-Detective Inspector Holroyd would not be attending any PMs in the near future.

He gunned the engine and drove back to the station.

★ ★ ★

Superintendent Bairstow was standing at his office window gazing down into the courtyard below when Trevor Dickins knocked and entered with the intention of bringing him up to date with the Eddie Briers case. Douglas Bairstow was a tall, distinguished-looking man who could have been a colonel-in-chief or a naval commander. He was nudging retirement and fighting it strenuously. He was respected by most of the men working under him, who were not fooled by his aloof, soft-spoken manner. Very little of what went on in the busy station escaped his notice and he was insistent on being kept informed in great detail about all the current cases exercising his force.

Trevor Dickins made his verbal report, including the postmortem results, and Bairstow heard him out before commenting.

'You're convinced this is a gangland killing?'

'Yes, sir. There's been mounting aggression between his mob and the Wingate lot. He was trying to move in on Maurice Wingate's territory — muscle in on some of his protection rackets and hookers. It was waiting to happen. I'm only surprised they went straight for him and didn't take out one of his henchmen first as a warning.'

'Has his minder turned up?'

'Woken from his beauty sleep at his lodgings early this morning.'

'Could he have had anything to do with it?'

'I'm pretty certain not. He was shocked and affronted and almost resigned. Apparently Briers had been in the habit of visiting his mistress after he left the Golden Rooster and dismissing him. Rowe says he warned him only a few days ago that he was taking unnecessary risks. It looks as if his killer had had him under surveillance and knew that he could strike when Briers was out pulling pussy.'

The superintendent looked pained. He knew the language bandied about amongst his officers had reached what he thought of as scurrilous levels with the f- and s-words peppering every conversation, and he deplored it. Most of his men were only too aware of this and watched their tongues in his presence. It was a measure of Dickins' arrogance and self-confidence that he made no attempt to modify his speech. Bairstow steepled his fingers and stared levelly over them at his inspector.

'So who do you favour as Wingate's hit-man? Lofty Munson? Garry Hicks? Have you any evidence to connect either of them with this killing?'

'He didn't use his own heavies. They're skilful at putting in the boot but they stop short of murder. He put out a contract and this is who he got.'

Trevor Dickins produced a print which he handed across the desk. It was a photograph of the card left beside the body of Eddie Briers and Bairstow read it out loud:

' 'PETS. Exits arranged. Professionally, Effectively, Terminally. Apply: The Coil Shuffler.' We've come across this before. The Bentley case — wasn't a card like this left by the body?'

'Yes. We were always certain that the wife's lover arranged to have the husband bumped off but we could never prove it and we got nowhere investigating this Coil Shuffler. None of my snouts knew anything about it — they insisted he wasn't part of the local underworld.'

'There was another incident after that. Can you call it to mind?'

'Yes,' said Dickins reluctantly. 'Nick Holroyd reckoned a visiting card like this had been left by the body of the hotel chain owner John Houghton when it was found in suspicious circumstances, but he was never able to prove it wasn't an accident and the card disappeared. I shouldn't place too much reliance on that episode.'

Douglas Bairstow sighed. He was running a station with staff problems. A tricky situation involving a clash of personalities and egos. Two of his best officers had been unable to get on; rivals professionally and also out of hours if the rumours were to be believed. It had made for a bad atmosphere but had also achieved results in a dramatic crime clear-up

40

rate. The Big White Chief, who had got a whiff of it, had warned him that it was unhealthy and that they should be separated by moving one of them to another manor, but he had chosen to ignore the situation and you could say it had blown up in his face. After the terrible incident that had rocked the station earlier in the year Holroyd should have gone, shunted off in his demoted status to work in another area, but the man had refused and he hadn't insisted. He knew that Holroyd was determined to get back his former position and secretly the superintendent admired his guts and obstinacy, but at the moment the man was something of a loose cannon and Bairstow was monitoring the situation carefully. He decided to ignore the palpable contempt in Dickins' voice, and instead tapped the photo that was now lying face upwards on his desk.

'I don't like this one little bit. It seems we have a professional assassin living on our patch whom nobody admits to knowing and who appears to operate entirely independently. This is not good news. It is imperative that we get a line on this character and nip his activities in the bud. Get Croft in on this. As Intelligence Officer he can check through the records and pull out any other references that may be hidden in the files.'

Taking this as his dismissal, Dickins got to his feet but Bairstow stopped him before he got to the door.

'You know the significance of this name — Coil Shuffler — I presume, Inspector?'

'Sir?'

'We're talking Shakespeare, as in *Hamlet*. Hamlet talks about shuffling off this mortal coil when he is contemplating suicide.'

'We're talking about murder, not suicide.'

'Quite.'

3

Rachel Morland unlocked the vestry door
and stepped inside, snapping on the light
as she did so. It did little to relieve the
gloom of the dark-panelled room. Cost-
cutting decreed a 40-watt bulb but even
floodlights would have made little difference.
St Luke's was a monument to High Gothic,
a cavern of a place whose numerous pillars
and intricate stonework were stained by
age to a dark, sombre grey. She wrinkled
her nose at the faint musty smell that
clung to the heavy oak furnishings and
rows of vestments crowding the cupboard
and overflowing along pegs set in the wall,
and thought fleetingly and regretfully of the
modern, airy St Batholomew's Church where
Christopher had been the incumbent.

She left her bag on the table and went
through the door leading into the chancel.
The east window above the altar glittered
blackly and shadows shrouded the vaulted
arches and rood screen but a last ray of
sunshine striking through the rose window
in the apse threw splintered pools of ruby
light across the stone flags at the back

of the church. She unlocked the ambry in the side wall and took out the flask of consecrated wine and the casket of consecrated communion wafers and carried them through into the vestry, where she used them to top up the travelling communion set that had been inherited from her late husband's uncle. This done she returned them to the ambry, locked the door and went back into the vestry. She took her cassock out of her bag, shook it out and put it on. She didn't like driving across the city swathed in the thick black folds that hampered her movements but it prevented an undignified scrabble at a sickbed later, important if the patient was elderly and male.

She didn't always wear vestments when administering communion on house visits but ·it added to the solemnity of the occasion and she knew that Bert Pryke would appreciate it. He had had difficulty in accepting a female lay reader and the more ritual she could bring to the liturgy the better he was appeased. She wondered what sort of mood he would be in that evening. He was a cantankerous elderly man who bitterly resented the infirmities that accompanied old age. He had been in the merchant navy for most of his adult life, and when in the mood could tell fascinating stories of his travels round the world. Now in his seventies, he was suffering from diabetes, ulcerated legs and arthritis and was being looked after in the home of his niece and her husband.

The niece, Madge Porter, answered the bell when Rachel arrived at the house. She looked put out when she saw who it was.

'Oh, it's you.'

'I promised I'd come this evening. Is he expecting me?'

'He loses count of the days but perhaps you'll cheer him up. A right old misery he's been today.' She stepped aside to allow the other woman into the hall and took her coat. 'You know the way, or do you want me to come up with you?'

'You're very welcome to join in and partake of the sacrament too.'

Madge Porter looked embarrassed and said hurriedly: 'No, we're not church people. You go on up.'

Bert Pryke struggled to get to his feet when Rachel entered his bed-sitting-room but she waved him down.

'Don't get up, Bert, you look nice and comfortable in that chair.'

She didn't ask him how he was as she knew from bitter experience that she would be told in great detail exactly how badly he was faring in the health stakes if she did so.

'You look like an old crow in that garb,' he cackled. 'Put the overhead light on so we can see better.'

Rachel complied. 'That's not a very complimentary remark.'

'Look like the Angel of Death, you do, dressed like that. *She'd* like you to be.' He jerked his head towards the door.

'What?'

'She'd like you to be the Angel of Death come to get me. She wants to get rid of me.'

'Oh, Bert, I'm sure that's not true . . . '

'It is. I'm just a nuisance. Nobody wants to know you when you're old and helpless.'

'I do. I hope I'm your friend. Shall we start?'

She undid her case and poured the wine into the delicate fluted chalice and laid the wafers on the little patten which she had set out on the table by his armchair and then handed him a copy of the Rite A Communion Service. She went through the litany slowly so that Bert could follow easily and his wavering voice gained strength as he mumbled the responses. She administered the bread and wine and as always felt uplifted by the beauty and simplicity of the phrases and the sense of God's presence, but Bert spoiled the occasion by developing a coughing fit as the dry wafer stuck to his palate. He was still wheezing and clearing his throat when she said the final prayer.

'You'd better have a drink,' she said, handing him the glass of water that stood on his bedside cabinet. The elderly man took a couple of gulps and handed it back to her with a grimace.

'You need something stronger than that when you get to my age. Have one of those biscuits.' He indicated the box of fancy chocolate biscuits on the table. 'You look as if you need feeding up.'

'Not just now thanks, but they look good. Did your niece buy them for you?'

'She got them for me but I *paid*. I wouldn't put it past her to put poison in them!'

'Bert, you really shouldn't talk like that. It's not a very Christian attitude. She's given you a home and looks after you.'

'You don't believe me, do you? You think I'm going senile. Well, I'm not, I've still got all my marbles and I know what I'm saying. I've heard them talking — they're planning to do me in!'

'I'm sure you're mistaken.'

'No, I ain't. You wait and see.'

Rachel sought to defuse the situation. 'If you're not happy living here why don't you consider going into residential care? There are some very good homes in the area; I could probably help you there.'

'Oh no, that wouldn't suit at all. I'd move tomorrow, it would be good to have a bit of company and talk to people my own age, but madame won't have that. It's the money.'

'What do you mean?' Rachel felt that she shouldn't encourage him but she was intrigued in spite of herself.

'She wants my money, see. I never married or had any nippers and all my money will go to her. She's my brother's daughter and my only kin. I still own the bungalow I used to live in before I moved in here. It's a nice little place, over at Sowton, but if I went into a home that would have to be sold to pay for my keep and she don't want that. She's got an eye on it for her son Jason — a nasty bit of work, no respect for his elders — and she don't want all my savings swallowed up to help pay for a home either. No, she's got me here and the only way I'll leave is feet first.'

'Now, you don't really mean that, Bert. She probably grumbles at times and gets tired. We women often moan about our domestic responsibilities, but you've got a nice room and I'm sure she does her best.'

'You mark my words,' he persisted, 'they'll

be carting me out of here in a wooden box before long.'

Rachel decided to change the subject. 'Shall we say the Grace together?'

Bert looked stubborn but mumbled after her: 'The Grace of Our Lord Jesus Christ and the love of God and the Fellowship of the Holy Spirit be with us evermore,' then watched silently as she gathered up the communion vessels and packed them away in her bag.

'I'll try and get in to see you again the week after next. Is there anything I can get you?'

'No. You're a good young woman. Thank you for coming.'

Madge Porter heard Rachel walking down the stairs and came out of the sitting-room.

'You've finished, then. How did you find him?'

'He seems rather low today but I hope I've helped him. It must be difficult for you having to provide round-the-clock care.'

'You can say that again. It's a great tie and he's not the easiest of men to deal with; very pigheaded.'

'Have you considered residential care?'

'Chance would be a fine thing. He ought to be in a proper home where they've got the staff and facilities to give him the care he needs, but he won't hear of it.'

'Really? I know old people can be awkward about that sort of thing, but perhaps he can be persuaded?' Rachel picked her way carefully.

'Not him. He's determined he won't be shoved away into a home, as he puts it, and if he won't agree, there's nothing we can do about it.'

Madge Porter pursed her lips and handed the younger woman her coat. Rachel decided to abandon the subject for the time being, but as she drove away from the house she wondered at the discrepancies between the two conversations. Mrs Porter seemed to be providing for her uncle to the best of her ability, though she was obviously stressed by the situation, but Bert had been adamant about his point of view. Perhaps it was just the cantankerousness of old age. He *was* getting muddled and elderly people often did suffer from persecution mania. She decided to have a word with Pat Fenton. It was Pat who had first brought her and Bert together. As a district nurse she visited him on a regular basis to dress his ulcerated legs and give him his injections and when he had mentioned to her that he regretted having lost touch with his Christian beliefs and the Church of England she had introduced him to her friend and proxy membership of St Luke's.

Pat was a frequent visitor to the Porter household and would be a much better judge as to whether there was any truth in Bert Pryke's allegations or whether he was more senile than she had thought. She must discuss the case with her friend the next time she saw her, she decided as she let herself into her car. She must also tell her that her interview with the ABCM had been postponed for a few months. She had been very disappointed when she had first heard but on reflection she had realised that it gave her more time to prepare and sort out her misgivings.

★ ★ ★

Nick Holroyd had switched on the television to watch the nine o'clock news. A bomb scare in Northern Ireland accounted for the first part of the programme and he felt a horrible sense of déjà vu as he followed the action on the screen. Then the newsreader switched to the forthcoming Party conferences and the in-fighting amongst the backbenchers and he drifted off into a doze. He was awoken by a man shouting and the sound of a shot that cut across his uneasy slumber and brought him to his feet trembling. The noise echoed around inside his head and for a few seconds he was back inside the disused factory circling round the abandoned hulks of machinery as he closed in on his quarry. He felt again the excitement gripping him as he paused for his partner to catch up with him, and the excitement turning to alarm as he noticed the figure following Mike. A black shadow dodging between the serried ranks of rusting pipes, barely visible until it moved in front of a window and was momentarily silhouetted against the moonlit sky and he could see the gun raised to fire.

Abandoning his operation and all thoughts of secrecy he had leapt to his feet and shouted at the top of his voice to alert Mike and divert his pursuer but he had been too late. Even as his voice had rung out the gun had barked, the noise reverberating round the enclosed space, and Mike had thrown up his hands and crashed at the foot of the staircase.

The sound of thundering hoofs jerked him back to reality and he found himself staring at the posse of cavalrymen fanning across the television screen. The news had ended and a Western was now under way involving a shoot-out. He fumbled for the control and zapped it. His heart was pounding and sweat was pricking his scalp and the old horror flooded his body and mind, spiralling out of control as he went through, in slow motion, the sequence of events of that terrible evening.

He had flung himself towards Mike, heedless of his own danger and dimly aware of the sound of running footsteps receding in the background, convinced that his friend and colleague was dead. Mike had lain sprawled on his face, apparently lifeless, whilst blood from the gunshot wound just below his waist had soaked through his outer garments. He had searched for a pulse and eventually discerned a faint throb but his relief had quickly turned to dismay as he had realised that the bullet must have entered Mike's spine. Aware that he must not attempt to move him but afraid that he might bleed to death before medical care could arrive, he had summoned help on his radio and had crouched beside his friend's body willing the medics to arrive before it was too late. The memory of that short period of time, which had seemed like a lifetime but had actually been only minutes, would never leave him. The smell of cordite had hung in the air, mingling with the faint oily smell of the machinery, and from somewhere nearby had come the sound of monotonous dripping; a leaking pipe that had somehow metamorphosed into the sound of his friend's life-blood trickling away.

Nick shuddered at the memory and ran his fingers through his hair. If that scene was indelibly inscribed on his memory what had followed was a jumble of events that formed no coherent sequence. The ambulance had arrived simultaneously with the Force — or had one preceded the other? He remembered the blue light flashing round the dank walls like some alien arrival from outer space as Mike was carefully lifted on to a stretcher and eased into the back of the ambulance, attached to drips and oxygen cylinder. He heard again the wail of sirens and the slamming of car doors as reinforcements from the station poured into the building; teams of men who should have been with him from the start of the operation. The two men he had come so close to arresting had disappeared together with the vital evidence of their scam and he had a hateful recollection of Trevor Dickins looming over him as he had slumped on the stairs, shouting at him to pull his finger out and make sense.

Then had come the interrogation from the superintendent. It was one of many such interviews but it was the first that stood out in his memory. Had it actually taken place in the factory or back at the station? He couldn't remember but he still inwardly cringed at the memory of the verbal lashing he had received. For once, Douglas Bairstow had lost his cool and bawled him out.

'What the hell did you think you were doing going in there alone with Croft? Why was there no back-up team?'

'It was a delicate operation. I'd been monitoring their activities for some time and I got the tip-off that they were moving the stuff that night and I knew I could catch them in the act. A large police presence would have given the game away and we'd never have got them.'

'Did you know they were armed?'

'No. Brad and Billy Stone weren't into violence. They never carried firearms.'

But he had lied. Joey Wilson, his snout, had warned him that the Stone brothers had been joined by their cousin, Gerry Baldwin; recently out of quod after serving a long sentence for GBS and known to be into shooters. And he had been found out. Trevor Dickins, who also used Joey and saw this as a means of grinding his old rival into the ground, had arrested the informant. Poor old Joey, thought Holroyd. Puny in body and spirit, he had been terrified at the turn of events and bleated to save his skin. He, Nick

Holroyd, had knowingly taken his partner into danger without any reinforcements, let alone the firearms team which the situation had called for, because he had hoped to grab all the glory for cleaning up his particular cell himself. It had been a matter for the disciplinary board.

At first he had thought he would be chucked off the force. The mini-court where he came up before the Complaints and Discipline Board, the charges of neglect of duty, the ghastly wait whilst his future was debated; all these events had swept him towards a future he had never envisaged. Instead of speeding up the professional ladder he was seeing things from the other side of the fence. *He* was the one on trial, he was the one awaiting a verdict and facing an uncertain future. This was how it felt to be the hunted rather than the hunter. He hadn't been thrown out of the force but his career had received a severe check: reduced in rank from inspector to sergeant and back in uniform. Officially it wasn't demotion to be moved from plain-clothes to uniform branch, but every CID officer knew different. They were the élite, a cut above the woodentops, and the humiliation had bitten deep. He could have saved face by transferring to a different manor but he had refused, his pride demanding that somehow he claw his way back to his former position and his guilty conscience and affection for Mike dictating that he hang around to look after his friend.

Although the court martial and its ramifications had been a terrible thing to live through, far worse had been his fears for Mike. The news that his colleague would live had been quickly overtaken by the knowledge that he would probably be paralysed for life. The bullet had missed severing his spinal cord by a miracle but had damaged vertebrae and surrounding flesh and he, Nick Holroyd, must bear the responsibility for this. The fact that Mike himself bore him no ill-will and did not blame him somehow made the situation worse. He should be reproached and railed against; God knows, he deserved it, but that wasn't Mike's style. He had put the accident behind him and concentrated on fighting back to full health, and he had made it to the extent of holding down a responsible job on the force, albeit no longer an active one.

Nick Holroyd sighed and looked at his watch. Nine forty-five in the evening and here he was, alone, spooked and afraid of his own company. He'd call round and see old Mike, grab a pack of beer from the off-licence on the way and later they could order a curry or Chinky if Mike was so minded. He let himself out of the house and drove round to Belvoir Road. The wind was getting up and blew ragged scraps of cloud across the rising moon. It eddied through the heaps of leaves in the gutters like some subterranean animal heaving beneath the surface and snatched at a sheet of cardboard, bowling it down the road ahead of him until it got snagged on an abandoned supermarket trolley that leaned at a drunken angle against a traffic bollard.

Mike answered his knock with raised eyebrows.

'What's the matter? You look hassled.'

Nick had already admitted to him in a weak moment that he had horrible dreams about the shooting incident; there was no way he was going to admit that he also suffered waking nightmares.

'Nothing's the matter. I was at a loose end and I thought I'd drop in and see how you were.'

'Much as you left me a few hours ago,' said Mike drily. 'Come on in.'

'I thought we could share a jar or two.' Nick followed him up the hall and into the sitting-room.

'Beware a Greek bearing gifts, but I never

say no to a free drink. Has your date let you down?'

'I didn't have one,' said Nick shortly, 'but I wondered if you might have a woman here.'

'Are you referring to anyone in particular?'

'The God-slot woman — what's her name — Rachel?'

'You're being offensive.'

'Hell, yes I am. Sorry, only I don't want to see you taken advantage of.'

'For Christ's sake, Nick, you're not my keeper! You seem to think that just because, for some extraordinary reason, you feel responsible for my condition it gives you the right to interfere and order my affairs! My private life is *my* bloody business, not yours!'

'Sure. Sorry, I spoke out of turn.'

'So far Rachel Morland and I have met on a purely professional footing but I do intend to ask her out. Any objections?'

'Well, no. I suppose you know what you're doing.'

'Thanks,' said Mike sarcastically. He threw himself into a chair and released the ring-pull on his can. 'Now, suppose you tell me what you really came for.'

Nick took his time answering. He slopped beer all over himself and the chair as he opened his can and mopped at it with his handkerchief.

'We do run to glasses, you know.' Mike eyed him quizzically.

'No, it's fine like this.' Nick waved the can airily and shot some more over his hand. 'You're in a unique position — everything that goes on in the station is monitored by you as a collator.'

'I hope you're not thinking what I fear you are.'

'All the information that filters through the station passes through your hands as CID Intelligence and Liaison Officer. You know the details of every current case, the progress being made, the lines of enquiry . . . '

'Leave it, Nick.'

'No, listen. What harm is there in you genning me up on some meaty case that's hanging fire?'

'Forget it. You're not CID now, you've got to accept that.'

'I'm not accepting it. I'm going to get back my rank and position. And don't tell me that if I keep my nose clean and be a good boy it will all come right because you know that's nonsense. I'll still be minding panda cars when I come up for retirement!'

'You think you can get back your CID Inspector rank by taking on single-handed and solving some case the CID has fallen down on? You're living in cloud-cuckoo-land!'

'No, I'm not. I was a damn good detective. You know that and I'm not going to rusticate just because some bloody police committee decided I needed my knuckles rapped.'

'Be serious. What could you possibly do on your own without any back-up? No Forensics, no SOCOs, no team to slog away on a house-to-house?'

'I've still got plenty of friends in lots of departments.'

'You're mad,' said Mike flatly. 'You're certainly not flavour of the month with those who count. You can't expect anyone to put their career on the line just to satisfy your vanity.'

'I'm not asking you to compromise yourself, Mike, only to . . . '

'We're not talking about us.'

'Yes we are. Wouldn't you like to do some real detecting again? We made a good team, we still could.'

'Christ, you don't give up, do you! Now you're trying to involve me in one of your mad schemes! No way, Nick, just forget it.'

'Okay. I can see your personality has changed too and your mental state.'

'What do you mean?'

61

'You didn't used to be so cautious, so keen to live by the book. You know a good detective is someone who doesn't always abide by the rules; who's not afraid of sticking his neck out when the occasion demands it. All right, I know you caught a packet by us doing just that but don't you ever get bored now? You're not a nine-to-five man.'

'I've had to rethink my life more than once. Just now I'm concentrating on getting back my physical health and I'm thankful I've got a job behind me. And I intend keeping that job.'

'Right. No homicides, no drugs, no large-scale embezzlement or larceny scams; surely there's some little poser we — I — can get my teeth into? What's this I've heard about a contract killer putting about for business?'

Michael Croft looked surprised. 'You don't need me. Seems you are your own little mine of information.'

'So it's true?'

His friend regarded him thoughtfully and came to a decision. Nick was a hot-headed idiot who would find himself in terminal trouble if he wasn't headed off. There was no reason why he shouldn't be given the known facts, such as they were, and the matter *was* intriguing.

'The Coil Shuffler's back in business.'

Nick's head jerked up and he leaned forward. 'Tell me more.'

'Eddie Briers' killing. Someone put out a contract on him and the Coil Shuffler picked it up. There was a visiting card left beside the body.'

'What did it say?'

Michael told him, hesitating as he tried to recall the exact wording.

'But that's — '

'Let me finish. Someone remembered coming across something similar on another case and the Super instructed me to check through the records. I've turned up three references so far. The Bentley case: there was an identical card left on Robert Bentley's body but we never got a conviction. The same card, in a slightly different version, figured in an enquiry into an elderly woman's death over at Balscombe. A friend of the woman was convinced the son had done her in or arranged her demise and produced this card which she claimed she had found in the house; but the autopsy that was ordered revealed that she had died from natural causes so the investigation was scrubbed. Then there was that business of John Houghton's death — the hotel chain owner. You investigated it and were convinced it wasn't suicide and you reported seeing a similar card at the scene of crime but it went missing.'

'There was something very fishy about that whole episode. It's a pity you weren't with me on that case — ' Nick broke off as he remembered that his friend had been on compassionate leave at the time following the deaths of his wife and son. 'Anyway, I quite definitely saw that card. It was tucked inside Houghton's breast pocket and I could read what was on it. Foolishly I didn't remove it at the time. I didn't want to destroy any evidence so I left it there thinking it could be checked by Forensics when the clothes were removed for the autopsy. It went missing between the scene of the crime and the morgue.'

'It must have slipped out and got lost somehow.'

'From a body zipped in a body bag? No way. I've always been convinced that it was deliberately moved by someone but I wasn't believed at the time. The Powers That Be were quite happy to get a verdict of suicide and didn't want me rocking the boat. They thought I was just trying to back up my suspicions of foul play so it was never properly followed up.'

'Well, there you have it. Four cases over a matter of two or three years. Of course, there may have been others that never came to the police's notice.'

'What's the feeling amongst the criminal fraternity? Do they know who this Coil Shuffler is?'

'Now that's where it gets really interesting. From the feelers put out amongst our snouts we get a complete denial, but they know something. You get the impression that this assassin is operating outside the known underworld and they are as baffled as we are; but they've closed ranks and are denying any knowledge of him, and that in itself is suspicious. They're trying too hard to get across to the Bill that no such person exists.'

'Whoever he is he must have contacts; some way of promoting his dubious business.'

'Maybe he advertises,' Croft said facetiously, leaning back in his chair and folding his arms behind his head.

'Maybe he does just that. It's somewhere for us to start.'

'We?'

'You're as intrigued as I am — come on, admit it. There's nothing to stop us two poking around and finding out if this bod really exists.'

'I thought you were already convinced?'

'I am, but we've got to have proof if

anyone else is to believe us. If we can unmask this person we'll end up in the CC's good books and clear up several outstanding cases in the process. What do you say?'

'You're on — against my better judgement. I shouldn't encourage you.'

Nick grinned. 'We must plan our strategy. But first I'll pop down to the take-away. What do you fancy?'

★ ★ ★

The following week Michael Croft quite accidentally stumbled upon the Coil Shuffler's advertisement. After a hectic morning inputting information into the computer he was taking a break, drinking cups of dubious coffee from the vending machine whilst reading the newspaper. The newspaper in question was the weekly freebie published by the local press and he was flicking desultorily through the pages when his attention was grabbed by the small boxed advert in the personal column. Hardly able to believe his eyes he read it through a few times to make sure he wasn't hallucinating. 'PETS: Exits arranged — Painlessly, Efficiently, Tastefully. Apply: The Coil Shuffler.' There was a box number underneath. He hastily called up on screen the information he had already collected on the Coil Shuffler. As he had thought, the advert was identical to the wording on the card found in the house of the elderly woman whose death had been queried.

He exited and left his desk to go in search of Nick Holroyd. He ran him to earth in the canteen, sitting alone at a table in the corner, spearing chips off a sauce-splattered plate. He slapped the paper down in front of him.

'Read that. I can't understand why no one else here hasn't noticed it before or why a dubious advert like this hasn't been investigated.'

Holroyd read it through out loud, his voice gaining in satisfaction as he did so. 'It's a very ambigious advert. PETS . . . Anyone glancing at it would probably think it was something to do with animals. A vet advertising a putting-down service for family pets or something similar.'

'That could be a cover in case it is investigated.'

'It should be easy enough to check. Someone must have placed the advert in person originally and presumably someone collects any replies sent to the box number. What are we waiting for?'

'Hang on, we've got to go public on this. This piece of information is vital to Bairstow's probe.'

'Shit! Give us a break, Mike. As you say, it's a miracle some smart-arsed dick hasn't noticed it already. It's going to be picked up sooner or later by one of our mob; in the meantime here's our chance.'

'It's out of order . . . '

'Look, forget you've seen it. You know nothing about it — I'M the one who found it — okay? Just give me time to do a little snooping and see what I come up with.'

'You win. When are you going to start?'

'There's nothing like the present. I'm off to the *Clarion's* office right now.'

'Okay. We haven't had this conversation. I'd better get back.'

'Well, leave the damn paper with me.' Nick held out his hand as his friend started to limp away.

He discovered when he reached the Clarion building that although the *Weekly Digest* was printed by the Clarion Press it was produced independently by a team working out of offices a couple of streets away. He left the car where he had parked it and walked the short distance to the other building. A young blonde girl dressed in a skimpy T-shirt and an even skimpier miniskirt was seated at a desk at the back of the front office. When she saw him she got to her feet and took up position behind the counter, eyeing his uniform and person with predatory interest.

'I want to see the person in charge of advertising. Do you have an Advertising Manager?'

'Melvyn Jones. He's not in today, can I help you?'

'I want some information on box numbers. How they operate, et cetera.'

'I can tell you that, it's fairly simple.' She leaned over the counter allowing Holroyd to see that she was bra-less and had a large black mole just beneath her left ear. 'Is anything wrong?'

'That depends on what you tell me.'

'Shouldn't you have a warrant card?'

'Do you think this is fancy dress?' He fished in a pocket and produced his ID card which he flashed before her eyes. 'Now, suppose I'm a customer. I come in here wanting to place an advert using a box number — what's the form?'

'You tell me the wording you want to put, what section it's to go in and how often you want it repeated and I'll work out the cost — it's so much per word. There is a form in the paper you can fill in but you can do it verbally.'

'So, how do I pay?'

'Cash, cheque, PO, credit card . . . ' She shrugged. 'It's all the same to us.'

'And I'd have to give my name and address?'

'Yes. I'd allocate you a box number and you'd make arrangements to collect the replies to your advert.'

'I see.' He gave her an appraising stare. 'What's your name, love?'

'Penny. Penny Hooper.' She gave him a coy, sideways glance that would have done credit to Princess Di.

'Well, Penny, that all seems pretty straightforward but what if I'm up to no good?'

'What do you mean?'

He lowered his voice confidentially. 'Suppose I'm a villain. This advert I want to put in the paper is really a message to my fellow baddies so I want to remain anonymous.'

'You could give a false name and address. We don't check.'

'But you'd still have seen me and would be able to describe me and recognise me again, wouldn't you? Could I place this advert over the phone without actually coming into the office?'

She considered this. 'Yes, that would be no problem. You could phone and pretend you were ringing from another part of the country and say you wanted an advert to go in the local paper. We could quote you a price and you could send the wording through the post with a cheque or whatever.'

'A cheque would have my name and an account number on it.'

'A postal order doesn't.'

'No, good thinking. How about subsequent repeat adverts?'

'You could pay for a run-on, depending on how many times and how often you wanted it to go in.'

'Right, so we've got me arranging this advert completely anonymously. Now we come to the nitty-gritty. How do I pick up my replies?'

'You could have them posted on to you.'

'Then you would learn my real name and address.'

' 'Y . . . e . . . s.' She pondered this, catching her bottom lip between lipstick-smeared teeth and drumming her fingers on the counter. 'I know. You could have them sent Poste Restante to some post office. I'm not quite sure how it works but it would mean you could get your replies without us knowing who you were.'

'Good girl. That's useful, thanks.'

'Is there anything else you want to know?'

'There is, but I'm not sure it's fair to ask you . . . ' He let the hint dangle tantalisingly, thankful that Penny Hooper was one of that increasingly rare breed of young people who did not look on the police as pigs or filth.

'Try me.' She was hooked.

'We've been talking generalities. I need more confidential information.' He tapped the side of his nose.

'Such as?'

'Such as how . . . no, it's not fair on you. I'd better wait and see your advertising manager . . . '

'There's nothing he can tell you that I can't,' she said tartly. 'What do you want to know?'

'Can you look through your records and find out if any advert has been placed in the manner we've just been discussing?'

'I suppose it is possible, but it would take time. We cover a lot of adverts each week — pages of them.'

'I'm thinking of one particular one.'

'You mean, there's an actual advert in the current paper that's a con?' Her voice rose in excitement.

'Shhh. Can I trust you? This is very confidential. If my chief knew I was bleating to you he'd have my guts for garters.'

'I won't say a word to anyone, I promise.'

Nick decided to take a gamble. He opened the paper he had taken with him and showed her the PETS advert. 'That's the one I'm interested in. Do you know anything about it? It's probably genuine but I'd like to know who has put it in.'

'It's funny you should mean that one. My friend and I noticed it last week and she reckoned it was about a pets' memorial garden. You know, the vet puts down your pet and then you can have it buried in a proper pets' cemetery with a gravestone or a memorial tablet.'

'Really?'

'I think it's a nice idea, don't you? Someone once told me that they used to put the dead animals in polythene bags and throw them on the council rubbish tips. That's quite disgusting, isn't it?'

Holroyd nodded and steered her back to the subject in hand.

'Can you check this out? If you've got a name and address I should like to have them.'

'It's supposed to be a confidential list of subscribers but as you're the police . . .'

'Quite. We can make it official with a warrant but that takes time and I don't think it is necessary at this point. You can be my undercover agent — how about it?'

'What's the rate of pay?' She smiled provocatively at him.

'I'll meet you after work. You can give me

the gen and I'll take you out for a meal.'

'My boyfriend's picking me up from work.'

'Just my luck. All the nice girls are spoken for.'

'I could meet you in my lunch-hour tomorrow,' she said hurriedly.

'Done. How about the Blue Boar?'

'Pietro's is nearer.'

'Fine. I believe they do a mean pasta. I'll meet you there at one o'clock. There's just one more thing . . . '

She looked enquiringly at him.

'You may get other policemen round asking the same questions. Don't let on I've forestalled them. I'm after a promotion so I'm trying to earn Brownie points by getting in first.'

As he walked back to his car Nick Holroyd wondered if he'd blown his investigation before it had got off the ground by confiding in Penny Hooper. If he had read her correctly he hoped not. She was intrigued at the thought of helping the Bill, particularly as the policeman involved was fairly personable, was almost old enough to be her father, and had been at great pains to get across that he had found her attractive. The trouble was he hadn't. He unlocked the door and flung himself into the driver's seat. She would be easy enough to pull but he found the prospect a turn-off. She was young and pretty in a rather obvious way and probably very sexually active but he knew that he'd be bored to tears before they even made bed and he no longer found a purely sexual encounter satisfying. The trouble is I'm getting old, he thought savagely as he slammed the car into gear and pulled out from the kerb.

4

The hydrotherapy pool was warm and reeked of chlorine. Michael Croft floated on his stomach and clung to the handrail, beating his legs in a ludicrous imitation of the crawl. It was humiliating, like being a toddler again learning to swim and just as difficult. It was like wading through treacle; the water felt heavy and his feeble efforts to displace it only served to bring home to him how weak his leg muscles still were. Beside him bobbed Rachel Morland, encouraging and overseeing his exercises.

'You'd never think I was once the three-hundred-metre champion at my local swimming club, would you?' he gasped, forcing his legs down and pulling himself upright.

'Don't put yourself down all the time. You've improved immensely in the last fortnight. Lie on your back and we'll try the same stroke from that angle.'

'I like that 'we'. I'm doing all the work and you must be bored out of your mind.'

'I enjoy this part of my job. How many people get a dip in a private pool regularly

76

in the course of their work?'

'I suppose that's one way of looking at it. How many more of these do I have to do?'

'Your twenty minutes is nearly up. Just float on your back and relax. By the way, your minder has arrived.'

'Eh?' He twisted round in the water and followed her nod. On the other side of the glass panel that separated the pool area from the rest of the physiotherapy department sat Nick Holroyd, following the activity in the water with great interest.

'He's not supposed to be there, you know. This part is strictly out of bounds to the general public.'

'I don't know why he's come. I told him I didn't want a lift today — he must have forgotten.'

'Look, Mike, I'm looking forward to going to the theatre but we don't have to go out for a meal first. Perhaps you'd better go home with your friend now he's turned up.'

'I've booked a table at the Clarendon Hotel for six forty-five. It will give us time to have a decent meal before the theatre starts and we can go straight from here if you don't mind acting as chauffeur.'

'Of course not, if you're sure?'

'Nick's made a mistake. I'll just have a word with him and explain.'

Nick Holroyd watched his friend pull himself out of the water and pick up his towel. Standing still you would think there was nothing wrong with him, he thought. Then Mike turned round and he saw the ugly white scar tissue disfiguring his back and he grimaced and turned his attention to Rachel Morland, who had followed him out of the pool. Who would have thought she would have such a spectacular figure, he mused; what a shame to hide it under a cassock.

'Tell me, what do I have to do to get myself in this situation?' he leered at the physiotherapist as Michael limped up to him. 'What a pair of knockers!'

'What a one-track mind. You're out of bounds. You'll be getting yourself arrested as a Peeping Tom if you come in here.'

'Just checking out your treatment. How often do you do this?'

'I wasn't expecting you. I told you I didn't need a lift today, remember?'

'God, yes, I do now. It had completely slipped my mind, I've got a lot to tell you — I've been following up that advert.'

'I'm not sure I want to hear this. It can wait till tomorrow, can't it?'

'I suppose so. In fact, by tomorrow afternoon I reckon I may have some more information.'

'I can't wait,' said Michael sarcastically, towelling his shoulders vigorously, 'sorry you've had this wasted journey.'

'Don't tell me, you're wining and dining the lovely Rachel?'

'Got it in one. Any objections?'

'Hell, no. It's good to see you taking an interest in the opposite sex again, though you're certainly playing safe. You're not . . . '

'Yes?' said Michael ominously as his friend saw his expression and petered out.

'I was going to say, you're not exactly laying yourself open to temptation, are you? A woman priest . . . she'll be as buttoned up as you are.'

'Get lost, Nick.'

'I'm on my way. Don't mind me. Just have fun and don't do anything I wouldn't.'

'That gives me a free rein, doesn't it?'

As he dressed, Michael reflected on his private life. What Nick had just said was true. When Jane had died his sexual drive had died too. Apart from an abortive affair not long after her death, when he had tried to blot out her memory for fear he would go mad, he had lived a celibate life. And dating Rachel was not likely to change this, as Nick had also pointed out. That was fine by him. Rachel was an attractive woman; warm and sensible with a surprisingly quirky sense of humour and not at all what he would have imagined a devout churchwoman to be like — not that he really knew anything about religion — and he would enjoy her company. She wouldn't be expecting him to jump into bed with her at the end of the evening and if their friendship developed — well, he would take it from there.

It was funny how misfortune took people different ways. When Nick's wife had left him for someone else he had gone off the rails completely, behaving like a bloody tomcat and leaving a trail of unhappy affairs behind him. He was still looking for another woman to take Maureen's place, yet at the same time was equally determined that no woman would ever get close enough to hurt him again, treating all the females he came up against as purely sex objects. As they said, it took all sorts and Nick and he were a couple of mixed-up guys . . .

Later, as he and Rachel sat in the dining-room of the Clarendon Hotel enjoying an excellent meal, she brought up the subject of Jane. They had spent the first course, a spicy fish soup with garlic bread, discussing general topics and skirting round personal issues, and it wasn't until they were well into their *boeuf en daube* that she leaned forward and spoke gently.

'Mike, I know about your wife and son. Nick told me. I'm very sorry, it must have been terrible.'

'Yes, well, you've been there yourself. How did you cope?'

'I suppose I had more time to get used to the idea than you did. Christopher was ill for a long while and I knew he wouldn't get better, but when the end came . . . it was still a terrible shock.' Her face darkened as if at some terrible memory and he reached across the table and squeezed her hand.

'I know what you mean. I just couldn't believe it. I suppose I was in shock, I was displaying all the classic symptoms, but for ages afterwards I just couldn't take it in. I'd seen their bodies, I'd buried them, I'd dealt with all the sordid details but my mind couldn't accept that they were really dead. I'd catch a glimpse of a woman in the street, or hear a boy's voice and for a few seconds I'd think I'd found them again before reality set in . . . ' He grimaced at her. 'You never had any kids?'

'No, we always intended to have a family but Christopher was taken ill before it happened.'

'Wasn't your belief in a God shaken? Could you still go on believing after such a blow? Though they say faith can be a great comfort.'

'They say right. I was — am — blessed in having my faith, and at the time it stopped me from going mad.'

'You never really get over it, do you?'

'No. There is still a big black hole. You build bridges, lay splints over it, but it's still there, gaping underneath.'

'I know exactly what you mean. But you survive, don't you? You may not want to, but somehow you survive.'

'Yes, as they say, life goes on, you can't just opt out . . . But you've had a double tragedy. Your accident, coming so soon after the death of your family, must have seemed like the last straw.'

'Yes and no. In a way it helped. It snapped me out of my self-pity and made me face up to life again. I suddenly realised that I did want to go on living and that I had to overcome my injuries.'

'If you don't mind me saying so, you seem less fazed by the accident than your friend Nick does.'

'Nick has this crazy idea that my injury is his fault.'

'Is it crazy?'

'Technically, I suppose, as senior officer, the blame fell on his shoulders but I don't hold him responsible. We both knew the risks — I wasn't led into the situation blindly.'

Whilst their plates were cleared and they waited for their desserts, Michael refilled her glass and gave her a brief résumé of the shooting incident and its aftermath.

'So Nick lost rank,' said Rachel thoughtfully when he had finished, 'is that why he has such a chip on his shoulder?'

'I suppose he has. He was very cut up about it. He's determined to make it back to DI.'

'And will he?'

'*He* thinks so. Frankly, I think he should have cut and run, moved to another part of the country and joined another force. It would be far easier to get back his lost status under those circumstances.'

'And you would be free of him.'

'I didn't say that! He's my good mate, we go back a long way.'

'I'm sure you do. Doesn't he have a wife and family?'

'He's divorced. His wife left him and there were no kids. Anyway, what are we doing discussing Nick and the past? Tell me about your future plans to become a priest.'

Rachel filled him in briefly about the intricacies and problems involved in becoming a Church of England priest, aware that he was intrigued and baffled in equal proportions.

The Theatre Royal was only a little way from the hotel, further down on the other side of the road. As they walked the short distance Rachel was very aware of the tall figure lurching along at her side. It was so long since she'd had an escort, been on a date, that she felt like a gauche schoolgirl. The guilt she had expected to feel didn't materialise; instead, she had the feeling that Christopher would approve, though she didn't think some of her parishioners would agree. This thought prompted another and she gave a little gasp.

'What's the matter, is anything wrong?' Michael looked at her curiously as she checked and hesitated on the pavement.

'I've just remembered, I usually meet up with a friend on Tuesday evenings and I forgot to let her know I couldn't make it tonight.'

'This is not a last-minute excuse to cut and run, is it?'

'No, of course not. It's not a definite arrangement but she'll probably be expecting me as I haven't been in touch. There's sure to be a public phone in the theatre — I'll ring her before the play starts or in the interval.'

The front entrance to the Theatre Royal

was up a broad flight of steps.

'Can you manage this all right?' she asked as Michael paused at the bottom.

'I thought going up and down stairs was part of my rehabilitation programme?'

'I'm glad you take my advice to heart. Move over to the side so that you can use the railing.'

'Look, I don't want to embarrass you . . . '

'Don't be ridiculous.' She took his arm and together they mounted the flight of steps. It wasn't until they were seated in the stalls and the lights dimmed that she remembered that the play they were about to see, *The Glass Menagerie*, centred round a woman with a limp.

* * *

Graham Scott would have lived longer if his wife had not insisted on a private bed. Not a great deal longer, perhaps only a few days until the Coil Shuffler worked out how to waste his victim on a busy hospital ward; but during those few days a public scandal might have been exposed. As it was his death came at an opportune moment for several interested parties.

Scott was a property developer who had made his fortune by buying up derelict real estate in rundown parts of the city, sitting on it until that area became once more a fashionable address, and in the fullness of time releasing his renovated and gentrified properties on to the market. His was a typical rags to riches story and if many of his dealings were somewhat dubious and there were hints that more than one planning officer on the local council was in his pocket, these were only rumours that had never been proved. He was a Mason, a prominent member of the Conservative Party and he enjoyed his new-found wealth. Although he still paid lip-service to his Methodist upbringing it did not prevent him from indulging himself in a hectic social life that resulted in high levels of cholesterol and liquor intake, not to mention stress.

His doctor had warned him of the perils of his sedentary life style coupled with his overeating and drinking but he had laughed at his concern and insisted that he was as fit as a fiddle. The fiddle had bowed to a stop one Sunday morning when a massive heart attack had felled him as he propped up the bar in the golf club, a G & T in one hand, a King Edward cigar in the other. He had been rushed to St Crispian's hospital where he had spent several days in intensive care before being pronounced out of danger and moved to one of the heart wards. Although Scott himself quite enjoyed the company of the other patients and the general bustle, Doreen, his wife, had demanded he be given a private room more in keeping with what she thought of as his elevated status. So he was wheeled into his solitary room where he lay, wired up to monitors and drips, staring at the blank white walls and ceilings, bored out of his mind.

The figure insinuated itself into the room not long after visiting hours. Scott, who had pretended to fall asleep during his wife's visit because she bored him as much as his surroundings, had genuinely nodded off and surfaced to find a figure dressed like a hospital porter, complete with cap and badge, approaching the bed.

'What now?' asked Scott sleepily, expecting another visit to X-ray. The figure didn't reply but reached over the bed and snatched at the wires attached to the prone body, tearing them away. Scott's gurgle of alarm was cut short as he looked into the blank, impassive eyes hovering above him and saw the knife in the upraised arm. He struggled to move and shout but a second massive coronary struck him. He was dead before the blade entered his body.

As the alarm bleeped on the monitor

screen at the nursing station and the crash team rushed into action, the figure slipped out of the room and bowled down the corridor pushing a wheelchair.

★ ★ ★

'I'm sorry about yesterday evening, were you expecting me?' Rachel Morland stirred her coffee and looked apologetically across the table at Pat Fenton. They were seated in the staff canteen at the hospital where Rachel had arranged to meet her friend.

'I know it's not a definite arrangement but as I hadn't heard to the contrary I *was* expecting you.'

'Sorry, it was bad of me not to get in touch but it wasn't until I was in the theatre that I remembered that I hadn't rung you and then I couldn't find a phone.'

'You went to the theatre? Not on your own, surely? Why didn't you ask me, I'd love to have gone.'

Hearing the prickliness in her friend's voice Rachel inwardly sighed.

'I went with Michael Croft, my policeman patient.'

'Oh well, he was obviously better company than me.'

'Don't be silly, Pat. I know it was remiss

of me not to let you know I wasn't coming round, but as you say, it's not a definite arrangement that we always see each other on Tuesday evenings and this came up.'

'Which was far more exciting than spending the evening with boring old me.'

'Look, I've said I'm sorry but I'm not going to grovel. We've been friends a long time but we don't live in each other's pockets. I certainly wouldn't object if you went out on a date.'

Pat still looked mutinous so she hurriedly changed the subject.

'That reminds me. You visit old Bert Pryke regularly, don't you? I've been meaning to ask you how you find him. Do you think he's *compos mentis* and knows what he's talking about?'

'Bert Pryke?'

'Yes. The last time I went round to give him house communion he was complaining about his niece and accusing her of planning to do him in. He was really convinced about it and I couldn't shake him. What's the matter?' Rachel had noticed the expression on her friend's face.

'Bert Pryke is dead.'

'Dead! But how . . . ? When . . . ?'

'Two days ago. I'm surprised you haven't heard through the grapevine.'

'How did he die?'

'He wasn't murdered, I can tell you that. A massive heart attack.'

'Are you sure?'

'Of course I am. It's not my responsibility to give cause of death — his doctor did that — but I can assure you he died of a massive coronary. I was the one who found him.'

'Oh, Pat, how come?'

'I went round to give him his morning injection and dress his legs. Madge Porter was out but she always leaves the door unlocked for me so I went in and up the stairs to his room and found him dead in his chair. It must have happened just before I got there. Don't look like that. It was very sudden, he didn't suffer. A good way to go.'

'It just seems so . . . odd.' Rachel pushed her cup away and frowned. 'One minute he's telling me his niece wants him out of the way, and the next minute he's dead. He did actually say he'd heard them plotting to get rid of him.'

'You mustn't believe everything the old tell you. Apart from being muddled they quite often say the most outrageous things just to get a little attention and sympathy. His niece gave him a home and looked after him in his twilight years. He didn't know how lucky he was. Some of the cases I see . . . '

'So he just had a heart attack out of the blue?'

'He had a dicky heart. It could have happened at any time, and what with that and his diabetes and arthritis I reckon he had a good innings.'

'Poor Bert, let's hope he rests in peace, though he wouldn't be happy to know that his nephew will now inherit his property.'

'I didn't know he had a nephew or that he owned any property.'

'He told me that he still owned the bungalow he used to live in and that Madge wanted it for her son, who apparently didn't see eye to eye with Bert. I must go round and see if she wants any help with the funeral arrangements. I'm sure Bert would have wanted a service in St Luke's.'

★ ★ ★

'He's cocking a snook at us.' Superintendent Bairstow shuffled his papers and glared at DI Trevor Dickins, who was hovering on the other side of the desk. 'Not only does he carry out a brazen killing in a tightly secure unit, but he makes sure we know who is responsible. Sit down, Trevor, and give me the facts such as they are.'

'It happened at 4.45 p.m. Scott was wired up to a cardiac monitor and when the screen suddenly blacked out the alarm was sounded and the resuscitation team went into action. They found him lying back against the pillows with a single stab wound through his chest. All the wires had been pulled off his body and the drip out of his arm.'

'So whoever did it knew exactly where to strike.'

'Quentin has done the autopsy but he says there was little bleeding although the knife actually penetrated the heart and there should have been copious bleeding.'

'What does he mean by that?'

'He thinks Scott must have seen his assailant approaching and the shock precipitated another heart attack, a fatal one this time. He reckons he was dead before the murderer struck.'

'It was still murder.'

'Yes. The general alarm was raised but there was no sign of his attacker anywhere on the hospital floor.'

'But you said the crash team were on the scene only seconds after it happened — how could he have got away so quickly?'

'The staff nurse has vague memories of seeing a hospital porter wheeling a chair down the corridor as they scrambled, but in the general kerfuffle no one took any notice.'

'Diabolical in its simplicity.'

'Yes. You expect to see porters in hospital corridors, most people wouldn't even register it. He chose his time well; after visiting hours and before the evening meal. Plenty going on in the hospital but no one likely to be in the victim's room. He must have gone into the hospital with the visitors, hidden himself in a bog and put on a porter's uniform and then helped himself to a wheelchair and walked down to Scott's room as bold as brass. If anyone *had* seen him he'd have had to abandon it then and try again later. No one would have challenged him.'

'And no fingerprints, of course,' said Bairstow heavily.

'No, he wore gloves and presumably pocketed the knife after using it. It was only after we were called in that the sister noticed the Coil Shuffler's visiting card pushed into the frame above the bed where the consultant's name should have been.'

'It points to someone familiar with hospital routine. Are we looking for someone in the medical profession?'

'No, I don't think so, sir. Anyone could familiarise themselves with the set-up after a few visits as a *bona fide* member of the public. Our man is quick and audacious but I don't think he needed any specialist knowledge to carry out his execution.'

'What about the knifing itself? A single stab wound right through the heart points to someone who knew what he was doing and where to strike.'

'His victim was a sitting duck, lying there with his chest exposed, completely helpless. You don't need to be a surgeon to realise that any deep wound in the heart area is going to kill.'

'I don't agree. Put yourself in the killer's place, Trevor. You approach your victim and when he sees you he conks out. You don't know whether he's just passed out or died from shock so you stab him. How do you know you've killed him if he's already unconscious? Wouldn't you make sure you'd finished him off by stabbing him a couple of times more? Unless you were quite positive your first thrust had done the trick?'

Trevor Dickins shrugged. 'I still think he's an opportunist who gets lucky.'

'What about Eddie Briers? That was a professional job.'

'Again, you don't have to be an anatomy expert to cut someone's throat. It was a case of careful planning beforehand and then not hesitating when he got his chance. Our chappie's got iron nerves and he certainly isn't squeamish.'

'What about the knife — any luck with that?'

'Quentin says it was a single-edged thin blade about seven inches long. It could be the same one that was used on Briers but as it was a different action he won't commit himself.'

'Hmmm. That leaves us with motive. Who wanted him dead? What about the wife and family?'

'His wife seems genuinely cut up, likewise his two married daughters. I can't see a motive there.'

'He was well off, wasn't he? Threw his money about, from what I've heard. Where there's a sizeable inheritance involved there is always a motive. You should know that.'

'I've picked up hints of planning irregularities connected with his business.'

'Is that so?'

'Not directly involving him, but earlier transactions involving colleagues that he turned a blind eye to at the time but was now threatening to pull the plug on as a newly established pillar of society. It's strange, isn't it, how once they've made their pile they want to turn respectable? He was a Mason, wasn't he?'

'Are you asking me or telling me?' said Bairstow blandly. 'It certainly begins to look as if somebody could have wanted him out of the way and hired a contract killer. The first thing to do is to investigate his business associates and the members of the planning committee on the Council.'

'What, all of them?'

'If there has been any hanky-panky going on someone will have suspected something somewhere along the line and someone will bleat. I'm putting you in charge of this investigation and I want it cleared up quickly. There must be a tie-up with the earlier cases involving the Coil Shuffler. Go back over them and see if you can turn anything up but keep it low key. With prominent people involved this could provide a field day for the Press if they get their teeth into it. There's bound to be public speculation over both Briers' and Scott's deaths as they are so well known locally, but I don't want any mention of the Coil Shuffler to get in the papers. Now get moving and keep me up to date with every development.'

★ ★ ★

The *Clarion*'s front page the next day was full of the latest murder. There was no mention of the Coil Shuffler but veiled allusions to gang warfare and innuendos about the apparent impotence of the police in dealing with the Mafioso element terrorising the streets of the city.

Michael Croft was reading the report in the evening edition when Nick Holroyd called round.

'Have you read this? 'Council official silenced in Godfather stranglehold'? — how the hell did the Press get to hear of it almost before the police were called in?'

'Someone must have leaked it. I'm wondering if it will help or hinder us in our investigation,' said Holroyd, throwing his jacket on to a chair and helping himself to another seat.

'You're still determined to follow this up?'

'You bet, and I've had some success already. My contact at the *Weekly Digest* came up trumps.'

'No prize for betting it's a female?'

'How did you guess? She looked up the Coil Shuffler's advert and we now have a name, though it's a hundred to one against it being the real one. The first contact with the paper about the advert was made over the phone, but those details are not on record. The caller must have been told the terms and price and then sent a letter setting out the wording for the advert and enclosing a postal order to pay for it and a run-on advert for several weeks.'

'So what was the name and address?'

'The name was Jean Duclos but there was no address. The writer said that they were travelling about the country and hadn't got a permanent address at that moment but asked for the replies to be sent to Roseberry Road Post Office, marked Poste Restante, to await collection.'

'Jean — a woman?'

'Ah, but is it? Jean might be a Frenchman. Our Coil Shuffler's not stupid. With a name like that he could arrange for a man *or* a woman to pick up the replies if he didn't want to do it himself. As long as they had some means of identification that said they were Jean Duclos he could arrange for a man to do it one week and next time a woman as long as there was someone different on the counter serving them. That way no one would remember their identity if it was queried later.'

'So what did the staff of Roseberry Road PO have to say about it? I'm sure you followed it up their end.'

'Yes, but I wasn't so lucky there.' Holroyd grimaced. 'I couldn't make an official enquiry and it wouldn't have helped me if I had. To get any information out of them I'd have had to have had a warrant and go through their Post Office Investigation Division. What they did tell me was that the Poste Restante service is free of charge and as long as your name and the full address of the post office is on the correspondence you can pick it up at any time during opening hours as long as you can prove you are that person. However, you can only use it for three months. As my lass at the *Weekly Digest* told me, it's a service for people who are travelling or holidaying and are temporarily without a permanent address. I suppose after the three months is up the Coil Shuffler could arrange for his replies to be sent to another post office in the area.'

'You know Trevor Dickins has been put in charge of the case?'

'Yes, which makes me all the more eager to get in first before that smart-arse. What has he got so far on this latest killing — do you know?'

They were still discussing it a little while later when the doorbell rang. Croft answered it to find Rachel Morland standing on the doorstep.

'Hello, Mike, sorry to call round

unexpectedly like this but I need to see you.'

She was dressed in green cords and a scarlet anorak and her cheeks were flushed and her hair slightly tousled as if she had been hurrying.

'It's great to see you, but is anything wrong?'

'There's something I want to discuss with you. Something I think you should know.'

'Well come on in, but I think I should tell you that Nick's here.'

She hesitated and then said something that surprised him.

'He's a policeman too, so that's all right.'

She followed him into the sitting-room and Holroyd made to get up from his chair.

'You didn't tell me you were expecting company,' he accused his friend.

'Mike didn't know that I was coming.'

'Sit down, Rachel,' Croft waved towards the sofa, 'let me get you a drink.'

'I can't stay long. I've . . . I've got a problem and I decided the best thing to do was to tell you about it and you'd know what to do, if anything ought to be done.'

'Look, if this is anything personal I'd better love you and leave you.' Holroyd stood up properly this time.

'No, it's all right, Nick, this concerns the

police — or at least I think they ought to know.'

'This sounds ominous. You're not going to accuse us of falling down in our duty, are you?'

'Shut up, Nick. What are you going to have to drink?'

'A dry sherry, please.'

When she had taken off her jacket and was seated comfortably sipping her sherry she smiled apologetically at the two men who were waiting expectantly.

'I haven't made much sense so far, have I? I'd better tell you what's happened and you can decide if it should be taken any further. In my capacity as a lay reader I do a lot of house visiting — to parishioners who are too old or too ill or whatever to attend church. Sometimes it is just a case of calling in for a chat but I often take the sacrament to housebound people. One of my regulars was an old chap called Bert Pryke.'

She explained the set-up in the Porter household, wondering, as she saw the bored expression on Nick Holroyd's face, why she was bothering. As she faltered to a close he raised one eyebrow.

'So what's the problem?'

'The problem is that the last time that I saw him, which was about ten days ago, he was convinced that his niece and her husband were plotting to do away with him.'

Now she had their full attention.

'Did you believe him?' Mike leaned forward and a cushion fell off his chair. He picked it up and placed it behind him without taking his eyes off her face.

'*He* believed what he was saying. He was convinced he was in danger, but he was old and getting muddled . . . ' She told them exactly what Bert had said and then relayed her later conversation with Madge Porter.

'I don't see what the police can do. We can hardly mount a guard on the old boy or accuse his niece of planning his death just on his say-so.'

'If we interfered every time someone in a family threatened another member,' Nick intervened, 'we'd have practically every family in the land banged up.'

'You don't understand. He's dead.'

'Dead? Why didn't you say so! When was this?'

'Three days ago.'

'Then the police *have* been informed. We've got a homicide on our hands?'

'No. The doctor said he'd died from a coronary and signed the death certificate. He didn't suspect foul play and my friend, who is the district nurse who saw to him, agrees.

She can't understand why I am suspicious.'

'So why are you suspicious?'

'I don't really know,' confessed Rachel, opening out her hands. 'It's just that one day he's telling me someone is trying to kill him and the next he's dead. Wouldn't that worry you?'

'We policemen have very suspicious minds. But if the doctor is satisfied he died from a heart attack and there is no evidence to the contrary how else could he have died?'

'I don't know, but he was old and sick . . . You're policemen, detectives, used to dealing with this sort of thing, you must have a better idea than me how it could be done.'

'You *really* think he was murdered?'

'Put like that you make me feel that I'm over-reacting. It's been worrying me ever since I heard that he was dead but I thought if I reported it to you you'd know what action to take and I'd have an easier conscience.'

'You don't happen to know by any chance whether one of these was left by his bedside?' Nick Holroyd delved in a pocket, and pulling out a facsimile of the Coil Shuffler's visiting card he held it out for her to take. 'What's the matter? Is anything wrong?'

The card had slipped from her hand and it fluttered to the floor where she stared down at it in horror, her face blanching.

5

For a few seconds she thought she was going to faint, something she hadn't done since a teenager. There was an acid dryness in her throat and she could hear her pulse roaring in her ears. With a great effort she clawed her way back to reality and the two pairs of eyes facing her, Nick's suspicious, Mike's concerned.

'Sorry, I just feel a little dizzy. I must have overdone the jogging.'

'Have another drink.'

'No thanks. I've just remembered I've got another appointment. I must go.'

She got to her feet and managed not to cling to the chair back.

'Can't it wait? If you're feeling giddy you ought to rest.'

'It's all right, I'm okay now.' She fastened her jacket and tucked her handbag under her arm. 'Are you . . . Can you . . . do anything about what I've just told you?'

'Quite frankly, I don't see what the police can do,' said Mike, heaving himself out of his chair. 'I can understand you being concerned. It's a worrying coincidence whichever way you look at it but unless we've got some concrete evidence we couldn't justify postponing the funeral and ordering a PM.'

'No, I suppose not. I've probably over-reacted.'

Somehow she got herself out of the house and back to the car. She slid behind the wheel and drove home on automatic pilot. Afterwards, she had no recollection of the journey and had no idea what traffic she had met or how she had reacted to it but eventually she had found herself sitting in her garage staring at the blank end wall. Shivering, she got out of the car and let herself into the house. She hung her jacket in the hall cupboard and went into the sitting-room where she slumped in a chair.

Just when she had thought it was all over the old nightmare had surfaced again. The terrible questions concerning Christopher's death, which had never been properly answered, flooded back again. Christopher, who had been so sure in his faith until that last betrayal . . .

Against her will she left the sitting-room and ran up the stairs to the small back room which she used as a study. She unlocked the bureau and fumbled through the pigeon-holes and compartments. She knew she had kept it. In fact, she knew exactly where it was, she was only prevaricating. She opened the little drawer at the back of the writing flap and drew out the card.

* * *

Back at Belvoir Road the two policemen were discussing Rachel's odd behaviour.

'She'd seen the Coil Shuffler's card before, that was perfectly obvious,' said Holroyd, mooching round the room.

'I don't see how you can jump to that conclusion,' protested his friend.

'Oh, come on, Mike. You saw her reaction when I showed it to her. She bloody nearly passed out.'

'Look, she was feeling under the weather — she admitted it — and she was worried about that old boy. You producing that card like a rabbit out of a hat was probably the last straw. Anyone who is religious would be upset at reading something like that — an open invitation to euthanasia or worse.'

'I'm sure she recognised that card. She'd seen one like it before and it shocked her. I think your Mrs Morland has a past; she's not the innocent young cleric you think she is.'

'And I think you're obsessed with this Coil Shuffler. How could Rachel possibly be involved?'

'She admits she visits people on their deathbeds. Perhaps there was another suspicious death earlier that she was in on and this card triggered off the memory?'

'Why don't you ask her?'

'I may well do that.'

'You bloody lay off her! Just because you've got a one-track mind at the moment you're not going to bugger up my love life!'

'You really are smitten, aren't you? A woman of the cloth who's mourning a dead husband: I reckon you've got yourself an uphill job.'

'You wouldn't be jealous by any chance, would you, Nick?'

'Jealous? Now who's being fucking ridiculous!'

'You don't like the idea of me showing a little independence and getting myself another woman. Poor old Mike, lost out in the love stakes and his career, must look after him and stop him brooding — I know just how you feel. You think you've got to oversee my every move, run my life for me. Well, I'm grateful for your help but it's *my* life and you're not going to take it over completely!'

'Hell, Mike, I'd no idea you felt like this . . . ' Nick was flabbergasted. 'I thought you needed my support, I didn't mean to stifle you.'

107

'Well, enough said. We go back a long way and I've got used to seeing your ugly mug around but let's leave Rachel out of it, shall we?'

'Forget I mentioned her if it makes you happy.' Nick picked up his jacket and shouldered himself into it. 'I'm off.'

'Already? Aren't you organising my take-away this evening?'

'No. And not because of what you've just said. I've got some serious thinking to do.'

'Do you know, I get even more apprehensive when you go all cerebral on me.'

'Don't lose any sleep over it.' Nick slammed out of the door and poked his head back inside grinning nastily. 'By the way, do you still want a lift tomorrow?'

'Okay, get your own back and watch me grovel. Yes, please.'

'*Ciao.*'

Once back in his car Nick didn't drive off straight away. Instead he sat behind the wheel and went over in his mind the recent scene with Rachel Morland. Mike was obviously besotted with her and he'd have to tread warily but something was hovering on the edge of his consciousness. Something he ought to be able to recall but couldn't . . . It had nudged him when he had held out the Coil Shuffler's card to her and she

108

had let it drop. As the colour had drained from her face and he had seen the panic in her eyes he had had the sudden feeling that he had seen her before, somewhere in the past. No, that couldn't be true. If he had met her earlier he would have remembered as soon as Mike had introduced them. Yet that memory of her white face, momentarily frozen, haunted him.

He couldn't have actually met her in person before but he had seen a photograph — that was it! There had been a photo of her. Where? In the local paper? But in what context? Something had happened, some accident . . . He searched his memory. Something to do with her husband. He was dead . . . died from cancer, hadn't Mike said? The Reverend Morland . . . The name rang a bell. The Reverend Morland. He knew that he was on to something but there was nothing he could do that evening. As he drove back home he pondered on the elusive memory that was just out of reach.

Next morning he caught up with John Swinburn, the Coroner's Officer.

'Does the name Morland mean anything to you?'

'Morland? Just that — no first moniker?'

'He was a parson. The Reverend Morland. Died a couple of years ago.'

109

'Ah, Christopher Morland. I remember the case. He topped himself.'

'What! I understood he had died from cancer.'

'He was terminally ill and took an overdose. Understandable, poor bastard, but the wife kicked up a stink. Said it was impossible.'

'Rachel Morland?'

'That's right. What's all this in aid of? Do you know her?'

'I've met her and it triggered off a memory.'

'Attractive young woman, from what I remember, but so insistent he couldn't have committed suicide that if the Coroner had taken her seriously she could have ended up in court on a murder charge.'

'Can you dig out the details?'

'No can do, as you know full well. They're filed with the Coroner's records and you'd need official permission to see them.'

'Come on, John, you could look them up for me, just a peek.'

'I've got better things to do with my time and you haven't told me yet why you're interested in the case.'

'Idle curiosity.'

'Then I'm certainly not obliging you. I'll tell you one thing though — it was widely reported in the Press at the time.'

'Can you give me a date?'

'Two years ago is about right and it was this time of year. I remember it was during a cold snap and when the heating was turned on for the first time that autumn it was on the blink and the courtroom was like a morgue.'

'Thanks, John. Why do we need computer records when we've got you?'

He was busy sorting out schedules and writing up reports for most of the day and it wasn't until late afternoon that he managed to get away and visit the *Clarion* offices. The archives department was in the basement of the building and he was well acquainted with the man in charge, a middle-aged asthmatic whose work environs could hardly have been less conducive to bronchial health.

'Afternoon, Nick, how's tricks?'

'Overworked and underpaid. And yourself?'

'Could say the same. I've come to the conclusion the world would be a better place if there was less of the written word.'

'Then you'd be out of a job.'

'I knew there was a catch in it somewhere. What can I do for you?'

'I want to look at some back numbers of the *Clarion*.'

'Not pre-war, I hope.'

'Your luck's in. Only two years back. September and October of '95.'

'That shouldn't be difficult. Bear with me and I'll fish them out for you.'

A short while later Holroyd was poring over the relevant newspapers. The *Clarion* had changed from broadsheet to tabloid earlier that year and although thicker the volumes were easier to thumb through. He found what he was looking for in the fifth paper he opened. The photo jumped out at him, unmistakably Rachel Morland. Her hair was longer and worn in a different style but the face and haunted expression was the same. Underneath, the caption proclaimed: 'Vicar's wife denies suicide bid.' He settled down to read.

★ ★ ★

'Where's Holroyd?' Douglas Bairstow's voice was quietly ominous as he strode into Traffic Control and confronted the two young constables who looked warily at each other before denying knowledge of their sergeant's whereabouts.

'Right. When he deigns to report in or honour us with his presence will you tell him I want to see him in my office *immediately*.'

The superintendent stalked out and had only been gone a few seconds before Nick sauntered in.

'The Super wants to see you in his office, pronto.'

'Does he now. Well, we mustn't keep him waiting, must we?' But Holroyd pottered around, sorting out papers on his desk for a good five minutes before he answered the summons, to the secret admiration of his colleagues.

Bairstow looked up inscrutably from the report he was studying when Holroyd knocked and entered.

'You wanted to see me, sir?'

'Yes, Holroyd. How are you finding Traffic Control?'

'Sir?'

'Getting a little bored, are we?'

'Sir?'

'Is that all you can say? You're beginning to bore *me*, Holroyd.'

'I don't understand.'

'What are you playing at, man? You are section sergeant in charge of panda cars. I should have thought that kept you busy enough.'

'Yes, sir.'

'So why are you meddling in a case currently under investigation by the CID;

113

of which, may I remind you, you are no longer a member?'

'I'm sorry. I don't know to what you are referring, sir.'

'Perhaps if I mention Roseberry Road Post Office it will jog your memory.'

'Oh . . .'

'Well, Holroyd?'

'I happened to come across a reference to the Coil Shuffler and as I was in the area I thought I'd try and follow it up.' Nick Holroyd sought to defuse the situation whilst wondering just how much the superintendent knew.

'I will not have that name bandied around on every policeman's lips. This is a top-security investigation and there is to be no risk of a leak the Press could pick up on.'

'Sir, the entire station knows that there are two current murder enquiries plus several unsolved cases that involve a hit-man who calls himself the Coil Shuffler. I was involved in one of those earlier cases myself. Naturally, when I saw this advert in the local rag I felt I had to follow it up.'

'Words fail me, officer.' Bairstow pushed himself up from his desk and walked over to the window where he rested his hands on the sill behind him and leaned forward. 'You picked up a reference to the Coil Shuffler and

114

you felt you had to follow it up . . . Your duty was to bring that evidence immediately to the attention of the investigating officer.'

At that point Bairstow remembered the animosity between Nick Holroyd and Trevor Dickins but pressed on. 'One of my best men is in charge of this investigation and when he also came across this evidence and pursued it he found that someone had got there before him and muddied up the trail. A uniformed sergeant blundering about where he had no business to be, asking questions that put up the back of the Post Office staff. You didn't get anywhere with them, did you?'

'No, sir.'

'You are *not* involved in this case. If I hear of you interfering again you're out, do you understand? And that applies to any of my men found withholding evidence. You've been warned before and I'm telling you, this is your last chance. Do the job you've been given and leave others to do theirs. Do I make myself clear?'

A subdued but unrepentant Holroyd made his escape from the superintendent's office and went in search of Michael Croft.

'I've just been given a bollocking by the Super. That toe-rag Dickins found out I'd been nosing into the Coil Shuffler's advert and went bleating to him.'

115

'I warned you. I hope you didn't drop me in it?'

'You're pure as the driven snow.'

'Good. You're not on duty tomorrow, are you?'

'No, it's my Saturday off, why?'

'Rachel wants to see us. She's asked us to go round to her place tomorrow morning.'

'Us? You mean she wants to see me as well as you?'

'Yes. I can't think why. She was all mysterious on the phone but insisted on both of us. Said she had something to show us.'

'I bet she has.'

'And what do you mean by that?'

'Nothing.' Nick had been about to blurt out the story he had culled from the back numbers of the *Clarion* but in view of the invitation he decided to say nothing for the moment. 'Well, I'll pick you up tomorrow morning. What time have we been summoned?'

'She suggested ten thirty.'

'Let's hope she does a good line in coffee. I don't suppose there'll be anything else on offer, unless it's communion wine.'

'What do you know of communion wine?'

★ ★ ★

When they drew up outside Rachel Morland's flat the next morning there was another car already parked in the driveway.

'Looks as if she's got company. Very nice, a Rover 620 — maybe you've got a rival.'

Nick pulled in behind it. The two men got out and Mike rang the bell. Rachel opened the door almost immediately.

'Hello, glad you could make it.'

'This is not a coffee morning in aid of church funds, is it?' Nick indicated the other car.

'No, it belongs to a friend. I want you to meet her, she's in on this too.'

'You certainly know how to whet a policeman's curiosity,' said Mike, limping across the threshold. 'I take it we're here in our official capacity?'

'Oh, no. I mean . . . well, maybe.'

She led the way through the hall into a sitting-room that overlooked the back garden. It was furnished comfortably with an assortment of furniture that did not match. Vases and ornaments were dotted around and pictures hung on the walls in an attempt to make it more homely and to stamp her personality on the place, but Nick reckoned she had probably rented it furnished and not many of the contents actually belonged to her. There was a transient look about the

117

flat, as if it were a resting place rather than a permanent home. Still, he mused, if she was going to be a parson presumably she would inherit a vicarage or rectory; that went with the job.

She took their coats and waved them into chairs and as they sat down a small, plump woman appeared in the doorway leading to the kitchen.

'I've just put the kettle on, dear.' She beamed at Rachel and the two men.

'Pat, this is Michael Croft and his colleague, Nick Holroyd.'

'Pleased to meet you, I've heard a lot about you.'

'This is my friend, Pat Fenton. She is a district nurse.'

The two men acknowledged the introduction. Late forties or early fifties; competent, good natured and sexless, Mike summed her up quickly. What used to be known as the salt of the earth. Why had Rachel asked them both round and why did she want them to meet this Pat Fenton? She was in no hurry to enlighten them. It wasn't until some time later, after they had finished their coffee and the small-talk was petering out, that she seemed to come to a decision.

'I've got something to show you.' She picked up her handbag, which had been lying beside the television set, and abstracted her wallet from it. Out of this she produced a card which she held out to them. It was the Coil Shuffler's visiting card.

'Rachel! Where did you get this?' Mike snatched it from her hand.

'I . . . I found it after my husband died.'

'You mean after he committed suicide.' Nick couldn't keep the triumph out of his voice.

'How did you . . . know?'

'I've been checking up on you, Rachel. I'm a nasty, suspicious policeman.'

'Checking up on me? What do you mean? Mike, I don't understand.' She appealed to Mike, who answered grimly:

'Neither do I. What is this all about, Nick?'

'Suppose we let Rachel tell us. That's why she's asked us here, isn't it?'

She met the challenge in his eyes and turned to Pat Fenton, who nodded encouragingly. 'You'd better tell them, dear, get it off your chest.'

Rachel sat down slowly and stared out of the window as she started to speak.

'Christopher had terminal cancer. We both knew he wasn't going to get better and we faced up to it. He looked on it as his last challenge; overcoming the pain and distress and winning through to his eternal rest. Death wasn't the end but the beginning of his new glorious life with God. He looked on his cancer as his own Gethsemane, his crucifixion, and said if Jesus could win through His Passion to the other side the least he could do was to offer up his suffering to God and trust in a place by His side . . . Oh, you don't understand, do you? You don't know what I'm talking about.'

'Rachel, don't distress yourself.'

'It's all right, Mike, I've got to make this quite clear to you. He accepted his suffering and we both — at least, I — prayed that the end would not be too terrible and drawn out.'

There was pain in her fine dark eyes as she looked at the two men, and Pat Fenton put a comforting hand on her shoulder. She swallowed and continued:

'I nursed him at home. We hoped he would remain at home as long as possible, but although I hated leaving him alone, I obviously had to go out sometimes. I went into the city one afternoon. I had a dentist's appointment and some shopping to do and I was away longer than usual. When I got back he was dead. He was lying on the sofa and there was an empty pill bottle on the floor beside him — his painkillers.

I couldn't believe it . . . I still can't believe it. Christopher would never have committed suicide — I was sure of that.' She looked wildly at them, and Mike asked:

'What did you do?'

'I rang the doctor and then I rang Pat. The doctor was out on a call and Pat got there first, but before she arrived I found that card tucked under the cushion his head was lying on . . . '

As Rachel seemed loth to continue Pat Fenton took up the tale.

'I realised as soon as I got there that nothing could be done for Christopher and I was more concerned about Rachel. She was in a terrible state.'

'Were you surprised that he had committed suicide?' asked Nick.

'Yes, I was, but in a way I was also relieved, if you can see what I mean. He'd saved himself and Rachel an awful lot of suffering. Anyway, I gave her a brandy and was trying to calm her down when she showed me that card.'

'So what did you think?'

'Well, it was obvious, wasn't it? He was weak and debilitated and I suppose his resolve gave way and he contacted a euthanasia society. They must have supplied him with information about how many painkillers he needed for a lethal dose.'

'Christopher *didn't* commit suicide,' protested Rachel, her nostrils flaring.

'Then what do you think happened?' asked Mike, longing to put his arms round her but resisting the temptation.

'I don't know . . . I've gone over it again and again and I just don't know . . . '

'If your husband didn't take an overdose himself are you saying that someone else helped him to it?'

'You mean . . . killed him?'

'Yes.'

'No, that's an even crazier idea. Who could have wanted to kill him?'

'I kept telling her not to harp on about it so much,' said Pat Fenton. 'She kept insisting he hadn't committed suicide and I was afraid the police were going to think she had done it to put him out of his misery.'

'I presume the police were called in by the doctor?' interposed Nick, trying not to sound too eager.

'Yes,' said Pat Fenton, 'and there was a PM and an inquest but she persuaded me not to mention that card.'

'Why?' Nick challenged Rachel.

'Because I knew if they saw that they'd definitely think he had committed suicide and I didn't want that.'

'There was no suicide note. No coroner is going to bring in a verdict of suicide without a note. It was an open verdict, wasn't it?'

'Yes.'

'So the police never saw that card?'

'No. I meant to throw it away, destroy it, but for some reason I've hung on to it. When you produced that other one yesterday I thought for one moment that you'd somehow got hold of it and it was a terrible shock. Where *did* you get it from?'

'It turned up in another suspicious case.'

'Is it a euthanasia society advertising its services?' demanded Pat Fenton, eyeing the card warily.

'No, we don't think so.'

'Then what is it?'

Mike raised his eyebrows at Nick and receiving a shrug in reply he leaned forward and addressed the two women earnestly.

'This is strictly in confidence but I'd better put you in the picture as you're involved. We've got a hit-man operating in this area who appears to be running a one-man business in eliminating people.'

'You mean here, in this city?'

'Yes.'

'But that's unbelievable . . . like something out of an American movie.'

'It happens in every community where

there is a flourishing underworld, which means most places these days.'

'Those two murders — it said in the papers something about the Mafia and gang warfare. Is that what you mean?'

'You mustn't believe everything you read in the Press, but yes, we think they were both contract killings and this character is not just operating amongst the criminal fraternity; he's openly touting for business by advertising.'

'You mean he's advertising his services as a *killer*,' gasped Rachel. 'How horrible!'

'What are the police doing about it?' demanded Pat Fenton.

'So far we haven't got a line on him but we'll get him in time. He calls himself the Coil Shuffler and this is his calling card. As you see, it is very ambiguous and all kinds of meanings could be read into it.'

'How does he advertise?'

'We're following this up but I can tell you that it has actually appeared in a local newspaper.'

'How *can* someone go around killing people for profit?' cried Rachel. 'Is he a psychopath?'

'Not in the way you mean. As you say, this character is motivated by profit which is not what turns on most psychos. The way

I see it, he killed once and got away with it and realised he was on to a good thing and became a professional killer.'

'You make it sound like a career! It's not like stealing or embezzlement; it's the ultimate crime — taking someone's life.'

'Yes, but once you've killed you've put yourself outside society. There is no going back so you go on. It's a truism but it holds good; after the first time it becomes easier and eventually it means no more than swatting a fly or shooting vermin. Our Coil Shuffler is cold-blooded and calculating and completely without a conscience but he'll make a mistake and then we'll get him.'

'This is the case you're working on?'

'The CID is giving this investigation top priority.'

'But Mike and I are doing a probe around ourselves,' put in Nick giving her a wink.

'You mean you're doing it unofficially — is this a good idea?'

'We think we can contribute something to the enquiry,' he replied blandly. 'Officialdom doesn't always get results.'

Rachel shook her head and looked up at the photo displayed on the bookcase. 'How did Christopher come to get one of those cards?'

Nick followed her gaze. He saw a fair-haired, chubby-faced man in a dog-collar smiling easily at the camera.

'That's the million-dollar question.' He turned his attention to Pat Fenton. 'As a district nurse you must have dealt with many deaths. Have you ever come across any that were unexpected and surprised you?'

She considered this. 'Don't forget most of my patients are old and ailing, I'm just helping to postpone the inevitable end. Sometimes someone goes sooner than you expected, on the other hand I've known people to linger long after they should be dead according to medical lore. I can't say I've ever been suspicious and I certainly haven't seen one of those cards.'

At that moment a phone trilled and she reached inside the holdall beside her chair and took out her mobile phone. After a few monosyllabic replies she grimaced and pushed back the aerial. 'I've got to go. I'm wanted at the Carlton Road Clinic.'

'It's nice to know we poor coppers are not the only ones who have to work on a Saturday morning.'

'I sometimes feel I'm on call twenty-four hours a day.' Pat Fenton buttoned up her coat and rummaged in her bag for her car keys. 'It's been nice meeting you. Perhaps you can put Rachel's mind at rest. She's started worrying about that card again but I've told her there's not much you can do after all this time, is there?'

'No, the trail will be cold by now. However, you can help by keeping your eyes and ears open and letting us know if you come across anything suspicious in the course of your work — but don't let it go any further. This is strictly undercover.'

After she had left Rachel brewed up some fresh coffee and whilst they were drinking it brought up the subject of Bert Pryke again.

'I know I said I was uneasy about his death but I can't believe his niece would have hired someone to kill him.'

'You'd prefer to think that one of the family bumped him off themselves?' asked Nick.

'That sounds equally ridiculous. But I could understand, if she were really provoked, Madge Porter perhaps lashing out at him and knocking him over or some such scenario — but that would have been obvious to Pat and the doctor, wouldn't it?'

'Quite. It's not easy to commit undetectable homicide. If he was helped on his way it was done professionally. Your Mrs Porter could have seen the Coil Shuffler's advert and acted on it. She had a double reason, from what you've told us: gain and getting rid of an encumbrance. Powerful motives, both of them.'

'No, I can't take that on board.'

'You would if you'd had to deal with some of the situations we come across in our work. We believe the Coil Shuffler was active in another similar case; an elderly woman whose son wanted her out of the way and who died very opportunely.'

'Rachel, you didn't go round to the house after Bert Pryke died, did you?' said Mike, putting down his coffee-cup and helping himself to another biscuit.

'No, I told you, I didn't even know he'd died until Pat mentioned it.'

'How long ago was it?'

'Five days. It would have been this last Tuesday.'

'Could you go round? As his spiritual adviser could you think of an excuse to visit?'

'I was going to go round. I don't know what arrangements they've made for the funeral but I was going to call and see if they wanted someone from St Luke's to officiate at the funeral service.'

'Perfect. Once you're inside try and get a good look round.'

'What for?'

'Another one of these?' Nick held up the Coil Shuffler's card between his thumb and index finger.

'Surely if someone is going round killing people to order the last thing they'd do is draw attention to themselves?'

'You'd think so, wouldn't you? But not our Coil Shuffler. He wants the police to know he's responsible. This card is his signature to a crime. Not only is he cold-blooded and calculating — he has a monstrous ego as well.'

★ ★ ★

'He's being cremated. Next Tuesday morning at eleven o'clock.' Madge Porter regarded her visit with little enthusiasm.

'Have you arranged for someone to conduct the service?' asked Rachel, wondering if she was even going to get inside the house.

'They fix that for you at the crematorium. The funeral director said there was a duty rota.'

'Wouldn't you like someone from St Luke's to do it? Bert was a member.'

'Well, I don't know . . . '

'Look, can I come in and discuss it?'

Madge Porter led the way reluctantly into the sitting-room.

129

'He hadn't been to church for years.'

'No, we came to him, but he was still part of St Luke's family. You must miss him — how long did he live with you?'

'Three years. Miss him? I suppose I do but I don't miss the work. Still, I mustn't grumble. He wasn't such a bad old man and you couldn't wish him back. He hated being ill and he'd had a good life.'

The number of times she had heard these same platitudes, thought Rachel. Meaningless waffle.

'Could I go up to his room?'

'Whatever for?'

'To say a few prayers.'

Rachel felt sure she was going to refuse but at that moment the phone rang.

'Well, I suppose so. You know the way.'

Whilst she went into the hall to answer it Rachel went upstairs and into Bert's bedroom. It had been stripped. A single folded blanket lay on the bare mattress and his orthopaedic chair was pushed into a corner and denuded of cushions. All his personal belongings, his knick-knacks, books and photos, had gone and the heating had been turned off in the room. The fusty, old-man smell had been replaced by disinfectant and aerosol freshener. She didn't take long to remove all traces of poor Bert, thought Rachel, looking round in dismay. The idea of finding the Coil Shuffler's card was ridiculous, still she made a quick search of the room. She found Bert's walking-stick behind the curtain propped against the window-sill where it had been overlooked. She fingered it gently and then dropped to her knees and prayed for the repose of his soul.

When she returned downstairs Madge Porter had finished her phone call and Rachel tackled her again about the funeral service.

'You mean *you'd* take it?' said the older woman disparagingly.

'I could do, if that's what you would like.'

'But you're not a proper priest.'

'I'm licensed to conduct funeral services, but if you'd rather I can ask David Bell, our vicar.'

'Yes, that would be better.'

'I don't know if he will be available on Tuesday morning, but if not, perhaps Simon Protheroe, our curate, can do it. Look, can I phone him from here — it will save time.'

'Help yourself.' Madge Porter nodded at the phone which sat on an ornate wrought-iron shelf in the hall. 'I'm in the middle of cooking, so I'll leave you to it.'

And thank you for your gracious welcome and offer of a cup of tea, thought Rachel sagely as she picked up the receiver. Still, Christopher used to complain that he drank so much tea and coffee during his house visits that he might as well have been permanently on diuretics. She punched in the number of St Luke's vicarage and the phone was answered by Hazel, David Bell's wife.

'He's not here, Rachel. He's over at the Hospice and he was planning to spend the whole afternoon there; taking a service in the chapel and then visiting some of the patients. I can give you the phone number and you should be able to contact him there.'

'Just a moment whilst I find a pen and paper.'

Rachel looked amongst the papers and magazines stacked on the shelf and located the telephone pad. As she wrote down the number her elbow caught the pile and sent them tumbling to the ground. She thanked Hazel and replaced the receiver and bent down to retrieve them. Madge Porter was a hoarder. Old shopping lists, junk mail offers, even last year's calendar. She put them back in what she hoped was the right order and retrieved a newspaper that had skidded under the chair. It had been folded to display the advertisement page and one item had been encircled by pen. It jumped out at her:

PETS. Exits arranged — Painlessly, Efficiently, Tastefully. Apply: The Coil Shuffler. Box AJ 6108.

With shaking fingers she removed the page and tucked it into her handbag and then went to say her farewell to Madge Porter.

6

The next day being Sunday, Rachel hoped that Mike would be at home but when she rang early in the morning she only got his answerphone. Reluctant to go into detail about her find, she left a brief message asking him to get in touch and then got ready for church. After the service she excused herself from the usual Sunday morning ritual of coffee in the church hall, intending to rush home and see if Mike had left a message on her answerphone, but then she realised that she had to drive past the bottom of his road to reach her house so it made sense to call in person. He wasn't there and she guessed he must be at work so she turned the car round and drove to Brent Hill police station.

Although it was Sunday the station was in business. The visitors' carpark was nearly full and when she went into reception there were several people waiting on the benches lining the walls. The desk sergeant was coping with a nearly incoherent woman accompanied by a young toddler. At first Rachel thought she was reporting the loss of another child but it turned out to be the theft of a mountain bike from a son doing a paper round. By the time the harassed sergeant had taken down the details and dealt with the woman and the now screaming infant, Rachel was wondering if she had done right to go there or whether she should have waited and contacted Mike at home.

She asked to speak to him and the sergeant waved her to a seat and busied himself on the phone. A short while later Mike appeared. He limped over to where she was sitting, a worried look on his face.

'I'm sorry to interrupt you at work, Mike, I hope I haven't committed a gaffe.'

'No, it's okay. Any excuse to get out of the office.'

'This isn't a social visit. Can we talk somewhere?'

Nearby the toddler was still screaming and an old man in the corner was muttering and swearing between bouts of raucous coughing.

'Hang on, I'll fix something up.'

A few minutes later he showed her into an interview room and closed the door behind them

'Well, Mrs Morland?' He tilted her chin up with one questing finger and bent and kissed her full on the mouth. At first she froze with shock, then relaxed against him enjoying the long absent warmth and comfort of a male caress. After a few seconds she pulled away.

'I thought this was the place where you grilled your suspects,' she said shakily.

'You mustn't believe all you see on the cop-shop soaps. On the other hand, this is not normal procedure. Sit down and tell me what's up.'

'I've found something, Mike. I went round to where Bert Pryke used to live and I found this.'

She pulled the newspaper cutting out of her handbag and handed it to him.

'Christ! — sorry, Rachel — I never thought you'd actually get something. Where was it?'

She explained how she had found it. 'Would this count as proof that something fishy was going on?'

'This is the evidence we need to investigate it further. We've got something to go on now.'

'You'll really be able to do something?'

'Not me personally, I'm afraid, this will have to be taken up by the investigating officer.'

'I don't mind talking to anyone about Bert but I don't want Christopher's death brought up again. I don't have to mention the card I found then, do I?'

'No, that's history. Look, can you hang around a little longer? I'll try and have a word with the Super — I know he's in this morning — and he'll want to talk with you.'

'My time's my own until six o'clock this evening — Evensong,' she added as he looked perplexed.

'Good, I'll get you some coffee whilst you're waiting. Actually it's almost lunchtime — would you like something to eat?'

'Coffee's fine, I'm not hungry.'

'Are you all right in here? You can go back and sit in the waiting room if you'd rather.'

'No, it's quieter in here. I can look on it as a contemplative period. I'm always complaining that I never get the time.'

Michael Croft went off to find Douglas Bairstow, wondering if Rachel would be found on her knees praying when next she was interrupted and how it would be interpreted by the personnel of Brent Hill station.

* * *

By the time someone did come to talk to her Rachel had almost run out of patience. Mike had reappeared at one point with coffee and a packet of biscuits, regretted he could not stay with her and assured her she wouldn't have to wait long. It had started to rain, heavily by the sound of it. There was opaque glass in the window so she couldn't see the downpour but somewhere above was a cracked pipe or broken guttering and the water was gushing out and hitting the ground below like a miniature waterfall.

Trevor Dickins bowled into the room just as she was about to go out and explain to the desk sergeant that she couldn't wait any longer.

'Detective Inspector Dickins. And you're Mrs Morland?'

Rachel agreed that she was and he hitched a chair out with a foot and sat on it facing her.

'So you're a friend of Mike Croft?'

'Yes, and I'm his physiotherapist.'

'Putting him back together again, eh? Now, I think you've got something to tell me.'

'Haven't you already been told why I'm here?'

'Yes, but I'd like you to explain in your own words.'

Rachel felt herself stiffening. He had a cocky attitude that grated and he was talking down to her but she sensed he could be dangerous. She explained briefly about Bert Pryke's death and her suspicions.

'I can understand you having doubts. So you took your worries to your friend Mike.'

'Yes, and Mike said although it certainly seemed suspicious you couldn't do anything about it without some concrete evidence.'

'True, so how did you get your evidence?'

'I went back to the house to see his niece about the funeral arrangements.'

'I thought you said you were a physiotherapist? Don't tell me you're a funeral director on the side.'

Rachel explained her pastoral role and he pursed his lips and looked appraisingly at her.

'So I can rely on you telling the truth?'

'I'm not in the habit of lying,' she said coldly, 'are most of your witnesses?'

'Practically all of them. Even the ones with nothing to hide who are not being accused of anything. It is an occupational hazard but I am skilled at reading between the lines.'

I bet you are, she thought, and at twisting innocent statements to get the facts you want. He seemed to read her mind; his mouth moved in a sneering smile and he raised his brows above those protruding green eyes. 'We digress. You went back to the house where Bert Pryke had lived and had words with the niece you think did for him.'

Rachel started to protest and he interrupted. 'Okay, the niece who you think arranged his death. How did you find this?' He waved the paper at her and she told him how she had come across it.

'You saw this and immediately jumped to conclusions.'

'I told you — I was worried about his death and when I found that it seemed to clinch my suspicions. Wouldn't you have thought the same?'

'No, I don't think that I would. It's an odd advert open to all sorts of interpretations but I don't think I would have immediately thought that it was someone offering their services as a killer — unless I'd seen it before.'

'What do you mean?'

'Had you seen something like this before anywhere?'

'Should I have?' she countered.

'If I didn't know different I should say you went back to that house to look specifically for this.'

Just *what* had Mike told him? wondered Rachel, and she decided the only way to avoid mention of the Coil Shuffler's card was to mount an attack herself.

'Look, I don't know what I'm being

accused of. I came here in good faith to report a suspicious death and you're treating me as if *I'm* the culprit! Perhaps I'm wasting your time, in which case I'm sorry.' She got up and gathered together her handbag and gloves.

'Steady on, I'm not accusing you of anything, Mrs Morland. Rachel, isn't it? Well, Rachel, I just like to get my facts straight. Now, when Bert Pryke died the doctor was quite happy to sign the death certificate, wasn't he? He had no suspicions that the old chap had been helped on his way?'

'No, and neither had my friend.'

'Your friend?'

'She is the district nurse who attended him. She was the one who actually found him dead.'

'Really? Can I have her name and address? I shall want to speak to her and the doctor.'

Rachel gave him Pat Fenton's details. 'I don't know who his doctor was.'

'We can easily find that out.'

'What will happen now?'

'I think we've got grounds to postpone the funeral. We'll let the pathologist have a little look at him.'

'Will . . . Does Mrs Porter, his niece, have to know who . . . '

'Spilled the beans? Don't worry, I never

reveal my sources unless absolutely necessary. Thank you for coming in and keep on with the good work of getting old Mike back to normal. Hate to see him lurching about the place like a drunken sailor.'

It wasn't so much what he said as the way he said it, thought Rachel, as he ushered her out of the interview room. Sympathetic words but uttered as if he delighted in Mike's disability. As they were crossing reception the foyer door crashed open and Nick Holroyd swept in, divesting himself of his dripping cape and brushing his wet hair out of his eyes.

'Rachel! What are you doing here with this berk?'

'I might have known any friend of Mike Croft's would be pally with you as well. The terrible twins, we call them,' said Trevor Dickins to Rachel. 'She's been helping us with our enquiries,' he said to Holroyd, 'but I'm letting her go.'

'What's happened?'

'It's all right, Nick, I'll explain later. Goodbye, Inspector.'

'Goodbye, Rachel, and thanks for coming forward.' He tapped her proprietorially on the arm and left them.

'Rachel, indeed — do you know him?' snarled Nick.

'I met him for the first time this afternoon.'

'Why are you here?'

She told him the reason for her visit.

'You actually found something — brilliant. What a pity Dirty Dickins had to deal with it.'

'I take it you don't like him.'

'You can say that again.'

By this time they were in the foyer and Nick regarded her with concern.

'You're going to get soaked. It's chucking it down out there — have you got an umbrella?'

'No, but my car's parked nearby.'

'How long have you been here?'

'Since midday.'

'So you've missed out on lunch?'

She nodded.

'Well, we'd better go and get something to eat, I could do with refuelling.'

'It's okay, I can get something when I get home.'

'I insist. Mike would do the same in my place. We'll go in my car.'

He held his cape over their heads as they made a dash across the waterlogged courtyard towards the green Mondeo parked in the corner. He unlocked the passenger door and half helped, half pushed her into the seat, then flung the cape in the back and got behind the wheel.

'Where's it to be? In this godforsaken part of the city the only places likely to be open on a Sunday afternoon are pizza bars and the Chinese or Indian, if we're lucky.'

Rachel shortly found herself seated opposite him at a table in a Pizza Hut, eating garlic bread whilst they waited for their main order and wondering just how she had been manoeuvred into it. A busy pizza restaurant swarming with noisy teenagers was not the place she expected to be on a Sunday afternoon.

'What's the matter? You look bemused.'

'I am bemused. I seem to have spent the last few hours being manipulated by bossy men. I'm not used to it, I'm my own woman.'

By this time their pizzas had arrived and they ate in silence for some minutes and then Rachel brought up the subject of Bert Pryke.

'The inspector said the funeral will be postponed and a post-mortem will be carried out. How do you go about that?'

'The Coroner's officer will be asked to apply to the Coroner to authorise the removal of the body from the Chapel of Rest to the mortuary for an autopsy to take place.'

'Poor Bert.' She made a moue of distaste.

'That's the only way to find out. If he was killed the pathologist should be able to tell. Did Dickins give you a hard time?'

'He made me feel I was in the wrong all the time.'

'He's an officious little prick. You can make a complaint if you think you've got the grounds.'

'No, of course not. It's probably just his manner. Why do you dislike him so?'

Nick shrugged. 'We've never got on. I reckon he dislikes me even more than I do him. And I suppose he's got reason,' he added slyly. 'When my wife left me I had an affair with his.'

'Oh.'

'Is that all you can say? I thought you'd be deeply disapproving.'

'How you conduct your life is your affair. It is of no concern to me.'

'Aren't you going to preach about the sanctity of marriage?'

'You're the one who's doing the preaching.' She looked at her watch. 'I really must go. I have an appointment in a hour's time.'

'An appointment?'

'With God,' she said succinctly, aware that she had got in the last word.

★ ★ ★

145

The Coil Shuffler doodled on the telephone pad and pondered the latest developments. The police were hopeless, utterly useless. Two murder enquiries in progress under the baton of an astute man charged with running the Coil Shuffler to earth and he hadn't got a clue. The Bill was running around like a headless chicken desperately quizzing all known informers in the hope of revealing the under-belly of the criminal fraternity and identifying the Coil Shuffler. It was insulting, them thinking that their quarry was a member of the sordid, pathetic dregs of humanity that made the underworld.

The Coil Shuffler was a master, far more intelligent than your average Dick and operating at an entirely different level. If only those gormless, baffled cops realised the truth they would be looking nearer home. There was no fear of discovery but now another unknown had entered the equation and what was one to do about it? Ignore the situation and treat it with the contempt it deserved? Or take action and stop any further encroachment?

The doodling had developed into a series of gibbets complete with pin-men hanging from the nooses. It reminded one of the game played as a child. The Coil Shuffler smiled, tore the leaf off the pad, crumpled it up and threw it into the wastepaper basket.

'HOLMES has drawn a blank,' said Michael Croft, referring to the Home Office computer. 'Our Coil Shuffler, whoever he is, is not known in any other part of the country. There's no record of anything similar cropping up on other patches.'

'That's unusual in itself,' said Nick Holroyd. 'Professional assassins normally operate over a wide area, even using an international clientele.'

'So our man's not a professional.'

The two men were in Nick's flat, speculating on the case. The smell of fish and chips still pervaded the room from their supper and the plates and cutlery from this and earlier meals were piled up in the sink which had been filled with water to soak them. The tap had been left dripping and monotonous splashing competed with the rain sliding down the window panes and sweeping across the porch in fitful flurries. Nick unwrapped a Mars bar and flicked the paper into the hearth. He spoke with full mouth.

'I'd say his work was most professional.'

'What I mean is, he's an amateur in it not only for the money but for the kicks, not a professional contract man.'

'That sounds reasonable. What we've got is someone who has killed once, got away with it and developed a morbid taste for the thrill and excitement and decided to cash in on it. Let's see if we can do a profile.'

Mike sighed. Since going on a forensic psychology course a few years ago Nick now saw himself as an expert in that field. Forget Cracker, Brent Hill station had its own profiling doyen.

'Okay, so what facts have we got?'

'He's a local person who has another job. Somewhere in this city is an employee — a bank clerk, a shop assistant, an insurance clerk or whatever — who is not what he seems.'

'He's a schemer with great patience and devotion to detail. A perfectionist.'

'He's also skilled at surveillance. He must have kept tabs on his victims for weeks before moving in for the kill. He knew exactly when and where to strike.'

'He's certainly a cool customer.' Mike shifted in his chair to get more comfortable and beat a tattoo on the arm with one hand. 'After careful planning he seizes his moment and doesn't panic.'

'And above all else he's vain. He thinks he is invincible and, not content with doing a good job, he makes sure the police

148

know he's the one responsible. That's really unprofessional but it's how he gets his excitement. Quite a customer.'

'Let's go through his known killings and see if we can find a common denominator.'

Mike leafed through his papers and found the reports he'd culled from the computer, and the two men studied them in silence for some time. It was Mike who broke the quiet.

'You know what's significant? No shooters. Our Coil Shuffler isn't into firearms.'

'Either he can't get access to a gun, or — and I think this is the case — he's a hands-on assassin. He enjoys the actual killing, the physical contact with his victim. Let's see what we've got: Robert Bentley, found dead in the bath tub with his wrists slashed. The wife had been having an affair and we were sure the lover had arranged for his murder, but we couldn't prove it. The Coroner reckoned Bentley had found out about the affair and committed suicide because he couldn't face life without her. One important point about this one: the lover, Paul Flynn-Smith, was seriously rich. Into the gee-gees — racehorse owner, punter, shares in one of the biggest racing conglomerates — he could certainly have afforded to employ a hit-man. After the dust had settled he and

149

the widow swanned off to South America where I believe he is now into polo in a big way.'

'You're never going to prove anything after all this time.'

'No, nor with the others. John Houghton, the hotel owner, was found hanging in his garage. There was some takeover bid going on at the time which he, as majority shareholder in the hotel chain, was trying to block. With him out of the way, the deal went through smoothly. The whole thing stank and as I've always insisted there *was* a Coil Shuffler's card on his body when I found him although I was the only one who saw it before it went missing. Again, a verdict of suicide was brought in.'

'If he was murdered his killer must have rendered him unconscious in some way first to enable him to be strung up — didn't anything show up at the autopsy?'

'There was a cocktail of drugs in the body but as he was a known snorter who dabbled in all sorts of substances this wasn't thought suspicious. The other case was the death of an elderly woman where a card *was* found by a friend of the victim. This friend insisted that the son had arranged his mother's death to get his hands on her money but the autopsy revealed she had died from natural causes.'

'If the three were murdered they were all dispatched in different ways. Our Coil Shuffler doesn't use the same *modus operandi* but as you say, he doesn't mind getting close to his intended victim.'

'You've forgotten the fourth one. What about Rachel's husband?'

'He was either force-fed the overdose or the Coil Shuffler provided him with the lethal amount to do it himself.'

'Surely he would have had enough painkillers to do the job anyway?'

'Apparently not. I've gone through the transcript of the inquest and there were higher levels of drugs in his body than could be accounted for. The Coroner thought he had been stockpiling them although Rachel insisted this wasn't so, but as you know she was over-ruled.'

'So where does this leave us?'

'Someone with medical knowledge and access to drugs?'

'It certainly looks that way, and he must also be strong and agile. At least three healthy well-built men in their prime amongst his victims. Haven't Forensics come up with anything from the last two murders?'

'Very little. In Eddie Briers' case, no

unidentified fingerprints in the car and no one in the street, either resident or passer-by, saw or heard anything. The girlfriend was used to him leaving her before dawn and she heard the engine fire and the car drive off as usual as she was preparing to catch up with her beauty sleep. The wife had no idea he had a mistress and thought he was staying at the Yellow Cock on the nights when he didn't come home. As for Graham Scott: we know his attacker disguised himself as a hospital porter but again, no fingerprints. We've had it drummed into us over and over again that the murderer always leaves something of himself on his victim and vice versa but not a trace so far.'

Nick got up and paced the room. 'You've got to admire him. He's got the entire force stymied and he's going to go on.'

'He must be stopped. Some might say the likes of Eddie Briers and Graham Scott are no great loss to society but knocking off helpless old folk because they're not popping their clogs quickly enough is another thing altogether.'

'Has our dear friend Trevor got anywhere chasing up that advert?'

'Another dead end. We got the official co-operation of the Post Office to intercept and identify the person picking up the replies but nothing doing. He's got wind of our enquiries and he's lying doggo.'

'And are there any replies?'

'There's one letter waiting to be collected.'

'Which the police have not had access to? Some co-operation that.'

'Probably from some granny basher or business rival. Our only hope at the moment is Bert Pryke. If he was killed and it shows up in the autopsy we can put pressure on the niece to cough up. If she hired the Coil Shuffler to do the job there must also have been arrangements made for payment, apart from the initial contact. We should get a lead on him from that.'

'You mean Trevor Dickens will,' said Nick gloomily.

* * *

The next morning Trevor Dickins bounded up to the two men as they sat in the canteen. He clapped Mike on the shoulder.

'Your girlfriend was barking up the wrong tree. The autopsy report has just come through from Stock. Bert Pryke died from a massive coronary — which is what his doctor put on his death certificate originally.'

'Hell, she was convinced something was wrong.' Mike shook his head and opposite him Nick Holroyd stared out of the window and feigned indifference.

'Could well have developed into a homicide if he'd gone on living. The niece was obviously fed up with looking after him and prepared to do something about it but he obliged first by falling off the perch. His doctor will be pleased he is vindicated — he didn't take kindly to the idea that he might have overlooked an unnatural death. The nurse too; most indignant she was when I questioned her — thought I was casting nasturtiums on her professional integrity.' Dickins sniggered. 'Thought I'd just let you know.'

'Thanks. How is the case going? Any more leads?'

'I'm following up some promising ones but all strictly confidential.' He tapped the side of his nose and looked pointedly at Holroyd who was still pretending that Dickins wasn't there.

'Well, I hope they produce better results than this one otherwise your clear-up rate is going to take a nose-dive,' said Mike dismissively, picking up his knife and fork again.

Dickins shrugged and left them to get on with their meal.

'It's a bugger about that autopsy result,'

said Nick, rapping his teaspoon against the saucer and drawing squiggles in the spilt sugar. 'Where do we go from here?'

'That little line of enquiry has certainly come to a dead end. It was a right no-no.'

'I think I'm going to have a word with Quentin Stock.'

'The pathologist? You must be joking! Even you can't be daft enough to suggest to the great Quentin that he's made a mistake.'

'He could have overlooked something. I'll be very tactful — just have a general discussion on causes of death that are difficult to ascertain by post-mortem.'

'Rather you than me. Suppose he complains to Bairstow?'

'I'll cross that bridge when I come to it.'

★ ★ ★

It was with a sense of déjà vu that Nick Holroyd parked in the visitors' carpark and made his way round the back of the hospital to the mortuary. Although the inside had been gutted and modernised the outside looked much the same as when first built at the end of the last century. The grey bricks were dirtier and darker, the tall, arched windows looked like something out of a Victorian workhouse and the fluorescent lights behind them seemed out of place. It looked what it was — a morgue, and one that was familiar from films of Jack the Ripper and that ilk. He knew to the day how long it was since he had last attended an autopsy and as he pushed open the door and went inside the old familiar smell of formalin and chilled air assailed his nostrils and tightened his guts.

At first he thought the building was deserted, then he heard someone whistling and the sound of running water. Damien Winter, one of the mortuary attendants, was sloshing water down a drain. He looked up when he saw Nick and threw down the hose.

'It's a long time since we've seen you in here.'

'Yes. Still busy?'

'They keep dying, haven't found the cure yet.' He grinned and pulled off his gloves. 'Is the big man around?'

'Quentin? No, he's at a meeting.'

'I thought he was 'Mr Stock' to you.'

'Not when he's not here. Can I help?'

'I just wanted a few words with him, pick his brains.'

'He should be back at any minute. I was just going to put the kettle on — do you want a cuppa?'

156

Unlike many of his colleagues who would have died from thirst rather than drink anything brewed on those premises Nick accepted with alacrity and followed him through the swing doors. Winter filled the kettle at the sink, plugged it in and put teabags in a couple of beakers. He produced a packet of chocolate digestive biscuits from a drawer and pushed it across the table to Nick who took one and chewed it absentmindedly.

'You've had a customer in I'm interested in.'

'Who's that?'

'Elderly chap by the name of Bert Pryke.'

'That's right, we did him yesterday, coronary. The report went through to you people, what do you want to know?'

'Is it possible . . . ' Nick picked his way with care, 'that something was missed?'

'You mean he got it wrong? No way. It was a suspicious death, wasn't it? He always takes special care with those. Christ! I wouldn't like to be in your shoes if he thought you were accusing him of slipping up.'

'I just wondered.'

'What's your interest in this stiff, anyway?'

'Something I'm following up. Where's Freddie Bains today?'

'On holiday. Gone down to Cornwall to bury a sister.'

'Some holiday.'

At that moment the phone rang and Winter went off to answer it. Whilst he was gone Quentin Stock returned. He raised his eyebrows when he saw Holroyd.

'I thought you'd been moved to another section, or are you back in CID again?'

'Not yet. Had a good meeting?'

'Total waste of time. The powers that be have strange ideas about balancing quotas.' The pathologist removed his coat and hung it up and helped himself to a biscuit. 'I see Damien's been looking after you, is this a social visit?'

'I want your advice on an idea I'm working on. Your assistant thinks it's impossible but I thought the top man might not rule it out altogether.'

'If you told me what you're talking about I might be able to answer you. What do you want to know?'

Nick took his time in replying. He knew he had to present his query obliquely to avoid ruffling feathers.

'Is it at all possible for someone to be murdered and for it not to show up in an autopsy?'

'What do you mean, not show up?' Quentin Stock was already on the defensive. 'If someone dies and I am asked to ascertain cause of death I do just that.'

'This is just hypothetical,' said the other man hurriedly. 'Could a death pass as natural causes or heart failure when actually it was — say — drug induced?'

'You know perfectly well that if there are any suspicions along those lines the organs and samples are sent off for analysis.'

'But some sort of poison that couldn't be diagnosed?'

'Some obscure South American toxin stolen from a primitive Amazonian tribe that kills instantly if only one drop is taken and leaves no trace in the body?' The pathologist snorted. 'I'm surprised at you, Nick. This is the end of the twentieth century not Sherlock Holmes's England.'

'Are you completely sure that cause of death could never be misdiagnosed?' persisted the other man.

'Are you suggesting that morbid pathology is sometimes at fault?'

'I'm not getting at you personally, Quentin, I'm just asking if it is at all possible. If you wanted to kill someone and get away with it — how would you go about it?'

'This conversation is getting ridiculous. I'm a busy man, I really can't spend any more time in idle chatter.'

The pathologist took off his glasses,

polished them vigorously and put them back on, then looked at Nick who was waiting patiently and grinned. 'But to answer your question; there's a lot to be said for the old plastic bag over the head.'

'You mean . . . ?'

'I'm not discussing this any further. Why do you want to know? You're not writing a book, are you? I hear it's becoming quite common for ex-policemen to turn their hand to writing crime novels. I believe there's even a pathologist in America who is fictionalising her occupation and making a fortune out of it.'

Nick assured him he was not into crime writing. 'You did an autopsy yesterday on someone we were interested in: Bert Pryke.'

'Ah ha! Are we now getting to the real reason for your visit? You think I should have come up with a different result?' Stock said nastily.

'Don't get me wrong. *You* know he died from a coronary, I know he died from a coronary, his doctor knows he died from a coronary but a little bird had whispered so we had to follow it up.'

'I didn't know you were working on that case.'

'The entire force is involved. We've got someone going around knocking off people as a commercial venture — we need to investigate every possible lead, no matter how remote.'

'Well, don't come wasting my time. It's the police who are losing their grip, not my department.'

7

'I've had a rather disturbing phone call.' The Revd David Bell pinched the bridge of his nose and looked down it at Rachel. They were in the study of St Luke's Rectory. 'A Mrs Madge Porter rang up making a lot of wild accusations against this church and you in particular.'

'Oh dear,' said Rachel. She had been disappointed when Mike had told her the result of Bert Pryke's autopsy but she hadn't thought beyond that. She should have realised that his niece was bound to make a fuss. 'What did she say?'

'A great deal about how she had sacrificed her own life to support her uncle in his last years and how she had been rewarded by being accused of doing away with him by someone who was supposed to be a woman of God and should know better. Actually it was couched in stronger language than that.'

'I'm sure it was. I'm sorry she bothered you, David.'

'You know what it was all about?'

'Yes.' She told him about her suspicions

162

over Bert's death and the finding of the ringed advert. He listened thoughtfully and when she had finished he smiled sympathetically.

'I don't blame you, Rachel, you obviously had to do something. Did you actually go to the police?'

'I know a policeman. He's one of my patients and I told him. After that it was out of my hands.'

'You did right. Under the circumstances I can see you had to follow up your suspicions.'

'Do you think I should go and see Madge Porter?'

'I don't think it would do any good. She made it quite clear in no uncertain terms that she wanted no one from this parish to officiate at the funeral. Don't worry about it, Rachel.' David Bell patted her shoulder. 'Now, how is the sermon coming along? Have you plotted it out yet?'

★ ★ ★

Trevor Dickins was holding a team briefing at Brent Hill Station.

'We are not dealing with your ordinary criminal here.' The DI gazed at the men and women in front of him who due to the presence of Superintendent Bairstow,

163

who was sitting in on the session, were presenting a more decorous appearance than was usual. Instead of bums on desk tops and shoulders propping up walls, his colleagues were sitting or standing to attention and there was no surreptitious bantering or muttered conversation going on in the background.

'Our killer is a clever bastard who is milking two markets. On the one hand we have the granny basher; our man is preying on the old and helpless, the incurably ill, possibly posing as a mercy killer. On the other hand he is a hatchet man hiring himself out as a contract killer. To this end he has two visiting cards, each slightly different.' Dickins indicated the blow-up of the cards on the wall behind him.

' 'PETS: Exits arranged — Professionally, Effectively, Terminally. Apply: The Coil Shuffler.' This is the one left behind at the scene of crime of the recent murders and was also found on Robert Bentley's body. It is more bluntly worded and there is no contact advice. This one' — he indicated the photo on the right — 'is more ambiguous. 'PETS: Exits arranged — Painlessly, Efficiently, Tastefully.' ' It is open to many interpretations and a contact box number is given. Both cards are completely unidentifiable. They could be produced by anyone with access to a modern computer and printer. There is no way they can be traced back to the perpetrator. Any questions?'

'Which came first?' The speaker was Kevin Parker, a young constable recently seconded to CID who was ambitious to a fault and had already realised that the way to get noticed was to draw attention to himself. Trevor Dickins had already marked him out as a possible future rival and someone to hold in check.

'A good question,' he said blandly. 'As far as we know our Coil Shuffler has been working both ends of the market simultaneously. However, it is possible that he started with the latter form of liquidation first. There may have been deaths that were covered up and never brought to our notice. Even if he left cards behind with his victims they could have been, probably *were*, removed by the relatives who arranged their beloved ones' demise. Our killer wants to advertise his skills but his hirers certainly don't want to be identified.'

'Are we dealing with a psychopath?' This question came from another member of the team and Douglas Bairstow took it up.

'Your psychopath kills from compulsion, as I'm sure you all know. Whatever starts him down that path, whatever constraints, background, upbringing, genes combine to pressure him towards that first taking of life, we do know that he finds relief and fulfilment in the act. It gratifies and exhilarates him, like the sex act, and it becomes a drug. He has to kill again and again to get the same buzz and as his need becomes greater the killings get closer, the gap between each one narrowing as he feeds his lust. This is not the case here. Our man kills to order, and he doesn't use the same MO, which is another characteristic of the psychopath. But' — here the superintendent paused and swept the assembled company in front of him with a searching gaze — 'he is without compassion. He enjoys killing for killing's sake like your typical psychopath. One could say that he has all the attributes of a homicidal maniac but he is ruled by his head rather than his emotions. This makes him a very dangerous man. Carry on, Inspector.'

Trevor Dickins cleared his throat. 'We have come to a dead end with the box number in the *Weekly Digest*. With the eventual co-operation of the PO we have been monitoring the Poste Restante facilities at Roseberry Road post office but no go. Our killer has somehow got wise to this and hasn't picked up his mail. He is not likely to now. He has written that one off but he is going to find some other way of advertising his services. Which means you've all got to keep your eyes peeled. Scrutinise the adverts in the local rags, read the notices pinned up in the windows of the little corner shop, take note of the fliers plastered in phone booths — I take it you can all tell the difference between Gloria advertising French lessons and a tender for murder?'

A subdued ripple of laughter ran through the ranks and Dickins grinned back and continued.

'That's the first thing. The second is: put pressure on your informers. I can't believe your snouts are as ignorant of the Coil Shuffler's identity as they would have us think. They may not know his name or who he is but someone, sure as hell, knows how to contact him. You've got to dig and dig until you uncover that fact and we need to know soon. Not next week or the week after but *now*, before there is another killing.'

* * *

Rachel Morland sorted out the free-standing equipment in the physiotherapy department, checked the appointments diary for the next

167

day and decided to stay on late and catch up with some of her paperwork. It was after seven before she locked the office door behind her and made her way to the carpark. She had a meeting to attend at the sports centre on sporting injuries and their treatment and if she drove straight there she should be in good time for the opening session. She slid into the driving seat and switched on the ignition. The engine was dead and she realised in dismay that she had left her headlights on all day.

There was no one else in the carpark and she debated what to do. Should she go back inside the hospital and try to find someone who could start the car with jump leads, or should she call the AA? In the end she did neither thinking it would be easier to leave the car there overnight and deal with it in the morning and catch a bus to her meeting. When she reached the bus stop she discovered she had just missed a bus and there was a half-hour wait before the next one, so she decided to walk, taking a short cut through Northgate.

She hadn't gone very far before she knew that she had been foolish. This was the red-light district and although it was still early evening the hookers were already plying their trade. The lighting was poor but under the street lamps lounged figures skimpily dressed in miniskirts and shiny boots and the flare of a match to a cigarette revealed heavily made-up faces and dyed locks.

As Rachel walked quickly along the street she was aware of animosity radiating from these shadowy figures and realised that she was being mistaken for a rival muscling in on their act. She hurried her pace and a couple of women stepped out of a doorway and moved threateningly after her. At that moment a car accelerated round the nearby corner and drew up beside her and a voice spoke through the open window.

'Get in!'

Oh no! she thought. She'd escaped one hazard and now she was being propositioned by a kerb-crawler. She ignored the car and started to walk on but she heard the door open and the voice snarled again:

'Get in, woman. What the hell do you think you're doing?'

She swung round to find Nick Holroyd glaring at her, his furious face framed in the doorway of the police car he was driving.

'Nick! What are you doing here?'

'That's my question.' He thumped the passenger seat beside him and she slid weakly on to it. 'Are you all right?'

'Yes. It's my pride that's taken a battering rather than my physical self, but I'm glad you came along when you did.'

'Are you going to tell me what you were doing hanging around one of the most notorious areas of the city after dark and on your tod?'

'My car wouldn't start and I'm due at a meeting so I decided to walk and take a short cut.'

'You're crazy, do you realise that? If I hadn't come along you might have had your face carved up.'

'Thank goodness you did, but should I be in here?' Rachel had belatedly realised that she was sitting in a police car, white with toothpaste-red-and-blue stripe and complete with blue lamp on top.

'I'm in charge so I answer to myself. I'm rescuing a damsel in distress. Where's this meeting — or do you want me to take you home?'

'It's at the Riverside Sports Centre and I really must attend.'

'Right, we'll soon get you there.'

Holroyd drove the short distance in silence. He appeared to be deep in thought and when he pulled up outside the Riverside he was in no hurry to let her go.

'This is not a religious meeting, is it?'

170

'No, strictly secular. Why?'

'This religious business you're dabbling in; I suppose there's no harm in it, but . . . '

'But what?' Her voice was ominously quiet.

'Don't get me wrong. I'm sure it means something to you, to many people, but let's face it, it doesn't really have any relevance in the real world out there. We're talking poverty, unemployment, crime, ill-health — how can you address these problems with religious — '

'Mumbo-jumbo?'

'Well, you said it . . . '

'I was pre-empting you,' she said wearily. 'I've heard it all before and really, when it comes down to it, there's nothing to choose between you and the likes of those unfortunate women forced to sell their bodies.'

'What do you mean?'

'As you say, religion means nothing to them and nothing to you either, does it? You're just as unenlightened as the most ignorant and underprivileged person on your patch.'

'Okay, so tell me, what's in it for me?' he challenged.

'Wrong question, Nick. It's not what you can get out of religion but what you can put into it. Christianity is about selflessness and putting others first. About helping your fellow men and not deliberately harming anyone and also about worshipping and loving God who created you.'

'Right, I could go along with this helping old ladies across the street and not knocking off my neighbour's piggy-bank. That's known as the unwritten rules that govern any civilised society.'

'Not unwritten. It's all laid down in the ten commandments.'

'Yes, well . . . what I can't take on board is this mythical old bearded man in the sky who I'm suppose to kow-tow to. How can I, or any reasonably intelligent person, love some imaginary being who no one has ever proved exists? It's superstitious claptrap and you can't convince me otherwise.'

'Do you really want a sermon?'

'I bet you do a good line in sermons.' He grinned at her and raised an eyebrow.

'Find out,' she said tartly. 'I'm preaching at St Luke's Sunday week at morning Eucharist. Come along to the service. Mike is going to be there.'

'*Is* he.'

'You can always be his taxi service if you need an excuse.'

★ ★ ★

Pat Fenton was helping Rachel to wash up, and she registered the tense back bent over the sink and the jerky movements as her friend piled crockery on the draining-board, slopping water carelessly on the floor. She had eaten an enjoyable meal but was aware that although Rachel was trying to appear normal she was distracted and absent-minded.

'What's wrong, Rachel?'

'Wrong? There's nothing wrong, what do you mean?'

'You're worrying about something. It's no good denying it, I know you too well. Tell Aunty Pat.'

Rachel grimaced and emptied out the bowl and made a play of carefully drying her hands before answering.

'This business of the Coil Shuffler . . . '

'What about it?'

'I keep thinking of Christopher. I'm all muddled, Pat, and it's preying on my mind. I *know* that he didn't make contact with the Coil Shuffler and I know that I didn't, so who did? Who arranged for him to . . . die? Who could have done such a thing and why? I have to know.'

'We'll never know. No one will ever really know the truth of it and you've got to try and put it out of your mind. Let it go.'

'I *can't*. Don't you see? It's driving me crazy. I pray and pray and I end up in a greater muddle than ever.'

'I wish you'd never got involved with that policeman.'

'What's that got to do with it?'

'You were putting it behind you and getting on with life and now he's brought it all back and put ideas in your head.'

'They've always been there.'

'It's just a job to him, he's not personally involved like you. He sees things from a different angle and he's no right to drag you through it again.'

'Perhaps he's helping me to see things from a different perspective. You can't shuffle unpleasant things under the carpet. In the long run you have to face up to them.'

'I don't know about a different perspective — you're certainly getting things *out* of perspective.'

Rachel busied herself putting away the pots and pans. She shovelled cutlery into the drawer and hung up the tea towels to dry. Then she sat down at the kitchen table and spread out her hands.

'It's not just Christopher and this Coil Shuffler. I'm beginning to have serious doubts about my vocation.'

Pat Fenton put her elbows on the table

and stared earnestly at her friend.

'That's not like you, perhaps you've got too much on your plate. You're working full-time at the hospital holding down a responsible job, as well as giving your all to your church — you don't want any further distractions.'

'We're talking about Mike Croft, aren't we?'

'Well, yes. You can't afford to take on anyone else at the moment.'

'I'm not sure he would appreciate your turn of phrase, but Mike *is* part of my life now, Pat, whether you like it or not.'

'You said yourself that he knows nothing about Christianity.'

'He's open to enlightenment and he's coming to hear me preach next Sunday week.'

'Do you think that's a good idea?'

'Why shouldn't it be?'

'No offence, but he'll put you off.'

'He'll put me on my mettle. Are you going to come?'

'I suppose I must support you.'

'Who knows, I may have better luck converting him than I have with you.'

★ ★ ★

The envelope was addressed to DI Trevor Dickins at Brent Hill station and had been opened by the time he arrived in the general CID office. Some of his colleagues were poring over the contents making ribald remarks as he walked into the room and flung his coat over a chair back.

'You've got an admirer, sir,' said a young WDC with a grin.

'Didn't know you were AC/DC, you've been holding out on us, sir,' chipped in one of his sergeants.

'What are you wittering on about? Haven't you got any work to do?'

Dickins stalked over to the desk and was handed the photograph which had come in the envelope. It showed a blond-haired man dressed in doublet and hose toying with a dagger.

'Where did this come from?' he demanded.

'Came through the post addressed to you.'

'What the hell . . . Why should someone send me a photo of some berk poncing about in tights?'

'Your secret life's catching up with you, sir.'

'Hah.' Dickins studied the photo in disgust. 'Someone's got a warped sense of humour.' He flicked it towards the wastepaper basket where it hit the rim and fell face upwards on to the floor. 'Now, could we try exercising our brains on more important matters?'

'That's Laurence Olivier.' DC Bains had been struggling with a jammed filing cabinet drawer over on the other side of the room and now he walked over and looked at the photo as it lay on the floor. 'As Hamlet,' he added.

'*Hamlet?*' said Dickins sharply.

'He directed the famous film and took the starring role. Years ago.'

Dickins took out his handkerchief and bending down he carefully wrapped it round a corner of the photo and picked it up.

'Where's the envelope?'

It was rescued from the wastepaper basket in a very crumpled state.

'A fine chance there will be of any fingerprints after all your filthy little mitts have been mauling them about.'

'What's this about, sir?'

'The Coil Shuffler coined his name from *Hamlet*. This has to mean something, it's not just coincidence. I'll show this to the Super and then we'll get the photo and envelope straight over to Forensics, though it's probably a waste of time.'

Bairstow was in his office and examined the photo with interest.

'You say it came addressed to you?'

'Yes, there's a local postmark but there was nothing else in the envelope, no message or anything and it was handled by too many people before we realised its significance so I don't think Forensics will get any joy.'

'Larry Olivier. Fine actor. I don't think the new Kenneth Brannagh version of *Hamlet* will better the original.'

'That dagger he's holding, sir. Do you think that's a message to us? Is he telling us that is his next choice of weapon?'

'Don't you remember the film? No, I suppose you're too young though I believe it's still doing the rounds amongst film societies. This, unless I am mistaken, is a still from the famous soliloquy 'To be, or not to be'.'

As Dickins looked blank he continued: 'The speech where Hamlet refers to 'shuffling off this mortal coil'. I suggest you get hold of a copy and study it, Trevor. If he's going to start sending us messages it will help if you can interpret them.'

'So what does this one mean?'

'This is probably his signing-on signal.'

★ ★ ★

The next day the first direct reference to the Coil Shuffler appeared in the local press. In an article purporting to warn the general public of the homicidal maniac on the loose, but actually slating the police, the *Clarion* mentioned him by name amongst a stream of innuendos and conjectures. This resulted in Trevor Dickins finding himself in the superintendent's office again facing an irate Bairstow.

'Have you seen this? It's outrageous!' Bairstow thumped the paper and read out loud: ' 'It is believed that the recent murders that have shocked our community have been carried out by a killer calling himself the Coil Shuffler. The police appear to be impotent in apprehending this villain although many weeks have elapsed since the first murder. We urge the public to be extra-vigilant and report any suspicious events so that this maniac can be stopped before he strikes again.' ' He threw the paper down and glared at Dickins. 'How did they get hold of this? Who leaked it?'

'I don't know, sir, but I'm sure it was not one of us. Rumours get around and perhaps someone put two and two together . . . one of the nurses at the hospital or someone at the Yellow Cock.'

'But how did they know about the visiting card? We put a strict embargo on that.'

'It doesn't mention the card. They haven't

179

got hold of that and they haven't connected the earlier murders with the two recent ones.'

'And I suppose we should be grateful for small mercies? I'm getting straight on to the editor of the *Clarion*.'

Bairstow picked up his phone and got a line to the *Clarion* offices.

'Put me through to Jack Breakspeare. I don't care if he is engaged. Tell him it's Douglas Bairstow — he'll speak to me! Jack? Where did you get this nonsense from you've got plastered all over the front page?'

'Superintendent. Good morning to ye. What are ye referring to?'

Jack Breakspeare, the editor of the *Clarion*, was a Scotsman with a penetrating voice. Dickins could hear every word coming down the line.

'I'm referring to your scurrilous article about a killer calling himself the Coil Shuffler. Where did you get your facts from?'

'You're not asking me to divulge my sources, surely, Superintendent. If ye read it carefully you'll note it is not stated as a fact but as a supposition, but thank you for confirming it.'

'Jack, we're dealing with two very nasty murders here. We're close to making an arrest but I will not have the waters muddied by

180

irresponsible articles like this one stirring up public fear just to increase your circulation. When I have some information that the public should know about I shall hold a press conference and you shall have the *true* facts. In the meanwhile — lay off!'

'You haven't arrested anyone, have you, so it's not *sub judice*. You can't muffle the voice of the Fourth Estate.'

'I know what I'd like to do to the Fourth Estate,' snarled Bairstow, banging down the phone. 'The *Clarion* gets more like the gutter tabloids every day.'

'Do you think it might work to our advantage to let them publish a copy of the Coil Shuffler's card?' enquired Dickins. 'It might jog people's memories and bring evidence of other deaths he's been involved in that we haven't caught up with.'

'No. We'd get all the weirdos on our patch producing their own version of the card and it could prompt a copy-cat killing. This is certainly not the time to go public. Whoever Breakspeare's informant was, we must hope he hasn't got any more titbits to leak.'

'We've had the report through from Forensics on that photograph. As we expected, there's a mass of fingerprints superimposed over each other on photo and envelope. They reckon the photograph itself is a photo of a film magazine original, developed in an amateur darkroom.'

'Which nips that little line of enquiry in the bud, though I suppose it tells us something about our Coil Shuffler — he's an amateur photographer.'

'It doesn't really follow, sir. He could have got the photo from anywhere — picked it up in a car boot sale or junk shop.'

'That's true. Any luck with the typewriter that was used to type the address?'

'They're still working on that but there are no obvious distinctive features in the print.'

'I suggest that any further unidentifiable post that arrives for you is dealt with with greater care.'

'Yes, sir.'

★ ★ ★

Michael Croft was still having three sessions of physiotherapy with Rachel each week; he had dated her several more times and now he was going to see her in her third guise as the dedicated churchwoman. St Luke's was three-quarters full; so much for the dwindling congregations one heard about, he thought, and there was a wide age range. Teenagers and young families were well represented as well as the older generation. Was it always like this or had they turned up to hear Rachel preach?

The pews were narrow, hard and uncomfortable and although all the lights were on it was still dark and unbelievably gloomy. When had he last been to church? It must have been at Jane and Andrew's funeral, though that had been in the crematorium chapel. He had been so spaced out that day that he really had no recollection of it at all apart from the hideous ordeal of shaking hands with his many colleagues afterwards as they had shuffled past muttering embarrassed condolences. He mustn't think of that now.

He tried to concentrate on the service and follow Rachel's movements in the chancel. Beside him Nick fidgeted uneasily and ahead of them and over on the other side sat Pat Fenton. She was dressed in her nursing uniform and her hat sat uncompromisingly on her short grey hair, managing to look like an upturned bowl. She had seen them arriving and had waved and indicated the pew beside her but they had ignored the invitation and settled further back.

The two hymns that had been sung so far had been vaguely familiar to Mike and the lessons had been read by an elderly man with his arm in a sling. As he walked away from the lectern Rachel moved to the centre of the chancel steps and read the Gospel. How small she looked in her cassock and surplice, he thought. This impression was heightened when she crossed to the pulpit and mounted the steps. She was almost swallowed up by the shadows but when she moved forward and looked out over the congregation she appeared confident and in no way intimidated by her surroundings. Was she aware of him and Nick, he wondered, or were they just part of the sea of faces upturned to hear her speak?

'For the New Testament lesson today you heard the parable of the talents and I am going to take that as the starting point for my sermon. Don't squander your talents. Every single one of you, every single one of God's children, which means everyone alive today, is different. No two individuals are alike, you are all unique and you have been given your own specific talents. So I am saying whatever you have a knack for, no matter how simple or ordinary you may think it, develop it and don't waste it. In developing it you will find fulfilment, and this brings me on to my main point: self-fulfilment *not* self indulgence . . . '

Rachel paused here and cleared her throat. She took a few sips from the glass placed strategically at her elbow, grimaced and continued: 'There is a mood abroad today that equates happiness with self-indulgence. It insists that to achieve contentment you have to put your self, your selfish needs, first, with no consideration of the effect on other people . . . '

It was hot in the church and the rising and falling cadences in Rachel's voice were having a soporific effect on Nick. A nudge from Mike jolted him back to reality in time to hear her touching on the sanctity of marriage. What she said grated on his conscience and he found himself seething. How dare she stand there and pontificate about marriage. She'd had a happy one apparently, though who knows how long that would have lasted if he hadn't upped and died. He glared in her direction but had to admit that she knew how to preach. She hardly referred to her notes though she was obviously nervous. She cleared her throat frequently and ran her tongue over her lips as if her saliva was drying up.

'One of the commandments says: 'Thou shalt not commit adultery.' ' Rachel leaned forward and swept the congregation with an accusing gaze. Nick felt she was singling him out and he turned his head away and studied the people sitting nearby, determined to listen no longer. He succeeded in cutting his mind off from what she was saying and the next thing he heard was:

'So use your gifts wisely, not just for your own good, but for the good of society and to the glory of God. And now, in the name of the Father, the Son and the Holy Ghost, Amen.'

As the congregation shuffled to its feet Mike nudged Nick and whispered:

'I think she's overstepped her terms of reference — look around you, some of them don't look too happy, do they? She's trodden on a lot of toes.'

'Never mind them — what's the matter with her?'

After finishing her sermon Rachel had given a dry little cough and drained the glass out of which she had been sipping. As she turned to descend from the pulpit she seemed to stumble and clutched at the rail. She swayed for a few seconds and then half fell down the short flight. At the bottom she steadied herself but when she attempted to walk back to her seat she staggered and collided with the end of the choir-stalls and knocked a pile of hymn books to the floor.

'She looks drunk. Maybe she was knocking back neat gin,' said Nick facetiously, but he half rose from his seat.

'She's ill! It must have been too much for her!'

'Something's wrong!'

David Bell had moved forward to say the Creed but as Rachel shuddered and collapsed on the floor he hastened to her side and bent over her. The two policemen hurried up the aisle at the same time as Pat Fenton squeezed out of her pew and rushed to join them. Rachel was shaking and twitching and the vicar crouched beside her and put his arms round her. He looked up in relief as the others joined him.

'Are you doctors?'

'No, police.'

'I'm a nurse.' Pat Fenton joined him on the floor and reached for her friend's pulse. 'Rachel, what's wrong? Can you tell me?'

Rachel grabbed at her wrist. She was flushed and breathing rapidly and her eyes looked enormous.

'Get her out of here, she's ill,' said Mike in concern

'Take her into the vestry . . . ' David Bell looked sick and flapped his hands towards the vestry.

'Right. Calm down the people out there and see if there's a doctor in the congregation.'

Nick bent down and scooped the ill woman up in his arms and carried her into the vestry with Mike and Pat Fenton at his heels. He laid her down on the settle which stood against one wall.

'Rachel, can you tell us what is wrong?' asked Mike urgently, reaching for one twitching hand and trying to massage it.

'I . . . can't . . . see . . . ' she managed to get out. 'So dry . . . the water . . . '

She was shuddering and gasping and her pupils had dilated to fill her eyes. In the enclosed space her heartbeat could be heard thudding away in her chest.

'I've seen something like this before,' exclaimed Nick. 'It was a long while ago but the symptoms were the same. It was atropine poisoning!'

'My God!' said Pat Fenton. 'Her pulse is very rapid and her heartbeat is accelerating terribly — she's going to convulse! We must get her to hospital!'

'Call an ambulance! Hell, there's three of us here and not a mobile between us just when we need one!'

At that moment David Bell hurried into the vestry.

'Dr Moore is not in the congregation this morning — how is she?'

'Not good. Where's the nearest phone?'

'Here, in my coat.' The vicar went over to his coat which was hanging on a hook in the corner and fumbled in the pocket. Nick snatched the mobile from him, dialled 999 and barked instructions.

'What's wrong with her?' asked the clergyman, taking back his possession.

'I think she's been poisoned. You want to get on your knees, Vicar, and pray!'

'You're our only medical back-up, Pat, can't you *do* something?' Mike was holding the twitching woman and he looked in desperation at the nurse, who seemed too shocked to function properly.

'If the ambulance doesn't get here soon she's going to need resuscitation, her heart — '

'Hang on, Rachel, can you hear me?' urged Mike. 'Help is on its way. We'll soon get you into hospital.'

8

After what seemed an age, in which Rachel's condition deteriorated, but was in actual fact only a few minutes since they were in the area, the ambulance crew arrived. She was strapped to a stretcher and rushed inside the vehicle. By this time she was unconscious and a tube was inserted into her airway to help maintain her breathing. She was wired up to a heart machine and a drip was set up into her arm.

'I'll go with her in the ambulance.' Mike heaved himself aboard, grim-faced as he wondered whether it was too late to save her.

'I'll follow in my car,' said Pat Fenton. 'Try not to worry too much. They'll phone ahead to the hospital and there will be a resuscitation team waiting to receive her. She stands a good chance.'

'I'll stay and cope with things this end.' Nick exchanged a meaningful glance with his friend and turned back into the vestry followed by the vicar. 'Are the congregation still out there?'

'Yes. They're praying. Do you think I

should resume the service?'

'Get rid of them. Someone's tried to poison your assistant. There is forensic evidence to be gathered.'

David Bell looked aghast. He opened his mouth to speak, shut it without uttering and hurried off to do the policeman's bidding. Whilst he waited for the church to clear, Nick went over the scenario in his mind. Atropine: he was sure of that and remembered the case he had been involved with when he was a young constable on the beat. A nine-year-old child had nearly died from eating deadly nightshade berries. The symptoms had been identical. The feverishness, disconnected movements and rapid pulse, with distended pupils. That child had been saved, would they save Rachel? Could she have taken it herself? Was it a suicide bid? No. She'd hardly be likely to choose this time and venue for such an attempt, and besides, she didn't believe in suicide and she could surely have no grounds for wanting to do away with herself now. She'd got over her husband's death and had taken up with Mike. God! Another blow for poor old Mike. The stuff must have been in the water she had drunk during and after her sermon. He seemed to remember that she had drained the glass but there might be some dregs left. Whoever had put it in there had probably been careful not to leave any fingerprints but it must be checked.

The only people in the chancel besides Rachel and the vicar had been another man in a cassock and two youngsters in robes who had carried candles around. He wondered if any of them had noticed anything. The choir had been housed at the back of the church beside the organ, instead of in the original choir-stalls.

The congregation had all left. The babble of voices had risen and died away as the last people filed out through the porch. As Nick went back into the chancel David Bell hurried back up the aisle to him.

'Is there anything I can do? I can't believe that Rachel has been deliberately poisoned. Was it something she ate, do you think?'

'Whatever it was, was in the water she was drinking and if she didn't put it in there somebody else did.'

The vicar looked even more shocked. 'This is terrible.'

'That glass and the remains of its contents must be analysed by the lab. Where is it?' he asked sharply. 'It was on the edge of the pulpit — has anyone removed it?'

The two men dashed over to the pulpit.

They found the glass lying on its side on the floor.

'She must have knocked it down when she stumbled,' said David Bell. 'There's nothing in it now.'

Nick bent down, and inserting his fingers, lifted it up then wrapped it carefully in his handkerchief. 'Who would have filled it and put it there in the first instance?'

'Well, Rachel herself, I suppose. We always keep a carafe and a glass in the church in case someone is taken faint. She probably put it there before the service began.'

'Is it possible to get a list of all the people who were here this morning?'

'If it had been later in the service and they had been up to the altar to receive the Sacrament I would have remembered everyone. As it is — the church-wardens and sidesmen between them can probably tell you who was in attendance. You surely can't think one of the congregation tampered with the glass?'

'Get that list for me and make sure the church is locked securely. The team will be in to check everything.'

'The police have to be involved?'

'Vicar, if Rachel dies there will be a full-scale murder enquiry in hand!'

David Bell moaned and sank down on

his knees behind the rector's stall, bowing his head and praying in anguish. Nick left him there and walked down the aisle and through the porch. As he pushed open the heavy oak door he heard footsteps clattering up the path. Pat Fenton was rushing towards him, a look of alarm on her face, her coat blowing out behind her like bat's wings.

'Quick! You're still here, thank God!'

'What's the matter now?' Surely she hadn't found a body propped up amongst the tombstones?

'Come and look at this.' Her breath came in gasps as she hurried him down the path towards the church carpark, which was at the bottom of the graveyard. 'I went to get in my car and I suddenly remembered that Rachel's would be here so I went to check if it was securely locked and . . . '

'And what?'

'Look for yourself.' She pointed at the red Fiesta that was parked in the corner near a stand of yew. With a feeling of foreboding Nick strode towards it. Something was scrawled across the back window. As he got closer the words leapt out at him. They said, in large, untidy capitals: THE COIL SHUFFLER.

★ ★ ★

The light beat against her eyelids, drawing her back to the surface, urging her to open her eyes, but she resisted, keeping them squeezed tightly shut. Here, inside her head, she had some control over her shifting vision. She could pretend she was dreaming, imagining things, that it wasn't really happening. How long had she lain like this, drifting in and out of consciousness? At first she had struggled to wake up, to break out of the trance that held her in its grip, but every time she had surfaced and forced open her eyes everything had spun out of focus. Faces had swum near and receded, hands holding hypodermics and medication had loomed over her and faded and curtains and light fittings had circled round her in a swirling pattern.

Through all of this she had been aware of the terrible dryness in her mouth and the periods when she hadn't been able to see at all. But even that frightening phenomenon was better than what had gone before when she had been in church. She had horrible memories of standing in the middle of the chancel whilst the carved figures on the rood-screen had come alive and danced round her in a macabre dance. Her heart had thudded away in time to the beat, threatening to burst out of her chest, and her arms and legs had surely twitched and jerked in imitation?

She swallowed painfully and remembered tubes being forced down her throat and being dreadfully sick. A nightmare that had seemed to go on and on . . . She gasped and snapped open her eyes. A window was close by and she could see a flock of pigeons winging its way across the sky. It flew in a straight line, neither dipping or turning as she eyed it. She drew her gaze back to the bedside locker. The water jug and vases of flowers were stable on the top. She could see them distinctly and they didn't move.

'How are you feeling, Rachel?' A nurse was bending over her.

'Dry . . .'

'Here you are.' The nurse held out a glass of water and helped her to sip. 'You're looking much better. You've got a visitor — do you feel up to seeing him?'

Rachel nodded and the nurse went over to the door. Through the glass Rachel could see her talking to a tall figure. It was Mike. She knew he had been in before. His face had been one of those that had hovered out of the nightmare, concerned and anxious. There had been other men too, policemen she was sure, who had tried to question her but she had shied away from the facts they were trying to make her recall and had feigned sleep.

Mike limped into the room smiling.

'How are you?'

'Much better,' she croaked. 'I can see properly. There's only one of you today.'

'That's good, I don't like being cloned.' He sat on the edge of the bed and leaned forward and kissed her. 'Nick sends his regards.'

'Mmm. What happened, Mike?'

'Do you remember anything?'

'I . . . I was poisoned, wasn't I?' She appealed to him to deny this but he nodded his head slowly.

'Yes, you were.'

'But how?'

'It was in the water you drank. Did it taste funny?'

'It was very bitter. I thought . . . I thought Bill Cardwell the verger had forgotten to put fresh water in the carafe. What was it?'

'Belladonna — deadly nightshade, we think.'

'The water hadn't just gone off, then — got contaminated?'

'No, it was deliberate.'

She gave a little moan and turned her head aside and he grasped her hands and stroked them. She twisted back to face him.

'But why, Mike?'

'We're not sure but we think it could be a warning to the police.'

'I don't understand.'

'There is a big operation on at the moment to try to track down this Coil Shuffler, uncover his identity and get enough evidence to pin the murders on him. It's not just Nick and me having a go — the whole force is involved and it's got top priority.'

'You mean this person who calls himself the Coil Shuffler tried to kill *me*?' Her voice rose and cracked and he helped her to a drink. 'But why *me*?' she asked when she had taken a few sips. 'You're not saying someone wants me dead?'

'Not an unknown someone but the Coil Shuffler himself. He must know it was you who pointed the finger of suspicion over Bert Pryke's death. This may be his way of getting his revenge on you and the police.'

'This is horrible!'

'I know, but what other reason could there be? You don't make enemies in your line of work, do you, and it's hardly likely to be one of your St Luke's crowd giving notice that he doesn't hold with woman priests.'

She smiled weakly. 'What did you think of my sermon?'

'It was riveting. It will long be remembered,

and not just because of what happened afterwards.'

'I think I got rather carried away and expressed my own opinions too strongly.'

'Don't let it worry you. Nobody knew beforehand what you were going to preach about, did they? So they could hardly have spiked your drink in anticipation of hearing something that incensed them.'

'The Coil Shuffler,' she said slowly. 'There wasn't a . . . a card left anywhere?'

He debated whether to tell her about the message scrawled on her car window but decided it would only worry her further.

'No. Now don't fret over this. We're going to catch this Coil Shuffler and he's certainly not going to lay another finger on you, I can promise you that. I wouldn't have told you only there will be some more of my mob around asking questions. How long have you got to be in hospital? Have they told you when you can come out?'

'The doctor said something about the middle of next week if all goes well.'

'When they discharge you I want you to go away for a holiday. Get out of this.'

'You think I'm still in danger?'

'No. I just think you need to get away and recuperate. For one thing the Press may make a nuisance of themselves. I'd go with you only I know I can't get any leave at the moment. Have you some relatives you could go and stay with away from this area?'

'No. Don't fuss me, Mike. I shall be all right and I've got to face up to things, I can't run away.'

'You wouldn't be running away, just making a sensible decision. You deserve a break.'

'I could go on a Retreat. David Bell has been suggesting it for a long while. He thinks it would be good preparation for my coming selection interviews.'

'Yes, well . . . ' He wasn't really sure what going on a retreat meant but he had some idea that it involved shutting oneself away in a religious house for a short period. If that was so at least she would be safe even if it wasn't exactly the convalescence he had envisaged.

'That might be a good idea. You think about it.'

★ ★ ★

Douglas Bairstow was holding a briefing to which Mike Croft and Nick Holroyd had both been summoned as well as Trevor Dickins and his team.

'We are here to discuss the attempted murder

200

of Rachel Morland.' The Superintendent paused and cleared his throat. 'The most important question we must ask ourselves is this: is it the work of our so-called Coil Shuffler? This name was written on Mrs Morland's car and we are clearly meant to assume this but I have my doubts. I think that either her attacker deliberately did this to shift blame on to the Coil Shuffler and throw us off the scent or someone else — possibly someone who was in the congregation at St Luke's that morning — scribbled it there later as some sort of sickening joke.'

'Excuse me, sir, but only a very short time elapsed between the congregation leaving the church and the message being found.' Nick spoke up. 'Hardly long enough for anyone to have got away from the crowd and done it.'

'What is Sergeant Holroyd doing here?' demanded Trevor Dickins, looking with hostility across the room at his old rival. '*He*'s not on my team.'

'I am a witness to the business,' drawled Nick.

'If it hadn't been for Holroyd's quick thinking we would be adding Rachel's photograph to these.' Bairstow gestured to the wall behind him which contained detailed photographs of the latest murder victims. 'I asked him to be present, and Croft.' He addressed Nick. 'I understand Mrs Morland's car was parked on its own away from the other cars in the church carpark?'

'Yes, it was tucked away in the corner under some trees. It is quite possible that the writing was done much earlier — I don't think anyone would have noticed it unless they had actually gone right up to the car.'

'Maybe Rachel did it herself,' said Dickins. 'Perhaps she took poison to attract attention and overdid the dose.'

Mike lurched to his feet knocking over his chair in the process. 'You're the one who's got the sick mind! Why the hell should she be an attention-seeker?'

'I don't know, you tell me, but she's already wasted police time investigating a natural death.'

'Nearly dying from a ghastly poison and suffering all the subsequent revolting treatment in hospital is hardly wasting police time!'

'All right, Croft, I'll deal with this,' said Bairstow firmly. 'You're out of order, Trevor. Rachel Morland quite rightly reported what she thought was a suspicious death and we looked into it. Is the Coil Shuffler targeting her as a result of this? Although we must bear this in mind we must concentrate on other angles. She works as a physiotherapist. Could she have had a patient, at some time in the past, whose treatment went wrong? Perhaps someone was permanently crippled as a result of it and they bear a grudge.'

'What about those Holy Joes she's involved with?' said Dickins. 'You get some real weirdos in religious sects.'

'For God's sake, this is the Church of England we're talking about!' snarled Mike. 'Rachel Morland is a licensed Reader at one of the most respectable churches in the area!'

'Come off it, Mike. We all know wars have been started in the name of religion and all manner of dreadful iniquities. What about the Spanish Inquisition?'

'The Spanish Inquisition has nothing to do with this enquiry,' said Bairstow firmly. 'We're straying from the point.'

'The point I'm trying to make is this,' persisted Dickins. 'I think she drank more than she was meant to. Someone spiked her glass with the intention of making her ill, for reasons suggested or unknown. She wasn't supposed to knock the whole glass back like that, only take a sip or two.'

'Oh, I think she was meant to have the full dose and it was done quite diabolically,' said Mike. 'She is comparatively new to preaching so she was nervous and probably started off with a dry mouth because of this. She took a couple of sips and naturally her mouth became even drier so she drank some more. Every time she tried to alleviate this dryness she made it worse and she ended up by downing the lot which nearly did for her there and then.'

'There were traces of poison in the carafe.' Bairstow cracked his knuckles and took charge again. 'The belladonna was put in there, not directly into the glass. This carafe was kept in the church porch, anybody could have got at it before the service. The verger says he refilled it before the eight o'clock communion service but as there was none left in it we must presume that the poisoner emptied some of it out leaving just enough to fill a glass when he added the potion.'

'How easy is it to get hold of deadly nightshade?' asked one of his audience.

'It is not all that common but it is around growing wild if you know where to look for it. The juice from the berries was used. So our poisoner, whether the Coil Shuffler or not, has used a substance that is available to anyone who would know and recognise its dangerous properties.'

'He hasn't used poison before, has he?'

'Not to our knowledge, but it is possible

that it could have been used in a death that slipped our net. Have Forensics reported on her car yet?' he asked Dickins.

'Yes, but nothing to help us. The name was scribbled with ordinary blackboard chalk but our chappie took care not to leave any dabs. Apart from a mass all over the outside of the car which must belong to Rachel — we'll have to check this when she's well enough — the only other ones belong to her friend, the nurse Pat Fenton. They are on the boot and side of the back window and are consistent with her leaning forward to get a good look when she first saw the writing.'

'Have all the congregation been interviewed?'

'There are still a few more we haven't caught up with but we should get the rest of them checked out today. As expected, no one admits to seeing anything unusual or suspicious.'

At that moment there was an interruption as the door opened and a young detective constable hurried in looking elated.

'What time do you call this, Willis? The briefing was arranged for nine o'clock, not' — Bairstow consulted his watch — 'nine thirty-eight.'

'Sorry, sir, I had car problems.'

There were exaggerated groans from around the room that turned to jeers when he added:

'I couldn't start. In the end I had to leave the old bus behind and come in by public transport.'

'You want to get a *real* car, Willis, not a Noddy toy,' sniggered one of his colleagues.

'It paid off,' continued Paul Willis, ignoring the interruption. 'Just wait till you hear this!'

'Well, Willis, we're waiting.' Bairstow folded his arms and looked pained.

'I walked across Thackeray Park to pick up the bus at Oldgate, there's a better service from there. While I was waiting I went into the newsagent to get a paper — that's the newsagent on the corner of Oldgate and Priory Street.'

'I presume there is some point in this preamble?'

'Yes, sir. When I came out there was still no sign of the bus so I looked over the adverts in the window. It was there, sir, the Coil Shuffler's advert!' His voice rose and there was an answering buzz from his audience.

'Go on,' said the superintendent sharply.

'It was the same as the one that was in the paper only instead of a box number there was a phone number.'

'Did you take any action?'

'No, I just made a note of it and came straight here.'

'Good. We're going to tread carefully this time and make sure we trace him.'

In the general excitement of the discussion that followed nobody noticed Nick Holroyd get up and slip out of the door. Mike realised that he was missing a little later when the meeting split up but he didn't see him again until later in the morning when Nick pounced on him as he was making his way to the canteen.

'Come on, the car's outside.'

'What are you talking about?'

'Your physiotherapy session. I'm driving you there.'

'Don't be ridiculous. Rachel's in hospital, it's been cancelled.'

'Yes, but they don't know that, do they?' Nick made a sweeping gesture with one hand embracing the entire manpower of the station. 'Officially you've been allocated to another physiotherapist.'

'Do you mind telling me what this is all about?' asked Mike as he stumbled alongside his friend across the carpark. 'Where are we going?'

'To my place. We've got to plan our strategy and I've got to check my answerphone. Now, don't argue, just trust Uncle Nick.'

'That fills me with confidence, I don't think!'

Nick grinned but refused to say anything more as they drove across the city to his flat. For once it was dry though very breezy. Wisps of ragged cloud tore across the sky, through which the sun shone fitfully, highlighting the damp, glistening rooftops and casting purple and grey shadows on the pavements below. Leaves whipped off trees and whirled like a caramel snowstorm across the windscreen and detritus from the market bowled along the road and clogged the gutters.

'Are you producing lunch?' asked Mike sarcastically as they drove past a fish and chip shop and the aroma fleetingly entered the car.

'I can heat up a can of soup and run to cheese on toast. Will that do?'

'It's no substitute for the steak and kidney pudding I had promised myself. I don't know why you're dragging me off, but it had better be good. And what happened to you this morning? You were actually allowed in on a meeting about the Coil Shuffler and you duck out in the middle of it. Don't you want to know what transpired after you disappeared?'

'Let me guess. Top priority is tracing that phone number to get a name and address — right? But information like that is covered by the Data Protection Act so there will have to be a formal application and that will take time. In the meanwhile I've rung that number.'

'You've *what*!!!! Nick, if you bugger up this investigation — '

'Keep your cool. Don't you want to know what happened?'

'Okay, what happened?'

'I got an answerphone telling me to leave my name and telephone number and an indication of my problem and I would be contacted. It was a male voice, pretty nondescript — no obvious accent and difficult to tell how old. I put the receiver down.'

'Knowing you I can't believe you left it there.'

'I thought about it and I concocted a message and rang again. I disguised my voice and called myself John Smith. I said I had an elderly mother who was incontinent and bedridden and whose quality of life was nil, and I needed help. Then I left my phone number. Hopefully by now there will be a message waiting on my answerphone.'

'So this is why we're going round to your place. You're rather optimistic, aren't you? Expecting a return call so quickly? How long is it — barely a couple of hours since you left your message?'

'We may be lucky. It's worth checking

so that we can get a piece of the action before the official investigation comes up with something.'

He swung the car round a corner into his road and drew up outside his flat. It was on the ground floor of an Edwardian house that had been divided into two apartments. The small front garden had once held a strip of lawn surrounded by flower-beds and enclosed by elaborate wrought-iron railings. These railings had never been replaced after World War II and the area was now paved in and a dying hebe in a plastic pot was the sole sign of vegetation. He unlocked the door and bent down to pick up the junk mail scattered on the doormat. A dark narrow corridor ran from the front to the back door and four rooms led off this, one behind the other, ending in a bathroom that had been made out of the original scullery. The rooms were high-ceilinged and narrow and he had once confided in Mike that it was rather like living in a lofty railway carriage.

As they went into the living-room the light was blinking on the telephone. Nick gave a grunt of satisfaction and loped across the room to activate the answering machine. There was a pause after Nick's voice invited his caller to leave a message and then a booming voice rang out. 'This is Bob

Marshall. I'm back in the area again for a couple of weeks on a course. How about cracking a bottle one evening? I'm staying at the Cat and Fiddle, give me a ring.'

Mike smirked. 'Is that the Bob Marshall who used to work for the Probation Service?'

'Yes. Sssh, there's another message.'

This time the voice was quieter and more deliberate. 'Calling John Smith in reply to his call of 10.15 a.m. If you would like to discuss your problem please ring this number at 6.30 this evening.' The number was repeated twice and then the line went dead.

'It's the same voice,' said Nick in elation. 'We've made contact with the Coil Shuffler!'

'You've got another phone number. He's going to make sure he covers his tracks. If you call at 6.30 this evening you'll just get another message.'

'I'm not going to wait until 6.30. I'm going to trace that call.'

'Oh, yes? And who is going to hand out that information to you when they won't give it to the official team without pressure?'

'I know someone who works for BT in Directory Enquiries. She owes me.'

'I might have known it would be a woman. You think you're just going to sweet-talk her and get the number just like that?'

'It's a local number. I'm sure she'll assist if I press her.'

'Nick, you can't do this. You're jeopardising the whole operation, quite apart from your career and mine.'

'Look, you go in the kitchen and start lunch whilst I have a go and then you can pretend you don't know what I'm up to.'

Mike shrugged and gave up the argument. In the kitchen he found a tin of soup in one of the cupboards, opened it and poured it into a saucepan and set it on the stove, lighting the gas underneath. As he busied himself slicing cheese and making toast he could hear Nick on the phone in the other room but couldn't make out what he was saying. He took two bowls from the draining rack and was pouring the soup into them when Nick joined him.

'She's going to ring me back.'

'Mr Fix-it himself. You always know a little man, or more often a little woman, who will oblige you, don't you? You're working on the wrong side of the fence, you'd really make it with the criminal fraternity.'

Nick grinned and took cutlery out of the drawer and laid the table before putting on the kettle. They had finished their makeshift meal and were drinking coffee when the phone rang. Nick leapt up and rushed to

212

answer it. He came back a few minutes later looking smug.

'What do you know — it's a public phone box. The one on the corner of Burleigh Road and Overton Street, at the edge of the Crofts Estate. This couldn't be better. We can stake it out; park the car nearby and sit in it and phone the box from my mobile and see who answers the call.'

'No, we've got to go public on this. We can't keep this information to ourselves, you've got to tell Bairstow what you've found out.'

'I can't, can I? Not without us getting it in the neck.'

'No, you bloody can't!' Mike lurched to his feet and pushed his stool violently under the table. 'Why do I let you talk me into these situations?'

'I don't know why you're getting so uptight. We agreed to try and flush out the Coil Shuffler ourselves and now we're getting somewhere you're getting cold feet.'

'Because it's my job on the line, that's why. You may not care about yours — I sometimes think you're actively trying to get kicked out — but I need *my* job and I enjoy it. Besides, if I'm out on my backside who is going to employ a cripple?'

'You're over-reacting. What harm is there

213

in just doing what I've suggested? After all, he may not turn up. The first phone number could have been traced by now and he may already be under arrest.'

'And what do you intend doing if he *does* turn up? Tap him on the shoulder and say, 'I believe you're the Coil Shuffler,' and arrest him?'

'We'll have to play it by ear. We've got no evidence to make an arrest, but if I can communicate with him on the phone I can tell him I want my poor old mother done away with and see how he reacts. With any luck we'll find out how he operates and actually plans a job and how payment is arranged.'

'He's not going to incriminate himself by handing out his name and address to a complete stranger, is he?'

'He's done this before. I'm sure he has what he thinks is a foolproof method of conducting his business but we'll have the advantage because he won't know I'm a police officer and not a genuine punter. Also, he may give a false name and address but there is nothing to stop us from following him and finding out where he hangs out.'

'And then you'll make an anonymous phone call to Bairstow and feed him the information?'

'Hell, I want to reap the benefit from this. I want to nail the bastard, not let Dickins get all the glory.'

'This is what it's all about, isn't it? Pipping Dickins at the post; that's all you care about! The fact that Rachel's husband may have been killed by the Coil Shuffler and an attempt has been made on her life are just incidental!'

'Hang on! It's those facts that are urging me on. Be honest, don't you want the chance of revenge for his attack on Rachel?'

'Don't tempt me.'

'So you'll back me up this evening?'

'You'll go ahead whether I'm there or not, won't you, so I'd better be around to hold your hand.'

'Thanks, pal. How *is* Rachel, by the way?'

'She's made a remarkable recovery and she's being discharged today.'

'They're letting her home already? Will she be okay?'

'She's going to Holgate Hall for a few days to convalesce.'

'Holgate Hall? Isn't that a monastery?'

'It was a nunnery. It is now an ecumenical centre where people go for quiet weekends and retreats and that sort of thing.'

'Retreats? What is Rachel retreating from — you?'

'Ha, ha, very funny. It is what she wants to do and peace and rest will do her good. David Bell was driving her over there this morning.'

'Granted she needs rest and relaxation but I should have thought she also needed cheering up. Sitting in a cell all on your lonesome contemplating your navel is hardly likely to buck you up.'

'You're mixing your religions, and anyway, what would *you* know about it, you ignorant heathen?'

★ ★ ★

Sitting on her bed several miles away at Holgate Hall Rachel's thoughts were echoing Nick Holroyd's. Perhaps it hadn't been such a good idea to insist on coming here. There was no doubt she needed the rest and a stress-free atmosphere in which to fully recover, but mentally it was a different matter. Contemplation and getting to really know oneself were traditional reasons for retreat but she was not sure she wanted to analyse her feelings. She had been acting out of character of late, experiencing emotions and doing things that were alien to her perceived nature. Her simple and straightforward life had been turned on its head and she was no

216

longer sure who she was or where she was going. As for contemplation, her thoughts were running riot, buzzing round her head like peas in a pottle, completely out of control. How did Christopher die? Why had someone tried to kill her? How did she really feel about Mike? What was she going to do about her supposed vocation?

She groaned and rested her head in her hands. She should be praying, asking for God's assistance in sorting out the chaos in her mind, but she felt unable to pray. She seemed to be living in some sort of limbo, not unlike the state she had been in immediately after Christopher's death, and the feeling of being cast adrift, of slipping the Church's anchor, was horrible. As least she was now sure of one thing — she wanted to live. When Christopher had died she had wanted to die too. She had known that this was impossible, that somehow she had to struggle on and fill the years that stretched before her until they were reunited at her death, but the future was something she would have passed on if she had been able. Her work as a physiotherapist and her Christian beliefs had fleshed out a framework within which to operate but there had been an emptiness, a hollowness that nothing could fill. But now she felt differently. As they had worked on her in hospital she had known that she did not want to die. She had wanted to recover and start living again. Was this because Mike had come into her life or because becoming a priest was now at last a real possibility? Or was it sheer cussedness brought about by the thought that someone had tried to kill her and she wasn't going to allow them that satisfaction?

She decided she needed distraction, not solitary confinement. She would go down to the refectory and get tea and then go to Evensong. Perhaps in the beautiful old chapel attached to the Hall she would find the sense of comfort and belonging that she seemed to be in danger of losing. It wasn't that her faith was at all shaky, she told herself as she very carefully descended the broad oak staircase. She was content in the knowledge that her beliefs were firm and unwavering; it was rather the channelling of this faith to render the best service to God and her fellow men that was worrying her. Did she really feel being ordained into the priesthood of the Church of England was the best way for her? Not but that she might have already blown it. That sermon . . . the sermon she had preached on that fateful Sunday morning . . . had it been too reactionary? Too slanted?

She had a vague memory of a sea of faces looking up at her as she had stood in the pulpit, the expressions ranging from annoyance to horror. Had this been because of the content of her sermon or because she had been starting to display symptoms of the poison? She had tried to bring this up with David Bell in the car earlier that day but he had turned aside her questions and urged her to concentrate on getting well. Perhaps her self-searching was all in vain and she was already *persona non grata* with the diocesan elders?

★ ★ ★

The two men waited in the car which was parked in the pub carpark across the road from the phone box. The Crofts Estate was a private housing estate that had been built in the sixties on a redundant playing-field belonging to a prep school that had gone bust. It consisted of half a dozen roads containing two-and three-bedroomed houses and bungalows covering a wedge-shaped area. At the narrow end of this wedge a road of bungalows met at right angles a row of shops situated on the main artery that led into the city. It was on this corner that the phone box was situated and the pub yard across the way made an excellent vantage point.

Mike shifted his aching back and tried to get more comfortable. 'I'm still not sure what you actually mean to do.'

'At six thirty we ring the phone box from the mobile and see who answers it, then we'll take it from there.' Nick squinted out of the window. 'We've got an excellent view of the two approach roads, if anyone goes near that phone we'll see them.'

'Have you considered that whilst we've been watching this callbox the Coil Shuffler could also be staking out the area and could have already spotted us?'

'I don't think so. We've been here a long time and we've seen nothing suspicious.'

'You can say that again.' Mike groaned and eased his cramped legs.

'He's not going to hang around the area drawing attention to himself and when he does turn up he's not going to see us. We're under cover here, parked right up against the wall, and if he does notice the car he certainly won't be able to see us inside.'

'He could be waiting in the pub already.'

'That's true, he'd have a good view of the box from the front bar. Perhaps we should have got here earlier and sussed out the pub's customers.'

'It's nearly 6.30.' Mike consulted his watch.

'Wait till it's spot on and then dial. We're lucky there are no pedestrians about to muddy the situation.'

Mike counted off the seconds and then raised his eyebrows. Nick nodded so he punched out the number on his mobile. From where they were parked they could not hear if the phone was ringing inside the box. Nothing occurred at first and then two things happened at once. The saloon door of the pub opened and a man stepped out on to the pavement and a car drew up adjacent to the phone box. It was a red Rover 620 and Mike knew he had seen it before somewhere. The driver's door opened and out stepped a dumpy, middle-aged woman clutching a mobile phone.

'That's Pat Fenton! What the hell is she doing here?'

'She'll bugger the whole thing up!'

The two men watched in frustration as she tapped her phone, shook it violently and then walked towards the box. The man who had come out of the pub and started to cross the road hesitated when he saw her, looked around him and then veered off to the right, hurrying down Burleigh Road.

'Shit! She's scared him off!'

'We don't know if he is anything to do with it. He could be quite innocent.'

'I'm going to follow him.' Nick slipped out of the car and disappeared into the shadows leaving Mike to deal with the phone call. He watched Pat Fenton push open the door and go inside the box. She picked up the receiver.

'Hallo?' Her hesitant voice echoed in his ear and he cut the connection with a curse. Of all the damn bad luck! As he watched she replaced the receiver looking puzzled and then picked it up again and punched out a number. She spoke briefly to the unknown recipient of her call and then hung up and went back to her car. She rummaged inside and backed out holding her nursing bag and, after locking the door, pushed open the gate of the nearby bungalow and walked up the path to the front door.

Nick flung open the door and slumped behind the wheel.

'I lost him. He had a car parked down the end of the road and he drove off in it. It was too far away to get the number.'

'Did you get a good look at him?'

'No, it was hopeless. He's about medium height, dressed in jeans and a dark jacket. I didn't see his face, and no, I wouldn't recognise him again. What happened here?'

Mike told him what had transpired and Nick thumped the wheel in disgust. 'That bloody woman! She's always popping up when she's not wanted!'

9

'The phone number is registered to a Miss Pat Fenton of 14 Bacton Road. We know her, she's already involved in this case.' Trevor Dickins couldn't keep the triumph out of his voice as he discussed with the superintendent the information obtained from BT.

'Refresh my memory.'

'She's a friend of Rachel Morland — the nursing friend — and she was there when the attempt was made on her life and she was the one who supposedly found the Coil Shuffler's name written on the car. And what is more, she was the person who found Bert Pryke dead and who supported the doctor in his diagnosis of heart failure.'

'Which it was.'

'I'm beginning to wonder what caused the heart failure.'

'You're saying this Pat Fenton is the Coil Shuffler? That our homicides were committed by a *woman*?'

'It is quite possible. She's strong as an ox, nurses have to be, and she's got the medical knowledge. As we've said before, our killer knew what he — or she — was doing. I've long had my suspicions that the Coil Shuffler is connected with the medical profession. She would be in a unique position to knock off unwanted wrinklies; a health visitor with access to the victim and the means of doing them in.'

'Bert Pryke . . . ' Bairstow tapped his pen on his desk and looked grim. 'There will have to be another autopsy. We'll get in the Home Office pathologist this time.'

'Too late. He's already been consigned to the furnace.'

The superintendent got to his feet and paced the floor. 'She could be responsible for deaths such as Bert Pryke's, I'll buy that, but Eddie Briers? Graham Scott?'

'We just took it for granted that it was a man, but there's no reason why they couldn't have been carried out by a woman; a reasonably fit woman who knew what to do.'

'Have you considered the possibility that she has an accomplice? That there is more than one person involved?'

'Rachel Morland herself could be involved. There was something fishy about the fuss she made over her husband's suicide. Perhaps she is in cahoots with Fenton and they've fallen out and hence the attack on her. And I'll tell you something else, sir, Fenton is in the money. Lives in a very nice, up-market bungalow and drives a Rover that she certainly didn't pay for out of her nurse's salary.'

'Mmm. This advert that was placed in the shop window — can we get an identification from the shop owner?'

'No. It was a postal job again. The card was mailed with a postal order to cover four weeks' advertising rate, it wasn't delivered in person.'

'So you have no proof if she denies knowing anything about it?'

'If we can get a search warrant and go over her house I'm sure we'll find something to incriminate her.'

'You won't get a warrant on such flimsy grounds. You'll have to come up with some more convincing evidence before a magistrate will grant you one.'

'Now we know where to look I'm sure we'll dig up something. She may panic and give herself away when she knows we've traced her.'

'You intend to face her with it?'

'Yes, sir. I don't expect we'll get a confession but her reaction may give us a lead.'

'Do you think this is a wise move? Wouldn't it be best to investigate her thoroughly before you show your hand? Try to come up with some more facts that tie her in with the case before you move in?'

'I'm hoping to panic her into giving something away. At the moment we haven't got enough evidence to support an investigation into her financial affairs but once she knows we're on to her she may go to pieces.'

'Are you going to bring her into the station for questioning?'

'Not straight away. We'll tackle her at home first. I intend going round about six o'clock this evening, she should be back from work by then. I'll take Coleman with me, he's good with middle-aged biddies.'

'Well, I suppose you know what you're doing, Trevor. Get results but make sure your chief suspect doesn't do a runner.'

★ ★ ★

'You're not going to believe this. That phone number in the advert is Pat Fenton's.'

It was the following morning and Mike Croft was bringing Holroyd up to date with what had transpired the day before with the official investigation.

'What! You're having me on!'

'I'm not.'

'My God! And we thought it was our bad

luck and timing when she turned up at that phone box! She really *was* going to answer the call — she's our Coil Shuffler!.'

'Don't get all excited. Don't you want to know what happened next?'

'Tricky Trevor has a plan of action — what is he going to do with this information?'

'Done. He's already made a move. She was questioned yesterday evening and she denied everything. Said she didn't know how her phone number had got on the advert but it was nothing to do with her.'

'Well, she would say that, wouldn't she?'

'There's more. She complained that a strange message was left on her answerphone that didn't make sense at the time. It was *yours*, Nick. It's all on record — you asking for help in dealing with your unwanted mother. Fortunately she didn't save it so they can't trace your voice. They're stymied unless they can dig up some other evidence and we've got that evidence. We must tell them what happened the evening before last.'

'No, wait. Apart from dropping us in the shit, she can deny that just as effectively. She can say that her mobile was on the blink and when she went to the public phone box to make a call the phone rang and went dead when she answered it. No one can prove otherwise. Look, she's under

228

suspicion, they're going to dig and dig until they come up with something else to really tie her in. Our little episode is not going to swing it.'

Mike shrugged and kneaded his forehead. 'I still can't take it in, that Pat Fenton may be the Coil Shuffler. I've been going over all the cases we know of and it still seems highly unlikely.'

'But possible.'

'What about Rachel's poisoning? That couldn't have been her, Rachel's her best friend.'

'Think it through. She's very possessive and now Rachel's met you and she thinks she's going to lose her she may have decided to kill her to get her own back on you, especially as she knows we're investigating the case.'

'But for Christ's sake, she was *there*, with us, when it happened. You saw how concerned she was.'

'She may have had regrets when she saw the poison actually working, but when you think about it, she wasn't much help at the time. It wasn't down to her that Rachel's survived. Also, she could easily have scribbled the name on Rachel's car when she went to get hers afterwards. There was nobody left in the car park by then.

She could have done it in the few seconds before she came running back to tell me about it.'

'She could have done in Bert Pryke. She was the one who found him but suppose he was still alive when she visited him and she killed him and pretended she had discovered him dead — but how did she do it so that it looked like a heart attack?'

'If anyone could, a nurse could, and just think of that business with Rachel's husband. She could have killed him and don't ask why. With him out of the way she may have thought Rachel would have more time for her, unless it was a compassionate killing.'

'She may have another go at Rachel — she must be warned!'

'I don't think so. Now she knows we're suspicious of her she's likely to lie low for the time being.'

'Still, Rachel must be told, to prepare her and put her on her guard. It's going to be a hell of a shock for her.'

'Once she faces up to the fact that her bosom pal has got it in for her she may be able to come up with some evidence to connect Fenton to the action.'

'You never give up, do you? Leave it, Nick, it's out of our hands now.'

'I'll drive you over to Holgate Hall this evening. You'll need a lift and I promise to stay in the car whilst you bend the lovely Rachel's ear.'

★ ★ ★

'I'm not supposed to have visitors, you shouldn't have come.'

'It's not a prison, is it? They're not going to wall you up or whatever they did in the olden days when a nun had truck with someone of the opposite sex.'

'Oh, don't be ridiculous. It's good to see you, but I don't know how you got in.'

Rachel had been to Compline. She had come out of the candle-lit chapel to find Mike waiting for her in the cloister. He had loomed up out of the shadows, startling her until she had recognised him.

'I had to tell them I was a police officer. I'm sorry if I've interrupted your meditation but there are things you need to know.'

'So this is an official visit? Well, I suppose it will give me a certain cachet, there can't be many visitors here who have the police on their tail.'

'How are you feeling?'

'I'm fine,' she said slowly, 'just a little spaced out still. I can't believe it really happened to me. Have the police found out who put the poison in the glass? Is that why you are here?'

'Can we go somewhere and talk?'

She considered this. 'The library would be the best place, we're not likely to be disturbed there.'

She took him through the main body of the Hall, up the front staircase and along a meandering corridor into the library. It was empty and in darkness and Rachel snapped on the lights to reveal a long rectangular room lined with bookshelves. They went towards the tables and chairs set out at the far end but before she could sit down Mike gathered Rachel in his arms and kissed her very satisfactorily.

'I don't suppose this room has seen much action along these lines,' he mussed her hair and ran a finger along her jaw, 'but I thought I had lost you. I want to keep you under lock and key.'

'I thought this was an official visit?' Rachel shakily disengaged herself and sat down abruptly.

'I got carried away.' Mike grinned and eased himself onto a chair. 'I suppose all those books are religious ones?'

'You'd be surprised if you looked closely. By the way, how did you get here?'

'Nick drove me over.'

'He's here too?' she asked sharply.

'Don't worry, he has strict instructions not to set foot on the premises. There's a very convenient pub just down the road. I shouldn't think he's the first escapee from this place.'

'We're not prisoners, you know. We come of our own free will and it's up to us what we get from it.'

'Sorry, I didn't mean to be facetious. You're certainly looking much better.'

'What has happened? What have you got to tell me?'

Looking at her composed, innocent face Mike didn't know how to break the news to her. How did you tell someone that her best friend was a murderer who had most likely killed her husband and made an attempt on her life? It was almost as bad as breaking the news to a relative that a loved one had been murdered or killed in a road accident. He approached it obliquely.

'How well do you know Pat Fenton? Have you been friends for long?'

'For several years and I suppose I know her as well as anyone. What's this all about? Why do you want to know about Pat?'

'I'm afraid you don't know her as well as you think you do.'

233

Briefly he told her about the latest developments in the investigation into the Coil Shuffler and she heard him out in stunned silence. When he had finished she shook her head in disbelief.

'You're not serious? You think Pat is . . . is the Coil Shuffler? That's ridiculous!'

'Is it? Just think about it.'

'Pat is a nurse. She's trained to *heal* people, not kill them! Apart from anything else what reason could she possibly have?'

'Money?'

'Oh, well, you're wrong there. She inherited a fortune a few years back. She doesn't need to work at all but she's such a caring, humanitarian person that she prefers to carry on with her nursing. What's the matter? Why are you looking at me like that?'

'Don't you see — you've just added another piece of evidence to the dossier building up against her. She's in the money.'

'But . . .'

'I don't think she inherited that money. I think she'd been earning it in a particularly diabolical way.'

'I just can't believe this.' Rachel got to her feet and walked over to a window pressing her forehead against the cold pane and staring out into the dark night. Mike watched her sympathetically, wondering how long she would take to relate what he had just told her to her own personal tragedies. He didn't have long to wait.

'What about Christopher's death? Are you saying that Pat gave him the overdose?' She spun round and plunged back to the table. 'Why should she do that?'

'Perhaps she was acting on compassionate grounds in his case.'

'I can't take this in but if what you say were true, how do you account for her trying to kill me? I presume you think she did that also?'

'I do. She doesn't like your friendship with me, does she? She's tried to put her spoke in there, you've told me so.'

'Yes, well, naturally she feels she's been rather sidelined.'

'If she's a killer she will have had no compunction about taking you out if only to revenge herself on us who are trying to track down the Coil Shuffler.'

'But this is ridiculous, Mike, she was with me in the church, *helping* me.'

'Was she? Granted, she was fussing round like a blue-arsed fly, she'd have had to, wouldn't she? But if Nick hadn't realised what was wrong with you I don't think she would have come up with the answer, do you? I think she would have soon been acting the part of the shocked, bereaved friend.'

'You think she may make another attempt to harm me?'

'She knows she is under suspicion so I shouldn't think she would be mad enough to try anything, but we can't take that risk. You mustn't see her, has she been to visit you?'

'I told you, they don't encourage visitors.'

'So she's had no contact with you since you came here?'

'She has phoned and she's offered to give me a lift back to my flat when I leave.'

'No, Rachel, you mustn't let her near you. I'll arrange transport for you.'

'A police car or Nick? Or perhaps both together?'

'Why do you dislike him so?'

'I don't dislike him, but he always seems to be around, hovering in the background.'

★ ★ ★

Pat Fenton loaded the dishwasher and switched it on and then swept the kitchen floor. This done she checked her fridge for supplies, wrote up her shopping list and then took off her apron and hung it up and went through into the sitting-room. She switched on the television in time to catch the second half of the early evening news bulletin and settled down to watch it. The knock on the front door startled her and sent a frisson of apprehension curling through her. Surely it wasn't the police again? She thought she had convinced them that they had got it all wrong and that she was entirely innocent of the allegations made. They had appeared satisfied at the time. She wondered whether to ignore the caller but another bout of knocking made her change her mind. They knew she was in, her car was in the drive, and they wouldn't go away. Sighing, she pushed herself up out of the chair and went into the hall. She fumbled with the lock and opened the door. There was nobody there.

The porch was empty and she peered out into the night but could see no one walking down the garden path. It was those damn children again. They knew she lived on her own and was an easy prey for their stupid games. Having got her out they were probably at the end of the road by now. She was about to turn back indoors when she heard a noise in the bushes over by the garden shed. The little devils were hiding over there. They'd wait until she went back inside and then come banging again. Well, she would soon sort them out. She strode across the lawn determined to flush out the miscreants. She didn't see the figure that had been lurking behind the holly bush at the side of the porch creep out and slip into the house.

There was no one in the bushes or inside the shed. Whoever had been there had disappeared. Grumbling to herself she retraced her steps and went back inside the bungalow. She locked the door behind her and shot the bolts and then bent down and took off her wet shoes. She padded down the hall and retrieved her slippers from the hall cupboard, annoyed that she had probably missed the end of the news and the weather forecast. As she went into the sitting-room her eyes immediately sought out the television screen. She did not at first notice the figure dressed in black waiting beside the chesterfield. When she did she gave a little scream and backed towards the door.

'Who are you?'

Eyes glinted at her behind the Balaclava mask.

'You know who I am, don't you?'

'The Coil Shuffler!' she gasped faintly as the figure advanced on her and she saw the hypodermic in the gloved hand.

★ ★ ★

Nick was chatting up the barmaid when Mike limped into the pub. He raised a hand and had a beer waiting by the time his friend had hauled himself on to a bar stool.

'Tina here says they often get refugees in from up the road. Even had nuns in full regalia.'

'Are you sure they weren't kissagrams?' Mike took a slurp out of his glass.

'You get all sorts staying up there,' Tina confided, leaning across the bar. 'I reckon they come in here for the company as much as the booze. They get pissed off being all on their lonesome. Still, they're never any trouble.' She spoke as if the guests at Holgate Hall might be expected to run amok under certain conditions.

'Having a centre like that in the village must bring in custom for the locals.'

'Well, as I say, you get the odd one coming in here but generally speaking they keep themselves to themselves. The management don't patronise the village shops, they bulk-buy in the city, but they do employ some of the locals for cleaning and in the kitchens. I'll tell you something — the vicar here don't have much truck with them, they don't go to his church.'

'They have their own chapel.' Mike set down his glass and shifted on his stool.

'Yes, well it don't seem right, do it? Mind you, the local chap is very low church — not that I go — and it's all crucifixes and statues up there, even incense I believe.' Tina flicked a cloth over the bar top and moved off to serve someone in the public bar and Mike stowed away that titbit to amuse Rachel.

'They let you in, then?' Nick regarded his friend with a grin. 'How is she?'

'Fine, but she didn't like what I had to tell her.'

'I bet she didn't. Did she believe you?'

'She thought I was out of my tree to start with but she's beginning to take it on board. At least I got through to her that Fenton could still be a danger to her.'

'Has Fenton made any attempt to visit her?'

'No, but she's arranged to give Rachel a lift home when she leaves on Sunday. I nipped that in the bud.'

'So Fenton's expecting to drive over here on Sunday and pick Rachel up? She'll have to be told she's not needed.'

'Nick . . . ' Mike spoke warningly.

'What better excuse could we have? We'll pop round early tomorrow morning — we're both off duty — and tell her that we are picking up Rachel and taking her out to lunch. It's a marvellous opportunity to have

240

a snoop round and get her talking.'

'Christ! If you muscle in on Dickins' case again you'll really blow it for both of us.'

'But this will be a social visit, it's nothing to with the official police enquiry. You're Rachel's boyfriend and you're just calling round to tell her that other arrangements have been made for bringing Rachel home.'

'And you?'

'I'm your chauffeur, aren't I?'

'But what do you think we're going to find? A bottle marked poison sitting on the table or a stash of Coil Shuffler's cards?'

'If she is the Coil Shuffler there must be some somewhere in that bungalow. I don't suppose we'll get a chance to search the place unless you engage her in conversation and I manage to slip — '

'Forget it,' cut in Mike before he could finish. 'She's not an OAP being bamboozled by a doorstep salesman.'

'All right, but we know her. We've got that advantage over Dickins and his team. She's a friend of Rachel, you're a friend of Rachel; it's only natural that we should discuss what's happened and mull it over. If we're clever we should be able to draw her out and with any luck she'll say something incriminating.'

'I take it we pretend not to know

anything about her being fingered as the Coil Shuffler?'

'Oh, I think so, don't you?'

* * *

He looked down at the figure slumped in the easy chair. She was not a pretty corpse. Her skirt had ridden up exposing her bolster legs sprawled open and her face was twisted in terror. He reached down and clamped her right hand round the syringe and then dropped it on the floor near her feet. The television was still burbling away and he switched it off and stood surveying the room. Her handbag was lying on the coffee table and he quickly searched through it, taking out the bunch of keys and the diary. He flicked through this but realised almost immediately that it contained nothing of interest. He returned it to the bag and prowled round the room.

There was an ornate bureau in one corner and he found the appropriate key and opened it, rifling through the contents of the drawers and pigeon-holes. There were bank statements and receipts and all the paraphernalia one would expect to find but not what he was searching for. The bookcase contained mainly paperbacks and book club editions plus a collection of nursing manuals and he moved on across the hall and into the main bedroom. This was frilly and pink. The duvet cover, valance and curtains, complete with drapes and bows, were a riot of shocking pink, magenta and cerise roses on a coral background. The carpet was crimson and the wallpaper carried the same rose motif in less strident pinks and peach. It was not the decor one would envisage for a plain middle-aged spinster and he recoiled from the onslaught to his senses. After a quick look through the wardrobe and drawers, which held only sensible, frumpish clothes, he went into the next room off the hall.

This looked more hopeful. It had been her study and the room was dominated by a large modern desk on which stood a word processor and printer. Good, that fitted in with his plans. The desk had three drawers down each side. They contained computer paper, disks and stationery apart from the bottom right-hand one, which was larger and locked. He found the key and opened it. When he saw the contents he grunted in satisfaction. He had struck gold. He had been sure she must keep records and here they were, together with a pile of Coil Shuffler cards.

He lifted out the files and looked through

them carefully. The bitch! How ingenious she had been but she'd nearly screwed it up for him. It was all there in detail, the police would be over the moon when they got their hands on this little lot. He searched through the file for two years ago and when he found the pages he was looking for he slipped them out of the binder and sealed them in an addressed envelope he had brought with him and put it in his pocket. He then carried the files through to the sitting-room and laid them on the coffee table, which he placed beside the chair holding Pat Fenton's body. From another pocket he took out a sheet of printed paper and, bending down, he lifted her limp hand and folded her fingers round it. When he relaxed his grip the paper fluttered to the ground and he picked it up again in his gloved hand and placed it on top of the files.

He made a return visit to the study and scooped up the pile of cards that had been in the locked drawer. He slammed the drawer shut, relocked it and carried the cards into the sitting-room where he scattered them on the floor around her feet. Then he took another card from his jacket and dropped this on top. That should puzzle them.

He checked round the room to make sure there was nothing he had overlooked and then went through into the kitchen, intending to go out via the back door. A wine bottle stood on the worktop beside the sink, still half-full of red wine. He picked it up and took a long swig at it, then wiped the neck and set it down again. He felt the old exhilaration coursing through his veins. Another successful operation, the only difference being that this one brought no monetary reward. It was a necessary execution and now there would be no check to his activities.

He unlocked the back door and slipped out, shutting it behind him but not relocking it. Only the crackle from a snapped twig betrayed his progress through the garden. Then there was silence.

★ ★ ★

When Mike Croft and Nick Holroyd drove along Bacton Road the next morning they found another car parked outside Pat Fenton's bungalow.

'Damn, she's got visitors.'

'It may be nothing to do with her. The curtains are still shut. She could be having a lie-in and that car belongs to one of the neighbours.'

'Maybe. Let's have a quick scout round

and see if she's about.'

Nick parked behind the green Fiat and the two men got out and went towards the bungalow. As they walked up the path a woman appeared from round the side of the building. She was wearing the navy coat and hat of a district nurse and there was a worried expression on her face which relaxed when she saw them.

'Is Miss Fenton in?' asked Mike.

'I don't know. I can't raise her, but her car's here . . . are you looking for her too?'

'We were hoping to have a word with her. Are you one of her work colleagues?'

'Yes. She didn't come in to the clinic this morning. We were supposed to have a case conference and it's most unusual for her not to turn up without a word. I wondered if she was ill — she's been looking very off-colour for the last few days — so I called round to see if anything was wrong.'

'Perhaps her car wouldn't start and she's gone off on foot.'

'I don't know.' The woman looked worried again. 'The curtains haven't been drawn back but I'm sure the lights are still on behind them.'

'We'd better have a look,' said Nick, thinking that Fenton had probably done a runner and wishing that they had come round yesterday evening.'

'Are you friends of hers?'

'We're police officers.'

'Then there *is* something wrong!'

'We're not here on official business, but here's my ID card.' Mike showed her it. 'This is a social call but it looks as if she may well have been taken ill. Have you tried the back door?'

'I didn't actually attempt to open it. I took it for granted it would be locked.' She followed them as they moved round the side of the bungalow and Mike tried to stall her.

'Why don't you wait in your car whilst we try and get in?'

'If she's ill don't you think I'd better be around? I am a nurse, after all.'

They had no answer to this so the three of them went to the back door. As the woman had said, the curtains at all the windows were still closed but there did seem to be chinks of light from behind some of them. A pint of milk stood in a holder beside the step. Nick squared up to the door expecting to have to break in but to his surprise it wasn't locked and it opened when he turned the handle. They stepped into a small, square lobby. A pair of wellies stood on the tiled floor and an old coat and anorak hung from the pegs on the wall. To the right a utility room led off this lobby and the door to the left led into the kitchen. The light was on and there was no sign that anyone had prepared or eaten a meal in there that morning. The central heating rumbled away but the kettle was stone cold when Mike put his hand to it. They moved into the hall and Nick pushed open the first door and poked his head inside. It was dark and he reached for the light switch and snapped it on revealing Pat Fenton's bedroom. The bed was made up and he was pretty sure it hadn't been slept in the night before.

'Is she . . . ?' The woman tried to see past him into the room.

'No, she's not in bed. It doesn't look as if she's here.' His experienced eye swept round the en-suite bathroom noting the clinical precision of the towels hanging on the rail and the lack of any steam or dampness in the atmosphere.

Mike had moved on to the next room. It was the sitting-room and as soon as he entered it he knew something was very wrong. The overhead light spilled down on the chair underneath it which was facing away from the door. It was occupied but all he could see was a head lolling at an unnatural angle against the left arm and a limp hand trailing on the floor. He lurched across the room and looked down on the body of Pat Fenton. There was no doubt that she was dead and when he laid a hand on her wrist it was as cold as the kettle next door.

'Oh my God!' The woman ran across the floor and dropped down beside her, fumbling for a pulse. 'She's dead! She's been dead a long time. It must have been her heart!'

She hadn't noticed the hypodermic syringe lying on the floor but both men had homed in on it and the cards lying face upwards around her feet bearing the Coil Shuffler's message.

'Leave this to us, ma'am,' said Nick, helping the woman to her feet. 'She's beyond help. We'll call the doctor. By the way, what is your name?'

'Bridget Green.'

'Well, do you think you could make us all a cup of tea whilst we're waiting, Bridget?'

She looked doubtful but reluctantly went back into the kitchen to do their bidding. As soon as she had gone the two men concentrated on the death scene. They immediately found the computer print-out on the coffee table.

'It's a suicide note.' Nick donned the plastic gloves he always carried with him and

249

picked it up. Mike looked over his shoulder and they read the printed message. 'I have reached the end of the road. I am the Coil Shuffler but now it is over. I cannot face the consequences so I am taking this way out. All the information is in the files. *Misere Mei.*'

'How odd, doing it on a computer instead of writing it by hand.'

'Right, I'm calling in,' said Mike, taking his mobile out of his pocket. 'You've got until reinforcements arrive to have a nooky at them,' he nodded at the files, 'but don't destroy any evidence.'

Nick was already engrossed in the top one by the time Mike had finished his call but he looked up as the rattle of crockery sounded from the kitchen. 'Keep her out of the way if you can. This lot is dynamite!'

Mike went into the kitchen where Bridget Green was struggling to open a new packet of tea-bags.

'The way they package things these days is ridiculous! How they expect old people with arthritis to undo them I don't know. Where are her kitchen scissors?' She fumbled in the worktop drawers and found the scissors but after a few abortive attempts to use them she threw them down in disgust. 'These are no good, they're left-handed ones.' Her hands were shaking and Mike was surprised at how upset she was. Surely finding a dead body was an occupational hazard for her the same as it was for policemen?

'Let me.' He took the box from her and managed to tear off the cellophane wrapping. 'Here you are.'

'It seems terrible bothering about things like tea when she's lying in there dead.'

'You've had a shock, we all have, and tea is the best remedy. The police will be here soon.'

'Police? I thought *you* were police?'

'I'm afraid she didn't die naturally. She killed herself.'

'Killed herself?' Bridget Green sank on to a kitchen stool and gaped at him in horror. 'How . . . how do you know?'

'It looks as if she's injected herself with something lethal. There's a syringe and she's left a suicide note.'

'Pat's *killed* herself? I can't believe it! Why?'

'No doubt we'll find out,' said Mike gently. 'The police surgeon will be along to confirm death and then there will be an autopsy and an inquest. Now, how about that tea?'

Bridget Green was still sitting dazed on her stool sipping apathetically out of her mug when the first police car drew up outside the bungalow. Nick hurriedly replaced the file he had been perusing and had a quick word with his friend as they went out to meet their colleagues.

'It's all there. She did do for Bert Pryke and a lot of others. But I tell you what — there's nothing there about Rachel's husband. I think some of that file is missing.'

10

'What the hell are you doing here!' Trevor Dickins bellowed in outrage as Nick opened the door to him and DC Coleman.

'We found the body, buddy, and watch that blood pressure or we'll have another stiff on our hands.'

'Just how do you always happen to be around snarling up my case?'

'Coincidence is a funny thing, wouldn't you say?'

Seeing the murderous look on Dickins' face Nick retreated and waved them inside. 'I'll leave Mike to fill you in but before you lose your rag completely there's an independent witness in here who doesn't realise the significance of Fenton's death, so watch your tongue.'

Mike explained the situation and after visually examining the body Dickins went into the kitchen to have words with Bridget Green. He was surprisingly gentle with her and turned aside her tearful enquiries as to what could have possibly made Pat Fenton take her own life. Time enough for the real facts to hit the public eye after the inquest, he reasoned to himself. Once the Press got their teeth into it the whole world was going to know that Pat Fenton was the self-confessed Coil Shuffler; in the meantime the police had to prove their case. In an effort to get rid of Croft and Holroyd as well as Bridget Green he managed to prevail on Nick to drive the nurse home and once they had left he sent for the police surgeon and SOCOs. Whilst he waited for their arrival a quick look at the top file on the coffee table convinced him that they had indeed caught up with their quarry. What a pity she had topped herself before they could bring a prosecution.

After dropping off Bridget Green and making arrangements for her car to be picked up Nick turned to his friend.

'What now? Do you want me to take you over to Holgate Hall? You'll want to break the news to Rachel.'

'No, I'll ring her from home. It's going to be a nasty shock. I wish I could leave it until she returns home but I don't want her to hear it from another source. She needs to be prepared before it's blared all over the local press and media.'

'It's a good job she was out of the way or Fenton might have attempted to take her with her. Christ! How I wish I was on the investigation team!'

'You need to keep a low profile at the moment. It's bad enough having to be called as a witness at the inquest.'

'Yeah. I thought Dickins was going to wet himself when he saw us on the doorstep.'

Nick drove through the Westgate interchange and negotiated the traffic in Belvoir Road. As he pulled into the kerb outside Mike's house a neighbour who was chatting with a friend on the pavement bent and waved, beaming, to his passenger.

'It's nice to see you're still doing a good public relations job. They'll have you on the local Neighbourhood Watch committee if you don't look out.'

'I am on the Neighbourhood Watch committee. Are you coming in for a coffee?'

'No. I'll leave you to make your phone call in peace. I have things to do. Are we picking Rachel up on Sunday?'

'I'll let you know.'

★ ★ ★

Rachel replaced the receiver and stepped out of the phone booth in a daze. It had been hard enough coming to terms with the fact that Pat Fenton was the Coil Shuffler; now Mike had just told her that Pat had committed suicide and left behind evidence of her crimes. It was unbelievable and she couldn't really take it in, but the fact was that Pat was dead so she went across to the chapel and prayed for the repose of her soul. She felt so troubled that she could find no comfort in her devotions and she suddenly realised how much she wanted to get back to work.

She decided she would definitely go in to the hospital on Monday. There was no reason why she shouldn't and her colleagues would be pleased to offload some of the extra work they had taken on in her absence. There was just the question of Mike. After lapsing for a week, he had returned to his physiotherapy sessions, working out with one of her colleagues. She decided this was a good time to make the arrangement permanent.

For some time she had been aware that her work with Mike had become increasingly difficult with the overlapping of her private and professional life. Of course, there was no question of unethical behaviour as there might be if she were a doctor and Mike her patient, but she thought it would be better if someone else took over his treatment. She was becoming too aware of him as a man rather than a patient. Apart from the scars from his injury and his temporary disability he was a fine figure of a man and her body betrayed her by reacting to his physical presence when she worked on his limbs or floated beside him in the hydrotherapy pool.

Was he aware of her in the same way? she wondered. Neither of them was overtly sexual or the type to jump into bed at the earliest opportunity, apart from any moral or religious restraints. Theirs was a comfortable relationship that was developing pleasantly and unhurriedly, which was how it should be. They were both victims of a tragic past and this provided a common ground on which to build their friendship. They were both past the mad passion of youth and even if some might call them emotional cripples, so what — this bound them together.

★ ★ ★

'There is something wrong.'

Trevor Dickins thrust his hands in his pockets and quartered the room, his shoulders hunched, his lips outthrust in a pout. He wasn't going to admit to the pricking of his thumbs to the superintendent; the intuition without which no fictional detective functioned, but that was what it amounted to.

'The results of the autopsy are quite

straightforward, aren't they?' Douglas Bairstow regarded him steadily.

'Oh, yes. A massive dose of codeine administered intravenously. The syringe was there and the puncture mark on the inside of her left elbow where she had injected herself.'

'So what is worrying you?'

'I'm not sure.' This was indeed an admission from the detective inspector which Bairstow listened to with raised eyebrows. 'The files, for one thing: case histories, I suppose you'd call them, of all the deaths she'd arranged. The elderly and terminally ill, including Bert Pryke, and how she'd done it. All the sorts of people she would have had easy access to as a district nurse, but nothing about the other murders we're investigating — Eddie Briers, Graham Scott or the Bentley and Houghton cases. I still don't see her as their killer. The others don't bother me — overdoses, plastic bag over the head, etc. — all what I would call women's crimes, but I can't see her sticking a knife into someone or stringing them up . . . There is a violence there that doesn't seem to match up with what I must call her more domestic crimes.'

'You're not saying a woman is not capable of knifing anyone?'

'Christ! No, sir. We know different, don't we? But we seem to have here two completely different murder scenarios. And another thing — those Coil Shuffler cards. They were scattered round her feet as if she had dropped them and they had the same wording as the adverts we've found but the one on top was different. This was identical to the card found beside Eddie Brier's body where the words 'professionally, effectively, terminally' are substituted for 'painlessly, efficiently, tastefully'. This one had blurred smudges on it as if it had been handled by someone in gloves; the others all had Fenton's fingerprints on them.'

'So what are you saying?'

'It looks almost as if someone had added this one afterwards. Someone who was first at the scene of crime.'

'I don't like what you are suggesting.'

'I'm sorry, sir, but I am in charge of this investigation and Nick Holroyd is obstructing me and the course of justice. Every time we get a lead or something significant turns up so does he, either before me or treading on my heels.'

'I think you are over-reacting. Why should he want to interfere?'

'Because he wants to discredit me and make me fall down on the job,' Dickins wanted to shout at the superintendent but he bit back the words and looked mutinous and Bairstow continued:

'He has become involved in this case through Croft's friendship with Mrs Morland.'

'That's another odd thing. There is nothing in those files about the death of Christopher Morland. I was sure there was a tie-up there with Fenton. Unless . . . '

Bairstow waited and Dickins plunged on. 'Unless Croft removed the relevant pages to spare Rachel's feelings. That file also appears to have less pages in it than the others so some could have been taken out.'

'That's a serious allegation you're making, Trevor. I should hope none of my officers would obstruct an investigation for personal reasons. Beside, from what I remember, Mrs Morland insisted all along that her husband wouldn't have committed suicide and if there is proof that he was killed by Fenton this would vindicate her and surely console her.'

Dickins shrugged and shifted ground. 'I'm also not happy about the suicide note. Why did she go to all the trouble of jacking up her computer, typing the message and printing it out when it would have been so much easier to write it by hand?'

'Was it definitely done on her computer?'

'I took it for granted that it was but we'd better run a check on it. One computer print-out is much like another but it may be possible to prove it one way or another. I'll get it over to Forensics straight away.'

'I've called a press conference for tomorrow morning.'

'Sir?'

'They are on our backs and we'll have to give them something. I think I had better handle it.'

'You're going to tell them we have fingered the Coil Shuffler?'

'A little subtlety is called for here. There's no way we're going to be able to keep it under wraps but we must play it down as far as it is possible until we are positive of our facts.'

'What I want to know is: what happens about the people who *hired* Pat Fenton to knock off their nearest and dearest? Will they be prosecuted?'

'This is a difficult one. With her dead and only those files as evidence it is going to be difficult to prove anything, especially as some of the incidents go back a long way. I should say it is going to be a nightmare for the Crown Prosecutor's department and keep the legal profession in work for years.'

'And in the money.'

'That too.'

★ ★ ★

In another part of the building Mike Croft stared out of the window and tried to snatch at the memory that was hovering on the edge of his consciousness. He had keyed in the report of the autopsy on Pat Fenton and something was bothering him. It all seemed straightforward enough, and yet . . . What was it that was prompting this unease? This feeling that something was not right? He read through the report again and something clicked. *That* was what he had heard and forgotten until this had jogged his memory. Well, it should be easy enough to check; Rachel would know.

As soon as his shift ended he tried to phone her flat but all he got was the answerphone. So she *had* gone in to work, he thought. It would be hopeless ringing the hospital. Even if they put him through to the physiotherapy department she would probably be busy with a patient. He looked at his watch. Maybe if he went over there now he could catch her in her coffee break. Cursing the fact that he was unable to drive he called a taxi and as he waited for it to arrive he wondered if his memory was playing him tricks or if he *had* fastened on to something crucial.

* * *

It had been a good idea to come back to work, mused Rachel. Her colleagues had been delighted to see her this morning and she had spent the hour since her arrival going through schedules and catching up with case notes. She was absorbed in this when Pattie Gordon, the secretary, pushed open the door of the cubby-hole Rachel called her office and sidled in balancing a cup of coffee in one hand and a packet in the other.

'I thought you'd be glad of a coffee,' she said, putting it down on the desk.

'Thanks, yes.' Rachel pushed a file aside and ran her fingers through her hair. 'You all seem to have managed admirably without me.'

'You're not back officially yet so ease your way in gently. It won't hurt them to have to cope a little longer.'

'I'm feeling fine, but I promise I'll be sensible.'

'This came for you in the post this morning. I haven't opened it as it's got Private and Confidential on it.' She handed over the bulky envelope and Rachel slit it open and drew out the sheets of paper from inside. She recognised the writing immediately and gave a little exclamation of dismay and the sheets slipped from her hands and scattered across the desk.

'Is there something wrong?' Pattie looked at her anxiously.

'No . . . no . . . ' She bundled up the sheets with shaking fingers.

'It's not an anonymous letter, is it?' Pattie was intrigued as well as being disturbed.

'No, nothing like that, just a voice from beyond the grave. I'll have my coffee whilst I'm reading it through. Can you make sure I'm not disturbed for a while?'

Fifteen minutes later she was still staring down at the sheaf of papers on her desk not knowing whether to cry or rejoice. One half of her wanted to laugh and exult, the other half was horrified. She had to get hold of Mike. He must see this and he would know what action needed to be taken. She rang the police station and was told that he had gone off duty and she had just missed him. She glanced at her watch and wondered whether he would go straight home and how long it would take him. She decided to wait half an hour before she tried to reach him there. Her coffee was untouched and now cold with a puckered skin on the surface so she went to get a refill. As she walked down the corridor she saw Mike limping across the entrance foyer at the far end. At first she thought she was hallucinating; that she had wanted to see him and therefore her mind had conjured him up. Then he pushed open the door and she saw that it really was him. She ran towards him.

'Oh, Mike, I'm so pleased to see you! I don't know why you're here — you're not scheduled for treatment today, are you? — but you're the answer to my prayer!'

'Well, I don't think divine intervention has anything to do with it,' he said, rather taken aback by her enthusiastic greeting, 'but it's nice to be wanted. What's up?'

'Come into my office. I've got something to show you. It came through the post and it's . . . horrible. Horrible and bizarre but I feel *vindicated*!'

'Rachel, are you all right?'

He was alarmed by her febrile state and sure that she was not far off hysteria. In reply she pulled him into the office and pushed the door shut and handed him the sheets of paper.

'Read this.'

He sat down and started to read. After a few seconds he looked up. 'My God! These are part of Pat Fenton's records. We thought there was a section missing.'

'She killed Christopher! I was right all along. I *knew* he wouldn't have committed suicide! *She* gave him the overdose — it's all there! She goes on about putting him out of his misery and . . . and having me to herself . . . ' Her voice faltered and Mike said quickly:

'You're sure this is her writing?'

'Positive. What did you mean about this being the missing section?'

'She kept records of everything but we noticed there was nothing about your husband in the appropriate file and it looked as if some of it had been removed. Most of the later stuff was typed but there were some handwritten entries. Have you still got the envelope this came in?'

Rachel handed it to him.

'This and the pages must go to Forensics.'

'I still don't see how she managed to get an overdose into Christopher.'

'It would have been simple. He was having regular doses of painkillers, wasn't he? She would have given him some and then when they took effect and he was dozy it would have been easy to feed him some more.'

'How could she pretend to have been so fond of me and then let me suffer like that, thinking he had killed himself?'

'She probably hadn't reckoned on you reacting so strongly.'

'I couldn't really bring myself to believe it

266

when you told me she was the Coil Shuffler, but now . . . ' She shook her head resignedly. 'How did she manage to kill all those people without anyone suspecting? How did she kill Bert Pryke without it showing up at the autopsy?'

'She injected him with a large dose of Adrenalin. It leaves no trace apart from symptoms of a massive coronary. As he was a diabetic and having regular insulin injections the pathologist wouldn't have been suspicious at finding syringe marks on his body. They were to be expected. It was well thought out, of diabolic simplicity and she had the medical knowledge and access to drugs to carry it out.'

'I suppose when you started investigating her she realised the game was up and couldn't face the consequences.'

'Ah, now that is what I wanted to see you about.'

'So you haven't got an appointment. This is a social call?'

'No, it's strictly police business, I'm afraid. Something I'm checking up on and I thought you would have the answer.'

'I'm intrigued. What do you want to know?'

'Was Pat Fenton right-handed or left-handed?'

'Left-handed.'

'You're quite sure?'

'Positive. She was very left-handed, if you know what I mean. Many left-handed people use their cutlery in the correct hands but Pat couldn't even do that. She used to look so awkward with her knife and fork in the wrong hands and she had to have left-handed tools — kitchen utensils and that sort of thing. Why do you want to know?'

'Because if she was left-handed it blows a huge hole in all the police theories.'

'How do you mean?'

'She was killed by barbiturates injected into her left arm. If she was left-handed it would have been in her right arm, wouldn't it? She couldn't have done it in the arm that was holding the syringe?'

'No way.'

Rachel suddenly realised the significance of these facts. She gasped and put a hand over her mouth. 'Are you saying — ?'

'Pat Fenton couldn't have killed herself. Someone else killed her, someone who didn't know that she was left-handed.'

'But who? And why?'

'I don't know. Detective Inspector Dickins thinks he has the case all tied up but this throws it wide open again.' Mike got to his feet and took a plastic bag out of his pocket into which he carefully put the sheets of paper and envelope. 'I'll take charge of this. You'll have to have your fingerprints taken for elimination purposes but I don't suppose there will be any unaccounted for ones. Still, it is often the ones that should be there but aren't that are important.'

'Mike, are you saying that Pat wasn't the Coil Shuffler?'

'I think there is no doubt that she carried out all the killings she'd recorded in her files but it is beginning to look as if there is someone else masquerading as the Coil Shuffler — a copy-cat killer.'

'This is horrible!'

'Yes, but try not to worry about it. You're not under threat any more, it was certainly Fenton who targeted you. Look, I must be going. I don't have to tell you to keep this to yourself. It mustn't get around. I'll be in touch later.'

'How did you get here?'

'Taxi. You see, I don't always have my minder with me.'

'I bet he doesn't know you're here.'

★ ★ ★

Instead of the neat suicide verdict that Trevor Dickins would have liked, the inquest on Pat

Fenton was opened and adjourned pending further police investigation into her death. At the briefing that followed the inquest other anomalies surrounding her demise were aired.

'I was unhappy all along about this death.' Dickins spoke with assurance and dared any of his audience to contradict him. 'Once the fact of her left-handedness came to light there was no doubt that Fenton could not have committed suicide, but apart from that there were other pointers to be taken into consideration. The pages from her files dealing with Christopher Morland's killing contained Fenton's fingerprints overlaid by those of Croft and Rachel Morland, but . . . ' he paused for effect 'there were none of Fenton's dabs on the envelope which there surely would have been if she herself had sealed it up and posted it. Also, if Fenton had posted that envelope off to Rachel Morland before killing herself, surely she would have sent it to her home address rather than to the hospital. This leads me to believe that whoever decided to send those notes to Morland didn't know her home address.

'Another fact has also emerged. The suicide note was not typed on Fenton's word-processor — the configuration is slightly different. Therefore I think we must assume she was not responsible for it. So . . . she didn't top herself, she was murdered.'

Dickins glared at his colleagues and snarled. 'Can I have some feed-back?'

'Are you saying there are *two* Coil Shufflers?'

'It is beginning to look very much like it. One of them is probably a copy-cat killer, but who came first is open to question. Going through the records of all known homicides, both appear to have started operating at about the same time; and to forestall the next question — we can be pretty certain who carried out which killings. The cards themselves are a clear indication. Eddie Briers, Graham Scott, John Houghton, Eric Bentley were all contract killings by the unknown person we shall call Coil Shuffler B. He is a professional assassin who likes to boast about his skills and makes sure we know who is responsible by leaving a card with his victim. This is the card which reads 'professionally, effectively, terminally.'

'On the other hand, Fenton — Coil Shuffler A — used her cards, the ones which read 'painlessly, efficiently, tastefully', to advertise her services, not as a signature to her crime. As far as we know only one of her victims had her card left with them and this may have just been an oversight on her part.

She didn't want to draw her attention to their deaths, they had to appear unsuspicious.'

'How did she manage that? Why were none of them queried?'

'Don't forget she was preying on the elderly and terminally ill. Their deaths wouldn't have been unexpected and of the ten homicides she carried out over the last four years, apart from Bert Pryke, only two were questioned — Christopher Morland's and the elderly woman from Balscombe and nothing came of it. She got away with it all that time because she used ingenious methods of doing in her victims, either by making it appear as suicide or natural causes, or by something that wouldn't show up in an autopsy if it got as far as that. I'm not going into details about this now, you can read the reports.'

'How is the pathologist taking all this?'

'Quentin Stock is not very happy that his professional skills are being queried but no blame can be attached to him. His autopsy findings ruled out foul play because Fenton had the medical knowledge to cover up her crimes.'

'Are we saying that Coil Shuffler B killed Fenton?'

'Yes, I think we can be definite about that. After all, he left his card, didn't he? Whoever he is, he knew about Fenton's activities and she was becoming a threat to his little operation so she had to go. He tried to make it appear as suicide but he didn't try very hard, did he? I think he likes making a monkey of us and wasting police resources. He knew we'd get there in the end and he's having a laugh at our expense. The question we must ask now is: what will be his next move? Will he carry on with his hatchet work or will he lie low for a while?'

★ ★ ★

The answer to this question came via the post a few days later. The envelope, addressed to DI Trevor Dickins, was picked up on immediately as being similar to the one that had come before, and was opened carefully by him when alerted to its arrival. It contained a photograph but no message and appeared to have come from the same publication as the previous one. He surveyed it intently through the polythene pocket he had tucked it into. It showed Laurence Olivier as Hamlet clutching a swooning woman in his arms. He arranged for both the photograph and the envelope to be sent to Forensics for testing but first he took the former to show Bairstow.

The superintendent studied it carefully.

'It would appear that our Coil Shuffler is a film buff with a ready supply of old movie magazines,' he said, laying it down on the desk.

'That's Hamlet again, isn't it, with some dame?'

'The *dame* is Ophelia. She was betrothed to Hamlet.'

'She doesn't look very happy about it, does she, unless she's passed out in delight. And why is he standing in a pit?'

'That's her grave?'

'Her *grave*'

'She's dead, Trevor. Hamlet is one of the great tragic dramas of English literature. We're not talking Mills and Boon here.'

'I don't like it. Hamlet and a dead woman. Is the Coil Shuffler telling us his next victim will be a woman?'

'So far as we know all his victims up to now have been men but there is nothing to stop someone putting out a contract on a woman. Have you made any progress over the last few days?'

'I keep coming up against a wall of silence. It's almost as if there is a conspiracy about. It all seems too close to home.'

There was a hesitant note in Dickins' voice as if he was not sure whether to unburden himself further to the superintendent, who looked at the baffled gooseberry-green eyes facing him and said quietly:

'Go on.'

'He's too well informed about our investigation. He knows exactly what we're doing and he's keeping pace with us, if not jumping one step ahead.'

'You're saying we have an informer amongst us who is hand-in-glove with the Coil Shuffler?'

'I'd go further than that, sir,' said Dickins, suddenly reckless. 'Supposing the Coil Shuffler is one of us? Take this business of none of our snouts knowing anything or not being prepared to pass any information our way. Apart from the criminal fraternity itself, who else has tabs on the Underworld and its goings on but the Old Bill itself? No wonder no one will squeal, when they've probably been promised immunity in return for their silence.'

'This rather narrows it down to the CID.'

'The current CID workforce or someone who has worked in the department in the past and still has the contacts.'

Bairstow regarded him thoughtfully but let this pass.

'I'm not shouting you down over this idea that the Coil Shuffler is one of our mob. I have been working towards that possibility too but the field is wide open. There is not a scrap of evidence pointing to any one particular person and you must be careful not to be blinded by prejudice.'

'Sir.' Dickins accepted the rebuke, satisfied that he had planted the seeds of doubt in Bairstow's mind. 'How do we play this one? Do we keep it under cover?'

The superintendent got to his feet and paced to the window where he stared out, unseeing, at the panoramic view of the city's roof-tops and landmarks spread out before him. This was every chief's nightmare; the discovery that there could be corrupt officer in his team. And it didn't end there. One rotten apple in the barrel could taint good honest men and pull them down with him. If the Coil Shuffler *was* a policeman the entire Brent Hill personnel was compromised. Public opinion and the Press would see to that without the horror of an internal enquiry. He swung round to face his inspector.

'No. I want every man-jack in this station to know that we may have a rotten apple amongst us. Each man and woman has to be on his or her guard, if they know they are under suspicion they may see their colleagues' actions in a new light. Something that someone did, or should have done and didn't may take on a different meaning under these circumstances and may lead to him being unmasked.'

'Spying on one's colleagues is not what policing is all about,' said Dickins, looking mutinous.

'Indeed not, but while the doubt is there we cannot ignore it. This is an added incentive for nailing the Coil Shuffler and I hope to God our fears are wrong.'

Taking this as dismissal Dickins picked up the plastic wallet holding the photograph and headed for the door. Bairstow waited until he was turning the handle before adding:

'By the way, Trevor, you and your team are not exempt from this, you know.'

11

This should have been a pretty corpse, would have been but for the method of dispatch. Strangulation did horrible things to the face, he thought, looking down at the bloodshot, bulging eyes and swollen tongue protruding through the lips. Still, this helped to balance things; no one should be as beautiful as this one had been, it wasn't fair. Her hair alone looked like an advert for some fancy shampoo and he was pretty certain that the colour was natural and hadn't come out of a bottle. Her figure too was quite something. He wondered what she had done to make someone desperate enough to arrange her death. He felt no compassion, no regret, just idle curiosity as to the reasons behind her squandered beauty.

He left the knotted scarf round her neck and bent down and picked her up. For all her voluptuous curves she was slight in build and he had no difficulty carrying her behind the screen of bushes and laying her in the gully that ran between the hedge and the boundary fence. She wouldn't remain hidden for long but this did not bother him. He wanted her to be found, so long as the discovery was delayed for a few hours to allow him time to get well away. He took the card out of his pocket and considered her thoughtfully for a few seconds, then he bent and crossed her hands across her bosom and tucked the card between the pale, lifeless fingers where it was clearly visible. He straightened up and grunted with satisfaction, then retraced his steps to where the attack had taken place and retrieved her handbag from the clump of dead bracken into which it had fallen. He intended throwing it into the canal on the way home and he picked up a couple of large stones and put them inside to weigh it down. He did not bother to go through the wallet and purse and abstract the notes and loose change.

This done he went back for one more look at the body and to check that he had left nothing incriminating behind. With a broken-off dead branch he churned up the muddy ground around the corpse obliterating his footprints, then he tossed this branch high up into the hedge and clutching the handbag in his gloved hands he started to walk away through the trees.

At the very last moment he changed his mind and turned back. He stooped over the body and very gently turned her head to one side and swept the fall of glorious hair over her face to hide the hideously contorted features. Then he padded silently away.

* * *

The handbag was found before the discovery of the body. It entered the water of the canal with a satisfactory splash and the Coil Shuffler loped on his way unaware that the long strap had snagged on a broken spar projecting from the bank and the bag hung suspended just below the surface of the water. He was also unaware that he had an audience.

Seamus McGinty, long-time vagrant and wino, huddled beneath the dubious shelter of a stack of corrugated-iron sheets, watched the incident with drink-sodden eyes. As the figure ran past him and he glimpsed the pale gashes of eyes and mouth in the Balaclava-covered face he almost gibbered in fright. He was back in Belfast, in the Shankhill Road enclave, and they were coming to get him. He drew his legs under him and shrank back in the shadows, whimpering in fear. The footsteps receded and after a long pause during which he muttered a string of prayers and blasphemies, he squeezed open his eyes and peered out of his lair. There was a half moon that night and in the diffused light that turned black to grey and substance to shadow he could see no movement, no sign of other human presence. In the distance was the subdued roar of the city's traffic but here the silence was absolute. Had he imagined the figure? Was it a trick of the memory or the drink talking? Had someone thrown something into the canal that oozed blackly alongside the embankment a few yards from where he crouched? There was one way to find out.

He staggered to his feet, knocking over the bottle at his side, and it clattered across the broken concrete.

'Oh, Holy Jesus, be quiet now! He'll be having us!' He plucked up the bottle and stared at it perplexed. 'Tis empty you are? Tat's not a nice ting to happen to a man, not a drop to steady his nerves.' Momentarily diverted from his purpose he twisted the bottle this way and that and upended it, staring despondently at it and shaking his head. Then he remembered his objective and setting it carefully down on the ground he shuffled towards the canal. The oily, opaque water glimmered like wet tar in the dim light and he squinted at it forlornly whilst teetering unsteadily on the bank. It was sheer chance that he happened to be looking in the right direction as the moon sailed out from behind a cloud, picking out the metal buckle on the leather strap that stretched from the spar down into the murky depths below. Holy Mother Mary and all the Saints, this was his lucky night after all! He staggered to the edge and tried to scramble down towards it but as he lowered his head a wave of dizziness swept through him and he toppled down into the water with a resounding splash.

It was his lucky night after all but not in the way he had envisaged. Two young police constables happened to be patrolling the old warehouses area at the time and heard the splash and ran to the scene. There was a commotion going on in the canal, a threshing about combined with gargled shouts. PC Daniel Webb swung the beam of his torch across the water and picked out the bewhiskered face of McGinty before his head went under in a cascade of bubbles.

'Hell, this is where someone gets wet,' he groaned, whilst his companion, Constable Kevin Lodge, was already kicking off his shoes and divesting himself of his outer jacket. After a disgusted look at the filthy water Lodge jumped in and struck out after the drowning man. He managed to grasp McGinty's neck and shoulders and, turning on his back, tried to tow him back to shore but the Irishman clutched him in a stranglehold and they both disappeared beneath the surface.

'I've got you, man, stop struggling or you'll drown us both!' gasped Lodge, resurfacing and spitting out water as he maintained his hold and tried desperately to propel him towards the shore.

Daniel Webb leaned out from his precarious perch on a rotten girder and grabbed them as soon as they came within reach. Somehow between them the two policemen manhandled the sodden, pathetic figure of Seamus McGinty to dry land. He was not at all grateful but continued to struggle and jabber incoherently.

'What's the matter with you, man? You're safe now.'

'Me bag — I tort I'd lost it! It's down there.' McGinty swung a wild arm in the direction of the canal and succeeded in catching Kevin Lodge on the side of the head.

'You're smashed, Paddy, give over.' Lodge regarded one of the city's down and outs with distaste and resignation.

'I only had a drop, but me bag's down there!'

Daniel Webb beamed his torch in the direction McGinty was pointing and saw the buckle gleaming as the Irishman had done earlier. He was more successful in reaching the handbag and managed to unhook it from the spar and drag it out of the water.

'This is not yours, it's a woman's handbag.' He opened the clasp to reveal the sodden contents. 'Where did you get it from, Paddy? Who have you mugged?'

'Sweet Jesus, I haven't mugged anyone!'

'Yes, you have. Where is she? Have you hurt her?'

'No, no, it's mine! The Holy Saints sent it to me!' McGinty was suddenly violently sick at their feet, spewing up the obnoxious water he had swallowed and the alcohol he had drunk.

'He's as pissed as a newt,' said Lodge in disgust. 'Let's get him back to the station.'

'I'll tell you what,' said Webb as they half dragged, half carried Seamus McGinty along the towpath, 'you may not get a medal for this rescue but sure as hell you'll both have to have your stomachs pumped out.'

★ ★ ★

Later that night at Brent Hill Station the duty sergeant was still trying to make sense of McGinty's confused ramblings. The Irishman had been locked in a cell on his return from

284

hospital and was entertaining them with mournful dirges warbled in a three-note range when he wasn't snoring deafeningly as he drifted in and out of sleep.

'Carolyn Hamblin.' The Sergeant read out the name from the wallet found inside the handbag. 'Where is she and how did this bag get into the possession of Pavarotti McGinty?'

'He insists that it was given to him by the saints,' said Daniel Webb. 'Nothing will shake him from that and he denies all knowledge of this Carolyn Hamblin.'

'Do you believe that?'

'He obviously believes every word he's uttered but whether it's the truth as he sees it or the drink talking is anybody's business. I take it she's not at the address given in the wallet?'

'No. I got a patrol car to check. It's a posh flat in that new apartment block over at Queensgate. There was no reply and the night porter said she was often away overnight. I've also checked casualty but no woman has been brought in suffering from the effects of a mugging.'

'If she was mugged why weren't the credit cards and money taken out of the bag before it was thrown away?'

'Quite. And I can't understand why

McGinty didn't ransack it either.'

'He may have been trying to open it and accidentally dropped it in the water, sloshed as he was. Then he fell in trying to retrieve it.'

'You may well be right but it doesn't look good for this Carolyn Hamblin. We'll have to wait until morning, then we'll put out a general alert and try and trace her.'

★ ★ ★

The body was discovered the following morning by a jogger out with his dog for an early morning run. The dog was first on the scene, diving into the undergrowth and barking voraciously until his master went to investigate. After he had got over the initial shock the man saw the card slotted between the stiff, dead fingers and realised the significance of it. He left the dog on guard and ran to the nearest phone to contact the police.

Within a short while a full-scale murder hunt was under way. The area was cordoned off, the police surgeon had certified death and hard on his heels came Quentin Stock, called out to view the body *in situ*. The SOCOs had carried out a preliminary examination and after the body had been photographed from every conceivable angle it was bagged and sent off to the mortuary to await the further attentions of the pathologist.

'Stock reckons she was killed between 9 p.m. and midnight,' said Trevor Dickins, holding court in the incident room that had been set up in a nearby redundant chapel. 'That bit of woodland where she was found is a no-man's-land between the official park and the Rutland Estate. It is used as a short cut and we think she was attacked on the footpath and then dumped a few yards away in the ditch. There had been no deliberate attempt to hide the body. She was meant to be found and we were meant to know who had done it.'

'Could it possibly be a copy-cat killing? Someone trying to make us believe it's the work of the Coil Shuffler?' asked one of his team.

'If it is he got hold of one of the Coil Shuffler's cards. It's the real McCoy. No, I reckon our man has struck again and this time he's taken out a woman. We have yet to identify her but she's young, well dressed and was quite a beauty before he throttled her. Someone is going to miss her and get in touch with us.'

'Was she interfered with sexually?'

'There's no evidence of it but Stock will

be able to tell us more when he does the autopsy.'

They didn't have to wait for a missing person report. Mike Croft plucked the incident of the handbag from the overnight computer input and the body in the morgue had a possible name. Trevor Dickins himself went to Queen's Court where the owner of the handbag lived and took with him Brian Coleman. The porter insisted that although there was still no reply from her flat and he hadn't seen Carolyn Hamblin that morning this was nothing unusual. He was persuaded to produce the master key to the flat and the two men rode up in the lift to the third floor.

'You don't live here for peanuts,' said Dickins as they trod the thickly carpeted corridor. 'This Carolyn Hamblin, whoever she is, was on to a nice little earner. She must have pulled in more in a week than you or I do in a month.'

'Or she was a kept woman and he wanted out?' suggested Coleman.

'You're jumping the gun,' growled Dickins, finding the right door and unlocking it. The two men stepped inside and looked about them. 'A *very* nice little earner if she paid for all this up front.'

The vestibule floor was covered by a thick

bronze carpet and an elegant rosewood side-table stood against the far wall supporting a magnificent floral display in a copper urn. The sitting-room opened off this vestibule and was carpeted in the same rich bronze shag. The three-piece suite was of cream leather and the curtains were olive-green velvet. Just the right colour scheme to set off a redhead, thought Dickins.

'Let's see what's in the bedroom,' he said, moving back into the vestibule.

The main bedroom was decorated in white and gold and managed to look very feminine without being too fussy. On the dressing table amongst the expensive cosmetics and toiletries was a brochure for Morden Hall, a very exclusive health and fitness club.

'Hey, look at this . . . ' Coleman flicked through the pages. 'That's her, isn't it? She was their receptionist.'

There was no mistaking the likeness. The Carolyn Hamblin smiling professionally at the camera from behind her desk was indeed the same person whose corpse now lay tagged and waiting in a mortuary drawer.

'No doubt at all. We've found our woman but we'll have to get a formal identification.'

The bedside table drawer revealed three packets of unopened contraceptive pills but no condoms. In the second bedroom they found a man's silk dressing-gown and a couple of shirts hanging in the wardrobe and the bathroom cabinet contained a man's razor and a bottle of aftershave.

'Well, she certainly had a man friend, and a wealthy one by the look of these.' Dickins fingered the designer label clothes hanging in the built-in wardrobe in the main bedroom. 'She may have earned a good screw working in that place but not enough for gear like this. I wonder what we'll find in the desk.'

The bottom drawer was locked but they found the key lying beneath a pile of travel brochures in one of the other drawers. When unlocked they found the usual documents: bank statements, cheque-book stubs, credit card accounts and a building society passbook.

'She was having regular large amounts paid into this,' said Coleman, looking through the latter. 'A fortnight ago three hundred went in and three hundred the fortnight before that and last month two and a half grand was paid in on the 18th.'

'There's nothing around to indicate who the boyfriend is and there seem to be no photographs or anything personal around which is rather odd. When we've had a chance to go through her diary we may get a lead; in the meantime we'd better find out what the porter can tell us about her. He may know who the boyfriend was and whether she had any family living locally.'

Initially the porter was not very forthcoming. He admitted to knowing that Carolyn Hamblin was employed at Morden Hall but denied any knowledge of her private life. He let them know in no uncertain terms that the residents of Queen's Court were respected professional people who guarded their privacy.

'Why are you so keen to see her? She's not in any trouble, is she?'

'Fatal trouble, my friend,' said Dickins heavily. 'Your respected tenant was found near Rutland Park this morning strangled and very dead. Not a pretty sight.'

The porter was shocked and sat down abruptly on the stool in his office.

'I can't believe it, you're having me on!'

'I'm certainly not, mate. You can come along with us and identify the body.'

'No, no, I can't leave here. Who would do that to her?'

'That's what we're trying to find out. Perhaps you can now remember who the boyfriend was?'

But the porter insisted that although he had seen her with different men there was no one he could single out as being the current escort. There were girl friends who had visited her but he couldn't remember seeing any possible parents. He thought she wasn't local but had come from Birmingham or Coventry but he didn't know from where he had gleaned this snippet of information.

'We'll be back. In the meantime you'll probably be over-run by the local newshounds when the story breaks. Don't let anyone else into the flat.'

'Right, next stop Morden Hall. Let's hope we get more joy there,' said Dickins as they got back into the car. 'She must have been friendly with some of her work colleagues. They should be able to fill us in with some details of her private life.'

'You reckon the boyfriend did it?'

'Don't be such a cretin, Brian. We know the Coil Shuffler did it but it's my bet he was hired by lover boy.'

Coleman didn't jump to conclusions. He worked things out slowly and conscientiously and they had almost reached Morden Hall on the eastern outskirts of the city before he spoke again.

'Supposing we do find out who the boyfriend was, how are we going to connect him with the Coil Shuffler? He's going to have an alibi for the time of the killing, isn't he?'

'Too true, but it's the only lead we've

got. Don't forget we weren't meant to find that handbag. The Coil Shuffler was careless there. We've got her diary and all those cryptic entries involving dates and meetings with people referred to by initials only. If we can marry them up with names we should be able to find out who he is and then we can lean on him.'

'What we need,' said Coleman, taking a corner with a screech of tyres, 'is a lead on how prospective punters get in touch with the Coil Shuffler.'

'We'll get it. He'll make a slip before long, he must do.'

'In the meantime, how many other bodies are going to end up in the morgue?'

* * *

Morden Hall Clinic occupied a manor house that had formally been the family home of the noble Broome family. In a more rural setting it could have called itself a country club, but the considerable estate that had formally belonged to the manor had been sold off piecemeal in the last hundred and fifty years as the Broomes had struggled in vain to hang on to the family home. The parkland and rolling acres had been overtaken by housing estates and now the city suburbs encroached and surrounded the house, although it still retained a fair-sized garden, part of which had been made into a carpark. This was divided by a tall evergreen hedge from an elaborate conservatory that colonised the east wall of the house.

They parked the car and walked round to the front of the building, entering through an imposing portico which led into a large foyer. A desk faced them and behind it sat a young, dark-haired girl who looked intimidated by her surroundings.

'Who is in charge here?' Dickins strode forward and slapped his hand on the desk.

'Dr Julian Porter.'

'Then we'll see him.'

The girl looked at them nervously. 'Are you members? Prospective members?'

'We're police.'

They flashed their IDs before her and she looked even more apprehensive. 'He is with a client at the moment.'

'We're busy men and this is important. Perhaps you'll tell him we're here.'

She disappeared through a door behind her and the two men paced the floor.

'Can anyone come here and use the facilities if they pay?' asked Coleman, examining one of the framed certificates on the wall.

'I reckon there is a hefty membership fee to keep out the likes of you and me. It's where all the rich biddies come to pamper themselves and stave off the ravages of time and the men try and fight off the effects of expense account meals and high living.'

The man who came across the foyer to greet them a short while later was a good advertisement for his establishment. He was tall and slim with muscles in the right places and carefully coiffured fair hair. He strode towards them confidently.

'Amy tells me you are police officers?'

'Detective Inspector Dickins and this is Detective Sergeant Coleman. And you are Dr Porter?'

The blond man agreed that he was.

'Are you a medical doctor?' asked Dickins.

'I have a Ph.D.' But he failed to elaborate in which field he had achieved this status. 'What can I do for you? We don't very often have a visit from the Force.'

'Can we go somewhere to talk?'

'My office.' He led the way through into an adjacent room. 'Now, gentlemen?'

'You have an employee called Carolyn Hamblin?'

'Yes, she's our receptionist. But she hasn't come in today. It's most unlike her not to turn up without warning us and her car is still here.' He paused and a look of dismay crossed his face. 'Dear God, she hasn't had an accident, has she? Is that why you're here? We've tried ringing her flat but there has been no reply.'

'Dead women don't answer the phone, Doctor.'

'*Dead*! Oh my God! What's happened? Has she been involved in a road accident?'

'The body of a young woman was found near Rutland Park this morning. She had been strangled. We believe her to be Carolyn Hamblin.'

Julian Porter looked stricken. 'I can't take this in . . . *Carolyn?* But why? How?'

'From what evidence we have gathered so far it would appear that the murdered woman was a Carolyn Hamblin who worked here at Morden Hall. Can you tell me anything about her family?'

After staring at them blankly for a few seconds Porter pulled himself together.

'She had no family, or certainly no close relations. She told me once that her parents had been killed in a car crash many years ago and that she had no siblings. I believe she came originally from the Midlands.'

'In that case, Dr Porter, would you be prepared to identify the body?'

'Is there no one else?'

'Well, you've just told me she had no family. Of course, if we knew who the boyfriend was . . . ?'

There was no reply from Porter and Dickins tried again.

'Surely an attractive girl like Carolyn must have had a boyfriend, plenty of admirers?'

'Oh yes, Inspector, she was a lovely girl, very attractive to the opposite sex, but I really don't know if there was anyone special.'

'I'm sure you look after your staff well, Doctor. You obviously know where she lived. I don't think she could have managed that rent on any salary *you* paid her, could she?'

'You're suggesting she was supported by someone? I don't know anything about that. I presumed she had inherited money and I'm sure she lived there on her own.'

'What about girl friends? Was she close to anyone else who works here? I'm trying to find out about her background and what made her tick.'

'Emma Pearson would be the best person to help you. She was very friendly with Carolyn. She'll probably be able to tell you as much as anyone but she is working with a client for the next half-hour and I can't interrupt her session.'

'What service does she provide?'

'She is a beautician. A highly trained

one who is much in demand with our members.'

'You said Carolyn's car was still here. What did you mean by that?'

'She has a BMW in which she usually travels here to work. However, on Tuesday evenings she works — worked — until seven o'clock and then went on to an evening class at the college. I believe she was taking a course in German, but the point is, the parking situation is very bad there and we are on a bus route that goes quite close so she used to bus in and then bus back and collect her car later in the evening.'

'The bus would have dropped her outside the main entrance to Rutland Park and presumably she took a short cut through the spinney, where her body was found, to Upton Road?'

'I expect so. I suppose in retrospect it was a foolish thing to do but Carolyn was not a timid person and she would have laughed at the idea of it being dangerous. Poor girl, to think there was a maniac lurking there waiting for some unsuspecting young woman . . .'

'She did this every Tuesday, you say? It was a regular thing?'

'Yes. You think someone knew this and followed her?' Julian Porter was deeply troubled by this thought.

'I don't think anything at this point in the investigation. I am just amassing what evidence there is so far and trying to make sense of it.'

A short while later Coleman had gone with Julian Porter in the doctor's car to the mortuary and Trevor Dickins was left sipping the coffee provided and waiting for Emma Pearson to put in an appearance. She didn't keep him waiting long. He studied her approvingly when she arrived in the foyer. She wasn't a beauty like her dead friend but she was expertly made up and coiffured, an excellent advertisement for her occupation. She was dressed in a neat white overall piped in pink and her glossy black hair was swept back in a French pleat.

'You wanted to see me?' Her voice was low pitched and pleasant.

'You're Emma Pearson? I'm Detective Inspector Dickins. Has your boss told you why I'm here?'

'He said that Carolyn had had an accident. Is it serious? Is she in hospital?'

'I'm afraid she's dead, Miss Pearson.'

Dickins broke the news to her as tactfully as he knew how and she seemed to shrink before his eyes.

'It's terrible! I can't believe it! Are you sure

it's her? Yes, you must be or you wouldn't be here ... Who could have done such a dreadful thing?'

'That's what I'm trying to find out. Dr Porter said you were her closest friend, so I'm hoping you can help me.'

'But I don't know anything about it!' Her voice rose hysterically.

'No, I'm not accusing you of that, but you can tell me about Carolyn, what sort of person she was, who her friends were, her hobbies and interests and that sort of thing.'

'I was her friend but I don't think anyone was very close to her. She was a very private person and I didn't really know her all that well.'

'How do you mean?'

'It's difficult to explain.' She wrinkled her brow. 'On the surface she was very outgoing and sociable but underneath ... she kept herself to herself. She was secretive and clammed up if you asked her any questions about her past or seemed too nosey about her affairs.'

'By affairs you mean her love-life?'

'No, I don't.' She was indignant.

'But she had a boyfriend, a lover?'

'Ye-es, there was someone ... '

'Who was he?'

'I don't know. That's what I mean about her being secretive. She'd had boyfriends in the past and was quite open about them. They weren't important to her and she'd laugh and joke about them but then she met the current one and it was different. She was really serious about him I think, very intense and involved, but she wouldn't even tell me his name or let me meet him.'

'A married man?'

'She never said so, but I reckoned he must be.'

'How long had she been going out with him?'

'About eighteen months. Certainly longer than a year.'

'And you never set eyes on him or got any clues as to who he might be?'

'No. I did try a couple of months ago to suggest she was on a hiding to nothing if she was dating a married man and she got very uptight and told me to mind my own business. She was quite cool with me after that until about two weeks ago when she suddenly seemed to want to take me into her confidence.'

'What happened?'

'She apologised for being so unfriendly and said she had been under some stress but that things had sorted themselves out and everything was going to be all right now.'

'He was going to get a divorce and marry her?'

'That's what I thought. I asked if she wanted to confide in me and she said to hang on a bit longer and soon I'd know all about it and meet him.'

'He was a well-heeled chap and he looked after her.'

'He was certainly very generous. She had some lovely presents.'

'She was a kept woman.'

'Oh, no. She was very independent and they certainly didn't live together.'

'You've been to her flat? You've seen her clothes and possessions? You couldn't have such a life style on what you earn here, could you? She may not have lived openly with him but he was supporting her financially. Would she have had any problems with that?'

'Not Carolyn. I don't think she had a very good opinion of men in general and she was quite happy to take what was on offer. She used to laugh to me about how different men had tried to buy her and whilst she accepted what was offered she secretly despised them.'

'In other words, she was an old-fashioned gold-digger? She screwed for profit?'

'No, you make her seem so hard and mercenary. She was light-hearted and carefree about these things. Said if men were so grateful for her love that they wanted to spoil her who was she to disillusion them?'

'And then she latched on to someone who was seriously rich and dug in.'

'You're twisting what I'm saying!' cried Emma in distress. 'This affair was different. I think she was genuinely in love and thought they had a future together.'

Dickins curled his lip in scorn and she hurried on.

'You think *he* killed her?'

'It usually is the lover in cases like this, but we've got to find him, haven't we? Could it have been someone she met here? A member of this place?'

'Well, yes, I suppose it is possible. She would have known everyone who came here and subscribed to the clinic.'

'You have some very affluent public figures amongst your members?'

'Yes. Morden Hall is in a class by itself when it comes to health and fitness clinics. It is the very best.'

'And Carolyn's fancy-man was probably top of the tree in his profession. Not someone who would like it known that his bit on the side was a Girl Friday at a health farm. Think about it, Emma, and if you come up with something let me know.'

12

'She was three months pregnant.' Mike was filling Nick in with details of the autopsy report on Carolyn Hamblin.

'So there's your motive.' Nick set down his pint and leaned across the table. 'She gets herself pregnant and tries to use it as a lever to persuade lover-boy to do the honourable thing but nothing doing. He's a married man and wants out.'

'Rather an extreme reaction, wasn't it, to have her bumped off rather than persuade her to undergo an abortion?'

'Perhaps she wanted to keep the baby. Let's say she refused to consider an abortion and threatened to tell his wife and kick up a stink. Whoever he is, it is pretty certain he is well-to-do and in the public eye with a reputation to preserve. He is quite happy to have a fling but nothing must disturb the status quo. When she gets out of line he becomes desperate and arranges to have her taken out. How am I doing?'

'Not bad. You're more or less following the official line. Two and a half thousand was paid into her building society account recently, which could have been payment for a termination but she had other ideas. Wanted to keep the baby or wanted to force his hand.'

'And have we any suspects?'

'We've got her diary — a lucky break — and Dickins is trying to marry up the initials written in that with the male clientele of the Morden Hall clinic. He is working on the theory that the boyfriend was probably someone she met through her work.'

'Any luck so far?'

'Yes, he thinks he's got a lead. One set of initials crops up over and over again in the diary and he thinks he has matched them with a member of the club.'

'You shit! Letting me theorise and shout my mouth off and all the while you've got someone in the frame!'

'Just testing.' Mike grinned at his friend. 'Does the name Stephen Longridge mean anything to you?'

'Stephen Longridge? Wait a moment . . . ' Nick wrinkled his brow. 'It rings a bell . . . I've got it! He's a company director, in the import and export business, something to do with computers. Isn't he big on the political scene also? I've seen his mugshot in the local rag on occasion.'

'That's the one. He's got his fingers in all

sorts of local pies and he's into the money, though rumour has it the money is his wife's and she holds the purse strings. There was some talk about him being adopted as the Conservative candidate for the constituency at the next election.'

'Christ! And they think he's the one who has been having it off with the dead woman and arranged her death?'

'Dickins is positive but he's got no proof, nothing to tie him in with it apart from the initials in her diary. Longridge denies everything and of course he's got an alibi for the time of the murder — he was at a Rotary Club meeting.'

'So we've got to find some connection between him and the Coil Shuffler.'

'I think that is going to be almost impossible because I have this theory that neither reveals his identity. The Coil Shuffler has managed to set up a scheme whereby he picks up a contract on a victim but he never knows who has employed him and, likewise, the person putting out the contract never finds out who he is.'

'There has to be some contact made in public, some initial meeting or message passing.'

'The trouble is you're not talking about the underworld here. Longridge is a respected member of the community and he's kicking up a stink about being a suspect. Bairstow is on the verge of a nervous breakdown — Longridge is a friend of the CC and on the Watch Committee and is threatening to sue.'

'Poor Trevor, I could almost feel sorry for him!' Nick folded his arms behind his head and tilted his chair back. 'He's not coming out of this at all well.'

★ ★ ★

Stephen Longridge was an arrogant man but beneath the self-assurance and hauteur he was scared and Trevor Dickins had sensed this when he had interviewed him. The detective was sure he was scared because he had something to hide. He was equally sure that Longridge was his man but how to prove it was another matter. Longridge had vehemently denied knowing Carolyn Hamblin, apart from a nodding acquaintance through the health clinic, and Dickins was determined to uncover some evidence that would tie him in with the dead woman. To this end he made another visit to Carolyn's flat. Longridge himself may have been very careful not to leave any proof of his affair around — no letters, photos, personal items — but surely Carolyn herself wouldn't have been so circumspect?

He struck lucky immediately he stepped inside the apartment. Amongst the post strewn across the doormat was a packet from Snappy Prints, a company that developed and printed films through a postal service. When opened he found twenty-four photos that had been taken at some social gathering. Seven of these featured Carolyn Hamblin and Stephen Longridge, talking, fondling each other and kissing.

'Got you!' he said out loud. 'Now try and talk yourself out of this one!' As he pocketed them he wondered who had been behind the camera. Maybe she had got a friend to deliberately compromise him by snapping them in intimate embraces as an insurance policy. Well, in a way it had paid off; although Carolyn was beyond help it might help to nail the man responsible for her death. Another search of the flat turned up no further clues to link Longridge with the place but Dickins was sure that if further evidence was needed fingerprints belonging to him would be found here and Forensics would probably find something when they examined the dressing-gown and shirts.

This time he had Longridge brought to the station for questioning. The company director took his seat in the interview room, flanked by his solicitor, protesting outrage at his treatment. He was a tall, handsome man in his mid-forties with dark, silvering hair and a patrician nose and brow. His beautifully cut suit and handmade shoes were witness to his affluence and he had a smooth tongue, used to charming and oiling his path. Nobody charmed Dickins and he made that clear at the outset.

'Nobody pulls rank in here,' he declared when the preliminaries had been gone through. 'No matter who you are outside this room, crook, tycoon, mugger or the Prime Minister himself, once you take up residence here you are a suspect helping us in our enquiries, so don't try and pervert the course of justice.'

'You'll be sorry for this,' snarled Longridge, ignoring his solicitor's restraining hand on his arm. 'I'll personally see to it!'

'I don't think so,' said Dickins blandly.

* * *

The Vanguard Club was a snooker club of mixed reputation. On the one hand it was known as a disreputable dive with a doubtful clientele; on the other hand, because of the excellence of its tables and facilities, it was sometimes used as a venue for tournaments organised by such as the local Rotary and Lions clubs. The police had held fund-raising tournaments there in aid of charity on more than one occasion and several policemen were members. One of these was Kevin Parker, an ambitious detective constable on Dickins' team. He frequented the Vanguard as much to communicate with his snouts as to play snooker. He was a canny young man who mentally noted the goings-on of the members of the underworld he came in contact with and stored them away to use against them later. He worked on the principle that rather than arrest someone for a minor infringement of the law it was to his advantage to lie low and then use the knowledge as ammunition to lean on the person concerned later with more benefit to him and his career prospects.

He knew that one of his informers, a part-time nightwatchman, was supplying details of security to a gang of safe-breakers; that Bill Watson, who owned and ran the Vanguard, ignored licensing laws and turned a blind eye to drugs changing hands on his premises. He knew that the man who now sat drinking with him in a corner of the bar was swindling the DHSS. Benny West was a ratlike little man who always looked as if his clothes were too big for him. Parker was convinced that Benny knew something about the Coil Shuffler; his emphatic denials of any such knowledge, out of all proportion to the original chance question, had made the detective suspicious right from the start. He decided that now was the time to put pressure on Benny and call in the loan.

'What have you got for me, Benny? You've not been very co-operative of late.'

'Nothing, nothing,' West whispered whilst his eyes darted round the room in panic lest they should be overheard. 'Everything's very quiet at the moment. It's the time of the year.'

'Don't give me that. You're active at the moment, moonlighting.'

'I don't know what you mean!'

'Let me remind you. You're drawing your giro each fortnight but you're also working on Danny Green's stall on the market.'

'Just helping out a mate for a couple of hours 'cos he got let down. 'E's not paying me.'

'You don't really expect me to believe that, do you? And what about your evening job at the stadium?'

'That's nuffink, jes peanuts. I haven't been able to work since I'ad me trouble.'

'I think it is time you were shopped,

311

Benny. It's my taxes we're talking about — going to line your pockets!'

'Now don't be 'asty, I'm getting myself sorted out but I might 'ave 'eard something you'd be interested in?'

'And what might that be?'

'This Coil Shuffler . . . '

'What about him?' Kevin Parker tried to be nonchalant and not let on to Benny how excited he was.

'You wanted to know how a person got in touch with 'im? Well, I've heard rumours that it happens here.'

'Go on.'

'There's messages left. In a cigar box.'

Parker made a rapid leap from this snippet to facts stored in his memory and connected.

'Hamlet cigars?'

'You know?' West was disgusted and disappointed.

'I'd like to hear your version. Spit it out.'

'That shelf beside the bar, with the photos and trophies on it — there's an empty cigar box kept there.'

Parker swivelled round to look at the shelf in question. It held framed photos of snooker players, two silver cups and a silver shield, and in the middle was a Hamlet cigar box.

'When someone wants to contact the

Coil Shuffler,' continued West, 'they put a message in it with a telephone number or contact address.'

'What happens then?'

'I don't know.'

'Come on, don't hold out on me, what is the next move?'

'Strikes me it's got to involve the landlord, hasn't it?'

Benny West refused to say any more and after a promise of further immunity from the vigilantes of the DHSS he scuttled off, and Kevin Parker interested himself in a game that was taking place at a nearby table and waited for the lunchtime trade to die down. When he decided he would get Bill Watson's undivided attention he sauntered across to the bar and went straight for the jugular.

'How's the trade in cigar boxes these days, Bill?'

The landlord was wiping the counter with a grubby cloth. He stopped abruptly for a few seconds and then hurriedly resumed his sweeping movements.

'What are you on about?'

'Cigar boxes. That one up there in particular. Hamlet cigars. They do a nice little advert for that on telly, don't they?'

'I don't know what you're talking about.'

'You're getting slack, Bill. You used to run

a tight little ship but you're getting careless. I can't turn a blind eye any longer.'

'Listen . . . '

'No, you listen to me. I saw you serve a couple of under-age drinkers only half an hour ago and what about the drink that was flowing in the small hours a couple of nights ago?'

'I can't ask everyone who comes in here for a birth certificate,' growled Watson, 'and that was a private party the other night.'

'I could overlook something like that but drugs is something else.'

'Drugs?' The landlord looked uneasy.

'Yes, drugs. There's dealing going on in this place.'

'I don't know anything about it.'

'You try telling that to a magistrate. If we carry out a raid on this place they'll close you down: the Vanguard — *kaput*, finished.'

Watson glared at him and flicked his cloth close to the edge of the counter, sending a shower of beer dregs over the detective's sleeve.

'You don't want that, do you, Bill? So let's discuss cigar boxes; in particular that one over there on the shelf.'

'It's empty.'

'Now maybe, but not always. I've been told

mysterious names and telephone numbers find their way into it from time to time. Now, I don't think you're running a dating agency, are you?'

Watson growled and looked mutinous. 'It's nothing to do with me.'

'Don't give me that. You're running a scheme putting a hit-man in touch with prospective clients. Who uses that box?'

'I'm not running nothing! I'm just the go-between.'

'That's better. Who set it up?'

'I don't know, I tell you.'

'Come on, someone must have put the proposition to you in the first place. How much are you paid for this little service?'

'I'm not paid nothing. I was threatened over the phone, told if I didn't do what he asked I'd be turned over and worse.'

'How long has this been going on?'

'Two or three years.'

'And you're still playing ball?'

'I know what's good for me.'

'So. That box is left there in a prominent position and if a person wants to get in touch with the Coil Shuffler he leaves a message inside. Who picks up the message?'

'I don't watch it, not me, mate. I jest have a flick round with a duster each day.'

'And?'

'If there's anything in it I move it, don't I?'

'You move it where?'

'Into the bog. There's no need to look like that, I run a high-class establishment here, no nasty third-rate urinals in this place. You've used them, could be the Ritz, couldn't it? Smells as sweet as a knocking shop.'

'Never mind the smell. Where do you put it?'

'On top of the condom machine. Every so often I check it out and if it's empty I bring it back in here. I don't know who removes the messages, I don't want to know.'

'Don't tell me he doesn't leave a sweetener in it for you?'

Watson didn't deign to answer this so Parker tried a different tack.

'You say you don't know who empties it, okay, but does it happen on a certain day of the week or at a regular time?'

'Look, you make it sound as if it's a regular pigeon post. It's happened less than half a dozen times and I never know when or how a message is going to be passed along.'

'You dealt with one recently, didn't you?'

'I can't remember.'

'You'd better try harder. Listen, Watson, you're in serious trouble, I wouldn't like to

316

be in your shoes. If you want to save your skin you'd better co-operate with the Bill. Not a word of this conversation must get out. If you attempt to warn this Coil Shuffler it will be your head on the block. Just carry on as usual for now but if another message is put in that box in the next few days we want to know immediately. Is that understood?'

Bill Watson agreed with bad grace and Kevin Parker hurried to the station to report on his breakthrough.

★ ★ ★

Back in the interview room at Brent Hill Trevor Dickins was becoming increasingly frustrated. On being confronted with the photos of himself cavorting with Carolyn Hamblin Stephen Longridge had admitted to having a fling with her, but would go no further. Even the other piece of information that had come Dickin's way was being turned against him. One of the uniformed sergeants who had recently moved to the city from the Midlands had recognised the dead woman as being a high-class prostitute who had operated in the Birmingham area in the early nineties.

'Your mistress, Longridge, was on the game. She was a hooker, well known to my colleagues in the Midlands where she came from.'

'She was not my mistress, how many times do I have to tell you that?'

'You're not still trying to persuade me that you didn't have an affair with her?'

'Not an affair, no. Just a brief liaison. As you say, she was a good-time girl and I took what was on offer.'

'You paid well for her services; setting her up in a luxury flat and showering her with presents.'

'Not me, Inspector. I was obviously one of many. Perhaps someone got upset at being two-timed and killed her in a jealous rage — a crime of passion.'

'Not so. She was killed by the Coil Shuffler who was paid to remove her from the scene when she got herself pregnant and became an embarrassment to her lover — *you*.'

'This is ridiculous. You're so keen to get a conviction because of your incompetence so far that you're snatching at straws. Well, you've chosen the wrong person to try to intimidate!'

'Was she threatening to tell your wife? I understand that Mrs Longridge is a very wealthy lady who has put a lot of money into your business and has a social position to keep up. As indeed have you. Wouldn't do for it to be known that a pillar of the Conservative Party and a prominent Mason has fathered a child on his mistress, a well-known call-girl, would it?'

'My client refuses to answer this ridiculous suggestion,' put in Longridge's solicitor smoothly. 'He has nothing to answer for. At the time of the murder he was in Germany on business. I suggest you stop wasting our time and concentrate on catching the real villain.'

There was an interruption at this point with the arrival of Kevin Parker, eager to impart his recently gained knowledge to his superior. He put his head round the door.

'Could I have a word, sir? Something has come up.'

Dickins temporarily halted the interview and joined Parker in the corridor outside. After he had heard Parker out he went back into the interview room hoping to surprise his suspect and force an admission.

'Well, Longridge, let's indeed stop wasting time. My time is as valuable as yours so let's stop buggering about and get down to business. What can you tell me about cigar boxes?'

★ ★ ★

Rachel had come to a decision. It had taken many hours of mental wrestling, searching her conscience and probing her motives, but now that she had made her choice she felt strangely light-hearted as if a burden had been lifted from her. She had decided not to pursue her admittance to the priesthood. This decision had been prompted by a letter from the Diocesan Board. She had suddenly known that she was not yet ready to take that big step, that her desire to become a priest had been motivated by the wrong reasons.

The most important of these reasons had been her overwhelming wish to take over where Christopher had left off. He had been plucked from life in the middle of his ministry and she had rushed forward to take his place, to continue his work in the way he would have done. But this was wrong, she had painfully concluded; she was a person in her own right with her own principles and methods of expressing her faith, not a clone of Christopher. Another factor in making this decision was knowing that she still hadn't managed to come to terms with the impact of Pat Fenton's treachery and death.

She had discussed all this with David Bell and surprisingly he had agreed with her.

'You have thrown yourself headlong into this but I have felt that perhaps the time is not right for you,' the vicar had said, regarding her sympathetically. 'Don't get me wrong, I think you will make an excellent priest, but you are still a young woman, Rachel, and you can always reapply later. The Church needs people such as you but as a reader you are already contributing greatly to this parish and your work as a physiotherapist is also fulfilling a need in the community.'

'As a non-stipendary priest I could continue this work.'

'Not so easily done as said. While non-stipendary clergy are a gift to the C. of E., particularly from a financial viewpoint, the stress on the individual person is tremendous. Trying to balance a full commitment to the Church with another career is no easy undertaking. Then there is your personal life to consider . . . ' He had paused delicately and she had said quickly:

'This has nothing to do with my friendship with a certain policeman.'

'No? Perhaps it should have.'

She had pondered this remark later, feeling stirrings of guilt. She still hadn't told Mike about her decision. She didn't want him to feel he was in any responsible for her change of mind. She didn't want him to take it as a sign that maybe she was ready to commit herself to him rather than to the Church. She wasn't. Not yet. She wanted their friendship to continue as it was for present. She enjoyed his company and his embraces but it was a strangely sexless affair with a reluctance on both their parts to become overwhelmed by passion. She knew that no relationship could stand still; it either had to develop or wither but for the time being she was content for it to continue as it was and she would try not to dwell on the knowledge that someone close to Mike harboured malicious feelings towards her.

Anyway, she told herself, becoming more involved with Mike didn't necessarily preclude her ambition to become a priest, did it?

★ ★ ★

Dickins has been forced to let Stephen Longridge go. Although convinced that the businessman had arranged the death of his mistress, Longridge had denied this and any knowledge of the Coil Shuffler and cigar boxes and he could not come up with enough evidence to back his belief and support an arrest. Instead, Bairstow had insisted that they now tackled the case from the angle of the Coil Shuffler, having at long last picked up on his method of communication. A cast round the station had revealed that besides Kevin Parker three other members of the local force were members of the Vanguard Club, including Nick Holroyd, so a trap was set up.

A cryptic message and a phone number were left in the Hamlet cigar box and Bill Watson was instructed to move this into the men's toilet when he 'found' it. With the aid of the security and electronic boffins a sophisticated device had been included whereby as soon as the message was lifted it broke a beam that activated a photoelectric cell and an alarm was sent through to the control bleeper held by the person on watch at the Vanguard. As the club was open from ten in the morning until after midnight it was not easy to keep a complete surveillance cover without the other habitués becoming suspicious. Bairstow fixed up a rota whereby one of the four police members was always on the premises, though as unobtrusively as possible. As there was an outer door leading from the toilets into the back yard where a gate opened on to the street, someone was also stationed outside in this yard.

Bairstow was aware as he made these arrangements that if one of his men was involved with the Coil Shuffler then his plans would come to naught. It was a risk he had to take. If the message remained in the cigar box and no one went near it he would know that he had a traitor in the camp.

Nick Holroyd was amused at being drafted on to the team and whilst he contrived to annoy Trevor Dickins as much as he was able in his new role he admitted to Mike that his snooker was coming on in leaps and bounds. It was, fittingly enough, Kevin Parker who was on vigil the evening that the Coil Shuffler made his move. The cigar box had been sitting on top of the condom machine for three days attracting no attention and Parker was trying to spin out his second pint as he sat in a corner from where he could keep an eye on the comings and goings to and from the toilet. He was also trying to avoid being cajoled into a game whereby he would have to move away from his strategic position. A young constable, seconded to CID for the operation and working in plain-clothes for the first time, hovered beneath the back wall of the club, nicely balanced between boredom and excitement. His leather jacket creaked as he shifted position and fiddled with the cigarette he didn't dare light.

Inside, Kevin yawned and squinted at his watch, wondering if the trap would ever be sprung. There had already been two false alarms caused by an inquisitive person investigating the contents of the cigar box. In both cases the message had been left inside and on the second occasion the box had been knocked onto the floor and left there.

'Fancy a game?' The voice startled him and he looked up at the man leaning on his table grinning down at him. He had noticed him earlier at the bar and recognised him as someone he knew and ought to be able to put a name to but couldn't.

'Damien Winter,' the man said as if reading his thoughts. 'I work in the mortuary. I've seen you there when we're carving up a suspicious death — you're a policeman, aren't you?'

Of course! As soon as the man spoke his memory clicked in.

'Yes. Sorry I didn't recognise you, you look different in ordinary clothes.'

When attending an autopsy Parker was so keen not to disgrace himself by throwing up or fainting that he would look anywhere but at the cadaver. He recognised this man as one of the two morticians who were usually hovering at Quentin Stock's elbow, clothed in gowns and caps and boots and more often than not with masks across their lower faces.

'How about it, then?' Damien Winter indicated the nearby table which was not in use.

'Not this evening, thanks. I played earlier and I'm definitely not on form. I'll give you a game another day. Are you a member here? I don't remember seeing you before.'

'Yes, I've belonged for several years but I don't get down all that often, although I try and make the effort. It's good to have a change of scene.'

'Do you enjoy your work?' asked Parker, overcome with curiosity as to how someone could work in the morgue from free choice. Freddie Baines, the other mortician, was old, probably couldn't get a job anywhere else, but Damien Winter was a relatively young man. 'Don't you get upset by what you see and do?'

'I could say the same about your profession. At least my lot are dead and can't answer back or turn on me.'

'True. I guess we both see the seamy side of life. What is Quentin Stock like to work for?'

'All right as long as you remember to treat him like a little god and don't step out of line.'

'Yes, I can imagine that. He's always struck me as a very cocky bastard. What's your shout?'

'Not for me, thanks. If I'm not playing any more I'll get off home and I'm driving.'

Winter picked up the sports holdall he'd propped against the table leg. 'You're the second copper I've seen in here this week. Nick Holroyd was sitting at this same table a couple of nights ago. How is the force using his talents these days?'

'Oh, they've found a niche for him. 'In my father's house are many mansions' — Hell! Where does that come from?'

'The Bible. They often quote it at funerals.'

'Well, I haven't been to one of those recently so I don't know why that popped out!'

'It's thinking about stiffs.' Winter grinned. 'See you.'

Kevin raised his hand as the other man moved off towards the door and settled back for another tedious wait. It seemed like only a couple of minutes later when the alarm in his pocket started bleeping. Shocked into full awareness he silenced it and dived for the toilet door.

The first thing he noticed was the darkness. Someone had switched off the lights. He fumbled for the switch and couldn't find it and as his eyes adjusted to the gloom he heard movement near one of the cubicles and then the back door was flung open. In the dim light that filtered through the gap he saw a figure hovering in the shadows, dressed in dark clothes and wearing a Balaclava mask. This figure moved across the doorway, completely blocking out the light for a few seconds, and then disappeared. Kevin shouted to alert his colleague in the yard and crashed after him.

There was the sound of bodies colliding and a muffled cry and then the thud of running feet receding down the street. Kevin pulled out his torch and swung the beam round the yard picking out the figure of the constable slumped near the gateway. He was groaning and clutching his shoulder and blood was seeping down the front of his jacket.

'Christ! Where did he get you?'

'I'm okay. Get after him — be careful, he's got a knife.'

'I'll summon help.' Kevin barked into his two-way radio alerting control that his colleague had been injured and their quarry was running down Brancaster Street, then he charged after him. For once the street lights were all working and he could see his man hurtling down the other side of the road, a bag swinging from one hand. There was a row of cars parked at the far end of the street and the man headed for a van tucked in behind the furthest one. He flung open the door and jumped behind the wheel, and Kevin, toiling down the road after him, groaned in frustration as the engine fired and the van swerved out round the parked vehicles and roared off towards the junction. He was too far away to read the number plate but he was able to radio through the direction in which the van was heading. This done, he leaned back against a fence and recovered his breath and then went back to join the injured constable.

The van headed towards the old Victorian district and within minutes had a police car on its tail. Aware that he was being followed the van driver took to the back streets hoping to lose his pursuer in the alleys and lanes that bisected this part of the city. He swung down narrow roads that ran between rows of terraced houses and doubled back on his tracks, screeching round corners on two wheels and ignoring one-way signs. After five minutes of this cat and mouse chase he became aware that the sound of the police siren was receding in the distance, going in the opposite direction to himself. He had eluded them. He turned down an alleyway that led past blocks of boarded-up houses, earmarked for slum clearance. With his lights switched off he cruised along looking for a gap in the buildings where he could get the van off the road and lie low until he was sure the pursuit had been called off. He was almost at the end of the road when a police car swung round the corner ahead and caught him in the full glare of its powerful headlights.

Startled and swearing, he slammed the van into reverse and roared back down the road, but in his mirror he saw another police car slip in behind him cutting off his retreat. Then another car moved in behind that and figures piled out and ran towards him. He drove the van on to the pavement and jumped out, flinging himself at the nearby wall. With a superhuman effort he scaled it and crashed down into a pile of cans and petrol drums. He picked himself up and hurtled through a maze of back alleys aiming towards the church that loomed up in the distance, its black spire standing sentinel against the night sky.

★ ★ ★

Rachel heard the sirens in the distance and wondered whether it was fire engines or ambulances. She had just read the evening office in St Luke's Church and before she got up from her knees she said a prayer for whoever was in danger. She switched off the lights in the chancel and walked down the aisle intending to let herself out of the main door. It was a shame the church had to be locked up when not in use, she thought, seeking out the large wrought-iron key on the key-ring she held. In theory it should be open day and night to offer sanctuary and support to anyone who came seeking it, but a spate of burglaries in recent years that had seen the disappearance of valuable silver plate and offertory boxes had ensured that the church was well secured.

She was just lifting the heavy latch when the door swung open and a figure cannoned into her, knocking her over. She sprawled across the porch floor and instinctively reached for the handbag which had shot away into the corner. A hand reached down and grasped her wrist, jerking her to her feet, and a voice grated in her ear: 'Lock the door!'

Startled, she nearly dropped the bunch of keys and gaped at the figure who still held her wrist in a painful grip. She saw the masked face and the eyes gleaming at her through the slits and cringed back in fright.

'Do as I say!'

She felt something cold and sharp prick her neck and with fumbling hands she put the key in the lock and turned it.

'Give them to me.'

She handed over the bunch and was released with a push. She skidded across the slippery flags and ended up against the notice-board.

'Who are you? What do you want?' she whispered.

'Why, Rachel, don't you know who I am? I'm the Coil Shuffler.'

13

'He's gone to ground in the church!'

The police pursuit homed in on the church, Trevor Dickins in the lead. Men fanned in from all corners of the churchyard and thundered up to the porch. The massive latch lifted easily but the door refused to budge.

'It's locked.'

'It can't be.'

'It damn well is. He must have got in and found the key on the inside.'

'Unless he's hiding in the churchyard somewhere.'

'The lights are on inside. It's my bet he's in there, but search the area and make sure he's not lurking behind a gravestone.'

'Maybe he's gatecrashed a service — there could be other people in there.'

'Hell!' Dickins thumped his fists together. 'Get hold of the vicar. The vicarage is over there if he's not in the church — and dig out the verger. There must be other keys.'

Whilst men rushed off to do his bidding, Dickins contained the scene by throwing a cordon round the churchyard. A thorough search amongst the ancient higgledy-piggledy gravestones revealed no hidden Coil Shuffler. The other door on the north side was also securely locked and looked as if it hadn't been in use for a very long time. While Dickins prowled round the walls more lights sprang to life inside, throwing fractured lancets of light across the black grass.

'Hell, I don't like this. Where is the damn vicar?'

As if on cue, David Bell came hurrying down the path from the vicarage. Dickins explained briefly what had happened and fired a volley of questions at him.

'How did he get in? Isn't the door kept locked?'

'Always, when there is no one there.'

'Well, he got in and he's locked the door behind him. Is there a key kept inside somewhere where he could have got at it?'

'No. I have keys to the main doors and the vestry and so have my verger and my curate.'

'There wouldn't be one of them in there, would there?'

'Not as far as I know. The evening office would have been read . . . ' His voice trailed away in consternation.

'Yes?'

'One of my readers — Rachel Morland — is

334

reading the evening office this week. She would normally do it much earlier' — the vicar glanced at his watch — 'but she could have been delayed. You don't think she's in there with him, do you?'

'If she is I don't give much for her chances. He's a professional killer!'

David Bell groaned. 'What can I do?'

'Try ringing her home number. With any luck she's back home safe and sound and he got in some other way.'

'My keys are here. Do you want to use them to get inside?'

'Not for the moment. He's armed and dangerous and I don't want to panic him if he has got Rachel Morland in there with him.'

Dickins radioed for reinforcements and with them came the superintendent.

'You think he's got a hostage in there with him?' barked Douglas Bairstow and Dickins explained the situation.

'Right, we'll try and flush him out.' Bairstow strode into the south porch and lifted a megaphone to his mouth.

'We have the place surrounded,' he bellowed at the door. 'You can't escape. Come out quietly and you won't be hurt.'

* * *

He laughed and to Rachel that was even more frightening than his snarled commands.

'You know my name?'

'Yes, I've made it my business to know all about you. How many doors are there to this place?'

'Just this one and the north door.'

'Both now locked and these are the keys?' He swung the ring in front of her.

'Yes.'

'So what is this key?'

'The key to the vestry.'

'Who else has keys?'

'The vicar and the verger and the curate.'

'Then we had better put these ones back in their appropriate locks so they can't use theirs. Take them off the ring.'

With shaking fingers Rachel did as she was bid and then he propelled her round the church and stood over her as she pushed the keys into the locks. She was very aware of the knife held in his right hand and knew he wouldn't hesitate to use it on her if the need arose.

'What are you going to do?'

'Sit tight for the time being. We're secure in here.'

'You won't get away with this, the police are on your tail.'

'The police don't know who I am either.

They are a bunch of bumbling incompetents. I've found it really amusing watching them go round in circles like blue-arsed flies.'

'They're closing in on you now. Listen, I can hear the sirens!' said Rachel recklessly.

'Don't forget we're in a church. I could be claiming sanctuary like they used to do in the olden days. They can do nothing, they're helpless!'

'I'm sure they won't let a little thing like sanctuary get in their way, it doesn't apply these days.'

'So what. I have a far more important weapon — you. They'll think twice before making a move that would endanger your life. How fortunate you happened to be around, Rachel, your god must be on my side — he's given me a hostage.'

At that point there was a thunderous knocking on the south door and Bairstow's voice, disembodied and distorted, floated through to them.

'You see,' cried Rachel when the voice died away, 'you're trapped. They know you're in here and they'll storm the place.'

'Then we had better make sure they know you're in here with me.' He raised his head and looked around the nave and Rachel watched his eyes probing the walls and recesses. They were dark eyes, opaque and strangely blank, and she didn't recognise them. Who *was* he? He knew her so surely this must mean that she had met him before? Who *could* he be? The very fact that she was familiar to him made him seem even more threatening. She felt that he was pulling strings; not just hers but of everyone who was connected with the case, and had been doing so for some time, manipulating them as he wanted and amused by the results. He was going to exploit her now, using her presence to coerce the police into doing his will, and she was helpless to prevent him. She would just have to play along with him and take courage from the fact that while she was useful to him she would be kept alive.

'What's that?' he snapped at her, nodding at a window in the south wall that was partially covered in wood panels.

'Vandals threw a stone through and broke it. It's been boarded up until the stained glass can be repaired.'

'Right, we'll open it up a little to get a message out. You can write it. Have you got paper and a pen in that handbag?'

The handbag was still lying in the porch where she had dropped it and she nodded and retrieved it from the floor. She took out her pen and tore a blank page from the end of her diary.

'Write: 'I am in the hands of the Coil Shuffler',' he commanded, ' 'if you attempt to break in or attack he will kill me' and sign it with your name. Sit down in this pew and do it and don't attempt to move away or I shall skewer you.'

She sat down and rested the sheet of paper on the pew in front of her, moving a pile of hymn books out of the way, and as she wrote out the message he climbed from the top of a pew into the window embrasure and used the knife to ease one of the boards away from the window-frame. His attention was distracted for a few minutes and she wondered if she could make a dash for it and get one of the doors unlocked before he caught up with her but she quickly dismissed the idea. She knew only too well how difficult it was to turn those old-fashioned keys in the locks and she would be dead before she managed it. He was a cold-blooded killer and would have no qualms at adding her to his tally.

He gave a grunt of satisfaction and jumped down and she looked at the small gap that he had wrenched open in the panels. Was it her imagination or could she feel the cold evening air seeping into the church? The sounds she could now hear outside certainly weren't a product of the imagination. It sounded as if there was a large body of people out there and she was comforted and alarmed at the same time. He snatched the note from her, checked it and then tucked it inside a small psalter he had picked up. He wrapped this inside a handkerchief he took from his pocket and then, climbing back on to the pew, he hurled it through the hole in the window.

'That will give them something to think about.' He slipped down and joined her in the aisle. 'They won't try anything now.'

'They don't have to do anything. They can sit it out until we starve to death or die of thirst.'

'You think I'm going to stay penned in here like a rat in a corner and not do anything? I shall set terms for my release and if they do not agree I shall persuade them by . . . by carving little bits off you and sending them out.'

He sounded almost dreamy at the thought and caught hold of her limp hand and studied it voraciously. 'Shall we start with a finger?' He splayed her fingers out across his palm. 'This one with the wedding ring? Or one of the others? Or shall we make it an ear first — like Van Gogh?'

She wrenched her hand away and the question burst from her lips: 'Are you a butcher?'

He chuckled. 'Not in the way you mean, Rachel, dear.'

There was a clunking sound and something shot through the hole in the window and clattered across the floor towards them. Rachel jumped and her captor quickly grabbed hold of her and she felt the knife at her throat. After a few seconds he let go of her again and bent down and picked up the tin that had come to a halt a few feet away from them. He examined it suspiciously and then eased the lid off. A piece of paper fluttered out and he grabbed it and read the message.

'They're sending in a two-way field phone. Good, that will make it easier to dictate terms. They're taking us seriously.'

A short while later the phone link had been established and the Coil Shuffler had made his demands: a car laid on to take him to the airport and a private jet, fully fuelled on stand-by to fly him to the destination of his choice. He described in minute detail just what he would do to Rachel if his conditions were not met. Rachel listened, sickened, knowing full well that he intended to carry out his threat if the police didn't agree to his demands and not believing his promise that she would be released unharmed once he got his transport. She tried to pray.

341

Whilst he arranged the telephone link, called in a trained negotiator and sent for marksmen from the firearms squad, Bairstow did a mental head count of his men and came to the conclusion that the Coil Shuffler probably wasn't a police officer. Most of his force could be accounted for and he had already noted that Nick Holroyd was part of the support team. He had been interested in his reaction when he had learnt that Rachel Morland was being held hostage inside. Holroyd had gone very white and then the colour had flooded back to his face and he appeared consumed by an intense anger. Of course, Rachel Morland was the girlfriend of his mate Croft, remembered Bairstow. Thank the Lord Croft was penned up, on duty at HQ. He didn't need an emotional overwrought presence handicapping proceedings still further.

When the Coil Shuffler issued his ultimatum Bairstow's lip curled cynically and he replied with his own demands.

'Before I agree to anything I need to know that Mrs Morland is safe and well. Let me speak to her.'

Inside the nave the Coil Shuffler handed the phone to Rachel.

'The superintendent wants to speak to you.

Tell him what he wants to know.'

'Rachel, are you all right?'

She forgot to keep her finger on the button and was cut off. When contact had been made again he repeated the question.

'Are you all right?'

'Yes.'

'He hasn't harmed you?'

'Not yet. He has a knife . . .'

'Who is he?'

'I don't know. He's wearing a mask.' As she spoke she was watching him, mesmerised. He was grinning at her and his lips looked fleshy and unnaturally thick protruding through the mouth slit in the black mask. There was a thunderous knocking on the north door over on the other side of the church. She nearly dropped the receiver and her captor spun round and made a move towards the door.

'Rachel?' The whisper down the line was commanding whilst being so quiet she could hardly hear it. 'Hang in there. We're going to get you out but it will take time. Try to distract him.'

'What is he saying?' The Coil Shuffler loomed over her and snatched at the phone.

'I was telling Mrs Morland that we agree to your terms,' said Bairstow smoothly. 'If you promise not to harm her we will lay on a car and a plane but this will take time to

343

arrange. You must be prepared for a wait.'

'I can wait as long as it takes, but no tricks or you won't see Rachel alive again.'

He laid the receiver down on a nearby pew and spoke to her.

'You see? If they know what's good for them, or rather *you*, they'll play ball. So what shall we do, darling, to pass the time until my transport arrives?'

'You'll take me with you?'

'Only as far as the airport. Once I'm ready for take-off I'll let you go.'

She didn't believe him. She also didn't believe that the police would supply his getaway. Perhaps they would mount an assault on the building. A locked church was a pretty impregnable building but there was always the windows. If they tried to break in she would be dead before they got inside. But what had the superintendent said? Try to distract him. They must have some scheme to try and infiltrate the place secretly, she must get him talking, keep his attention on her.

'Why do you do it?'

'Do what?' He deliberately misunderstood her.

'Go around killing people for money.'

'It's a business. And a very lucrative one.'

'But we're talking about people — human beings — not some sort of commodity without souls!'

'Don't come the God talk with me, Rachel. You may believe all the mumbo-jumbo that goes with this,' he gestured round the church, 'but I came to my senses years ago. I know it's all a big con.'

'You don't know what you're talking about.'

'Ah, but I do. I was smothered in it as a youngster. Baptised, confirmed into the Roman Catholic faith, schooled by monks, altar boy, acolyte — that surprises you, doesn't it? They had me marked down for the priesthood — *me*! But I got away. They're all a lot of fawning sycophants, corrupt and power crazy, imposing their will on the poorest classes and keeping them under by playing on their fear of an afterlife in hell. There is no afterlife.'

'That's not true!'

'Oh, yes it is. When you're dead you're dead. Dead meat, Rachel. When they carve you up they'll find no soul. No divine spark lurking in any of your organs. A scalpel through your heart will reveal no trace of God or Kingdom Come. You're just carrion: blood, guts, bones, tissues — like meat on a butcher's slab, and if you're snuffed out

345

sooner rather than later, so what?'

She listened, shrinking in horror. He was mad. Not in the accepted sense, perhaps, but he was utterly without conscience, a natural-born killer. But surely what he was saying was a pointer to his identity? Could he be a medical man? A male nurse or a doctor or even a surgeon? Someone who had tipped, for some unknown reason, from being a healer to a destroyer? If he worked at the local hospital as she did it would account for his knowing her. Something else was niggling at her too. His voice. It was anonymous, no discernible accent, but when he got swept up in his own rhetoric, like now, could she hear a slight Irish lilt in his tones? Who *could* he be?

'You've gone quiet, Rachel, have I convinced you?'

'You're crazy! Anyone who thinks life is not sacred is crazy.'

'Don't say that!' He grabbed hold of her and she felt the knife pressed against her throat. 'I'm not crazy, I know the truth! It's you who are crazy, thinking your God will save you. If I slice through your windpipe do you think you'll be swept up to heaven? No, you'll be *kaput*, finished. Rachel Morland will be no more.'

She felt the point of the blade pierce her

skin and the warm trickle of blood down
her neck.

★ ★ ★

'Sir, there's another door round the other
side. It's half below ground level and almost
buried in rubble.'

'What!' Douglas Bairstow bellowed at the
uniformed constable who had brought him
the information. 'Why wasn't it noticed
before? Where the hell is the vicar?'

He swept down the path towards the
gate where David Bell was huddled with
the verger and a couple of CID officers.

'I thought you told me there were only
two doors — this officer says there is another
one.'

'Beyond the boiler house,' said the constable.
'Is it a coal store?'

'Oh, that,' said the vicar, 'no, it leads to
the leper's squint. I'd forgotten about it.'

'The *leper's squint*?' said Bairstow
ominously.

'They had them in many of these old
medieval churches but this one is unusual,
almost unique I believe. You know what a
leper's squint is?'

'A hole in the wall through which the
lepers could look and watch the proceedings

inside,' said Bairstow heavily as they walked round the tower after the constable. 'So, why the door and where does it lead to?'

'It doesn't now. I told you this is most unusual. Instead of your usual hole in the wall a little gallery was built in the upper part of the nave. It was enclosed by a carved stone screen through which the lepers could peer but not be seen and it was reached by a staircase that led up directly from outside.'

By this time they had reached the concealed door.

'You're telling me there is a stairway leading up from this door to a gallery inside the church?'

'Not now. The stairs have partially collapsed. They haven't been used for years and the gallery itself is crumbling and unsafe.'

'Is it noticeable from inside the church? Will he be aware of it?'

'No. There's no lighting up there. Anybody looking up probably wouldn't see it at all and if they did they'd think it was just part of the decorative carving and wouldn't realise there is a little gallery behind the screen.'

'There's nothing else you haven't told me about, is there? No crypt?'

'No. I didn't mention the leper's squint because it's in such a bad state of repair it is unusable.'

'How bad are the stairs?'

'I really don't know. The door hasn't been opened for years. This fall of masonry outside happened about four years ago and we left it here as it makes a good barrier to prevent kids getting inside and having an accident.'

'Right. We'll get that unblocked and then see what state the stairs are in.'

'He'll hear you, won't he — you can't do it silently? You can't risk him harming Rachel!'

'Rachel Morland's safety is of paramount importance. Now, I suggest you let us get on with our work and you get on with yours. How about getting down on your knees and praying?'

At that moment the negotiator arrived and Bairstow briefed him on what was happening. By this time powerful arc-lamps had been set up in the churchyard, flooding the church in a brilliant light that bleached the ancient stonework white and made the spire stand out against the black background like a fluorescent pencil. Bairstow had pulled out all the stops to preserve the scene. Extra manpower had been drafted in and all leave cancelled and a tight cordon of men surrounded the area, cutting it off from the outside world. As governor in charge of the operation he gathered his senior officers around him and discussed diversionary tactics whilst earth-moving equipment was put on stand-by.

★ ★ ★

The sound of pneumatic drills tore through the church.

'What the fucking hell!' The Coil Shuffler tightened his grip on Rachel and snarled into her ear: 'They're trying to break in!'

'No, it's further away,' she said weakly, convinced that at any moment she was going to meet her Maker.

With her clamped to his side he manhandled her across the aisle and picked up the phone, pressing the button.

'I told you no tricks! What the hell are you playing at?'

'No tricks. This is nothing to do with us. It's roadworks down on the corner of Epping Street. They're laying a new gas main and it has to be done at night to cause minimum inconvenience. We haven't the authority to stop them.'

'Who are you? I want the superintendent!'

'He asked me to speak with you. Now, calm down and we'll talk this through sensibly. There is no need for anyone to get hurt. We're laying on the transport you've requested but in the meantime why don't you release Mrs Morland? She is nothing to do with this, just an innocent person who happened to get in the way. This is between you and the police. Let her go and they'll see you get away safely and won't try and stop you.'

'Like hell they will!'

'You're upset and you're not thinking clearly. Harming Rachel will not do your cause any good at all. You know you don't really want to hurt her.'

'Try me!'

'Listen, I know how you feel. You feel that the whole world is against you but it isn't true. I'm your friend, believe me, but it's so impersonal, speaking to someone whose name you don't know. Tell me your name and then we can get better acquainted.'

'You must think I was born yesterday. Who the bloody hell are you?'

'I'm Jeremy Burnham. I'm not on anyone's side. I just want to help you.'

'I don't want any poncy psychobabble! You won't sweet talk me. Now put the superintendent on the line, or else!'

Outside the church, Bairstow grimaced and took the receiver from the negotiator.

'Superintendent Bairstow here. I'm afraid

351

I can do nothing about the noise, it's beyond my control.'

'Where is my transport?'

'We've fixed up the car but the flight will take longer to arrange. We have to clear with customs and air traffic control. Shall we send in food and drink?'

'No. You stay where you are. I'm not being tricked into unlocking the door.'

'Let me speak with Mrs Morland again.'

'Why?'

'You may not feel the need for counselling but I'm sure Rachel does. Let me just have a few words with her to reassure her and explain what we are doing.'

The Coil Shuffler thrust the phone at Rachel and hissed: 'Tell them to hurry up!'

'He wants you to hurry up,' she said woodenly into the receiver.

'We're doing our best. The flight is a complicated thing to set up. It will take several hours to get clearance and fuelling for it organised.'

The sound of drilling echoed down the line, magnified and deafening and she winced. The superintendent's voice seemed to come and go, laying strange emphasis on the odd word.

'I'm sorry about the *noise*. Can't do anything about it. It's an unfortunate *distraction*. Can you hear me, Rachel? It's *making* a terrible *noise* — very *distracting*. We can't *divert* them. Your vicar is here — would you like to talk to him?'

'No, she wouldn't!' The Coil Shuffler snatched the receiver from her and bawled down it before cutting contact and throwing it down. He jeered at her: 'The forces of law and order and they can't even do anything to stop a racket like that. They've no bottle. All they're good at is beating up poor innocents in their cells and persecuting the motorists. I've got them running round in circles. I can do anything.'

He sounds really crazed now, thought Rachel, but her attention was not fully on him. Her ears were still ringing with the sound of the Superintendent's voice, with the odd words that had come in powerful bursts against the background cacophony: *noise, distract, divert*. She almost gasped and gave the game away as she realised their significance. He had been sending her a message. He wanted her to create a diversion inside the church, to make a noise, kick up a disturbance in some way to prevent her captor from realising what was going on outside the building. What could she do? She could scream, but she couldn't keep that up for long and he wouldn't let her.

She had the fleeting idea of getting to the bell ropes and trying to peal one of the bells but dismissed that on the same grounds that he would certainly prevent her from doing any such thing. The organ . . . could she play the organ? She suddenly knew what she could do. She put her hands over her ears and shook her head.

'I can't stand that noise, it's driving me crazy!' She pretended to look wildly round the nave and then started moving up the aisle.

'Where the hell do you think you're going? You stay right here. If you take another step I'll skewer you!'

'You're paranoid! You know I'm completely helpless. All I want to do is muffle that racket. We'll make our own noise — have some music. Come with me!'

With a great effort she turned her back on him and started walking towards the vestry and miraculously he went with her and didn't use the knife.

'What are you talking about?'

'You'll see.'

As they moved towards the chancel she hoped and prayed that the police were not trying to break into the vestry. They crossed in front of the altar and she genuflected and was jerked upright.

'He's not there, you're wasting your time!'

'Then why are you so bothered?'

On the shelf in the alcove beside the vestry door was a tape-recorder. She reached out and pressed a switch.

In an instant the church was flooded with sound. The crashing chords of Bach's 'Toccata and Fugue in D Minor' rolled round the lofty interior, reverberating off the walls; thunderous, majestic and utterly shattering. Even prepared as she was, Rachel was momentarily startled and for a few seconds the Coil Shuffler seemed to lose control. He reeled against the choir-stalls and clutched his head.

'Stop it! Turn it off! Turn if *off*!'

'It's better than the row outside. Don't you like it?'

'I hate organ music! I've always hated it! Switch it off!'

'You're frightened.' Although he had recovered and was now making threatening gestures with the knife she felt, for the first time, that she was in control of the situation. 'Listen to it. It's the wrath of God. There's no escaping it. You know that and it's your conscience speaking!'

'Hold your tongue! Your filthy lying tongue!' His hand reached out and scrabbled for the switch.

'Go on, then, switch it off if you're so frightened,' she taunted and he snatched back his hand.

'It doesn't scare me. Listen to it if you want — think of it as your requiem mass!' He lashed out at her with the hand not holding the knife and the power of the blow knocked her off her feet and sent her skidding across the chancel floor to end in a heap against the altar rail. She'd created the diversionary noise but had aroused him to a dangerous psychotic state. She must try and calm him down and occupy him in talking.

'Get up!' he snapped and she scrambled to her feet and gestured to the tape-recorder.

'The Bach lasts a few minutes but the whole tape runs for ninety minutes.'

'Then we shall listen to it all.'

'It makes talking difficult.'

'So you want to talk do you, Rachel? What do you want to talk about?'

Against the background of ascending arpeggios she told him.

'Why did you kill Pat Fenton?'

'Because she was squaring my pitch! I was the Coil Shuffler and she was muscling in on my act, copying my idea and arousing the suspicions of the Fuzz. I couldn't allow that — she was too much of a threat so she had to go.'

356

'You've got it wrong. *You* copied *her*. She started her murderous activities years ago.'

'So did I. The police didn't go far enough back in their records. Surely you don't regret her death — she killed your husband.'

'Not for profit.'

'He was the exception. She knew her victims, she exploited them — that is really sick. Mine is just a business arrangement.'

'Do you think a cold-blooded execution is less wrongful in the eyes of God?'

'Don't bring him into it! She became too greedy and got careless. I couldn't let her live.'

'So hers was the only life you haven't taken for profit?'

'So far.'

His eyes gleamed at her through the slits in the mask and a smile twisted his lips as she took his point. She wouldn't get out of this alive. He couldn't afford to let her go, she knew too much. Except that she didn't. She still had no idea of his identity, whether he was a medic or a policeman or someone she had met in some other walk of life. Surely he wasn't a cleric? The thought was horrendous. She *must* try to find out who he was and somehow pass this knowledge on to the police, then if he killed her at least it wouldn't have been in vain. By this time the

Bach had finished and the lilting melody of 'Greensleeves' was echoing round the walls; a tune she had always associated with balmy, summer evenings, not the starkness of a gloomy church in the grip of an early winter. She shivered and ignored his innuendo.

'I imagine you don't come cheap. What do you do with all the blood money you've collected over the years? Are you a millionaire — one the local population don't know about?'

'I'm not bothered by thoughts of the life style my money could buy me, my interest lies in something else — stamps.'

'Stamps? You mean you're a stamp collector? I thought that sort of thing went out of fashion years ago, along with train-spotting and collecting birds' eggs.'

'Fashion? What's fashion go to do with it? You don't know what you're talking about! Just a small piece of paper, often less than three centimetres square, but unique, romantic, mysterious — often priceless. And I have some of the most sought-after ones in my collection, world-famous ones. Soon I hope to acquire the — *What was that?*'

There had been a crashing noise outside like falling masonry. Rachel had heard it and tried to pretend she had not.

'What?'

'That noise — they're trying to break in!'

'I didn't hear anything. You're imagining it.'

'I don't trust them — they're going to double-cross me. Well, I shall have to show them I mean business and they had better not try anything.'

He twisted his hand in her hair and the knife flashed above her eyes. He sliced through a bunch of curls and shook them in her face.

'We'll send these out with a little note to say that if they don't get my transport laid on very soon the next thing they'll receive will be living tissue.'

14

The rubble and masonry blocking the door were painstakingly removed piece by piece in an operation involving manual labour rather than machinery. The team of workmen called in to create diversionary noise with their pneumatic drills was moved in closer to the church and large diggers and excavators rumbled up and down creating their own volume of sound. The door was locked and the key was missing. Force could not be used to blast it open and precious time leaked away as an expert in lock picking set to work. When he had sprung it the superintendent was faced with another snag. The door opened inwards and could only be moved a couple of inches. There was more fallen masonry inside preventing the door from opening properly.

'We'll have to take it off its hinges,' said Bairstow, eyeing the immense rusty hinges with foreboding. 'Get cracking on it and keep it propped up. For God's sake don't let it fall or he'll know what we're doing.'

As the men worked silently and sweating on the jammed door the swelling tones of organ music rang out on the night and freezing everyone in their tracks. Bairstow mopped at his brow and recovered first.

'Good girl, she understood what we wanted. She's playing the organ!'

David Bell corrected him.

'It's a tape. We recently did a pageant in the church representing the past five hundred years with a series of tableaux. That's part of the music tape that was set up to accompany it. It starts off with that — the famous Bach 'Toccata and Fugue'.'

'Well, it's noisy enough to cover up any little mishaps out here as long as he lets it play.'

To the accompaniment of Bach and Vaughan Williams the door was finally unscrewed and lifted away, precipitating a fall of masonry from inside that sounded to Bairstow like an avalanche. A light was trained on the doorway and he peered upwards.

'There seems to be a four- to five-foot gap in the stairs above head level but beyond that they seem to be intact. Do you know if that's correct?' he asked David Bell.

'Yes, that would be right. The last time it was inspected by the diocesan church architect he reported that the middle section was rotten and had collapsed.'

'How long ago was this?'

'We're about due for another inspection so it would be five years.'

'Didn't you have to repair it?'

'Normally anything wrong has to be put to rights but in this case, as the staircase was never used and could be sealed off, and the main structure wasn't affected, we were able to leave it and save money.'

'Right, let's get this lot out and see what the damage is.'

The men tackled the job with rubber-sheathed jemmies and formed a chain-gang along which each stone was manhandled to its new resting ground near the perimeter wall. They had nearly finished clearing it when Trevor Dickins hurried round from the other side of the church.

'Sir, he's sent another message out.'

'What did he say?'

'Not a verbal message, he didn't use the phone. He chucked our tin back through the hole in the window. It's not good.' He handed the tin over to Bairstow who read the note and viewed the lock of hair grimly.

'Time's running out. Get the rest of that rubble out and set up a ladder. I'll speak to him again and try and stall him.'

By this time it had started to rain and the chief constable had arrived. As he stepped out of his car the initial drizzle changed to a steady downpour, scything through the gravestones and quickly turning the ground into a quagmire. Bairstow brought him up to date with what was happening and the chief constable listened gravely.

'You'll have to take him out.'

'Yes, sir. The idea is to get a marksman up in the gallery inside the church but until we can get up that stairway we don't know what the circumstances are like up there. I've spoken to the Coil Shuffler in the last few minutes and told him that a plane has been commandeered for his use and is being moved to a private part of the airport to await him. I stressed that it would be another hour at least and he seemed to accept this.'

Not long after this conversation took place the bottom of the stairway was finally cleared of debris and a ladder installed to breach the gap. Trevor Dickins was elected to reconnoitre and he carefully heaved himself aloft. To the waiting policemen down below he seemed to be gone a very long time but eventually his feet appeared at the top of the ladder and he lowered himself to the floor.

'Well?' demanded Bairstow.

'It's not going to be easy.' Dickins rubbed grimy hands down his trousers and cleared his throat. 'It's very dark up there and the stone fretwork is in an appalling state. Any pressure on it will send the lot down. There are two openings in it which you can get a rifle through but one is very close to the floor. The bad news is the Coil Shuffler and Rachel are that side of the church. I could hear them talking, they're almost directly under the gallery so you can't get a sight on them and he's got her close to him.'

'We'll have to set up a diversion to get them away from that wall and split them up. How many people can we get up there?'

'Two at the most. Any more and they're going to be falling over each other and unable to operate, apart from the risk of their weight bringing the whole thing down.'

The chief firearms officer then investigated the situation and reported that he could take up position using one of the apertures in the grille but the other one was too low and almost directly underneath and of no use for a marksman.

'Ideally we should have at least four of you inside there covering different angles but it looks as if it's going to have to be a solo volley shot,' said Bairstow. 'Can you have someone beside you using that bottom aperture to throw a stun grenade through?'

'As long as he doesn't tangle with my

364

legs or come in contact,' said the firearms officer drily.

'I'll do that,' said Dickins. 'We'll get the bastard on the hop and you can take him out.'

'No, Trevor, I want you round the other side. You are responsible for getting him away from Rachel. As soon as the stun grenade has gone off at their feet he's going to move out into the middle of the church — it's a reflex action — and you then throw wailers and flash tubes through the hole in your window. He'll be deafened and disorientated and he'll release his hold on Rachel. Once he's down we'll go in through that window — we'll fix up an explosive charge to demolish it — and you grab Rachel and get her out. She's our priority.'

'So who is going up in the gallery with the marksman?'

'Sir, I volunteer.' Nick Holroyd had been hovering on the periphery of the group, desperate to do something constructive in the rescue of Rachel and now seeing his chance. 'I've done riot training and I know how to handle stun grenades and I have excellent aim.'

Dickins started to protest but Bairstow over-ruled him. He knew that Holroyd had nerves of steel and performed well in a crisis and was also anxious to redeem himself.

'Right, Nick. You shall be up in the gallery and remember, we only get one chance, nothing must go wrong.'

Whilst the chief constable waited in his car, Bairstow and his picked men retired to the operations van to plot their strategy in detail to cover every contingency.

★ ★ ★

It was very dark up in the gallery. The chandelier lights that served the nave and chancel were suspended from the hammer-beam roof and hung below the level of the gallery. Cobwebs and dust clung to every crevice in the stone screen and an unpleasant smell pervaded the air which Nick discovered, when he grovelled on the floor to get into position, was due to bat droppings. His ear protectors hung round his neck and he doubted whether he would be able to use them. It was vital for him to be able to hear what was going on below. His was the responsibility to launch the attack and he was in radio communication with Trevor Dickins and Matthew Longman, the firearms expert, who was poised nearby, his rifle in position.

The taped music had come to an end a few minutes earlier and the sudden silence had been disconcerting. He strained his ears trying to pick up sounds of movement or talk from below but could hear nothing. Surely they hadn't moved to another part of the church without the watchers being aware of it? Perhaps Rachel was already dead. Nick felt the sweat break out on his neck and shoulders and he jammed his face against the hole and tried to see further into the interior. The voices broke out again directly beneath him and he caught his breath in relief. They sounded quite loud but he couldn't make out what was being said. Suddenly Rachel cried out sharply, a cry that was instantly muffled, and he froze. Christ! The Coil Shuffler was carrying out his threat. There was no time to lose, this was it!

He alerted Dickins and Longman and activated the stun grenade. He thrust his arm out through the hole and hurled the grenade downwards. 'Go! Go! Go!'

There was a deafening noise and a blinding flash as it exploded, detonating a further nine bursts of thunder and light which leapt round the nave, shattering in their impact. The Coil Shuffler staggered into sight, pulling Rachel with him, and was confronted by the bombardment from Dickins's side. Rubber tubes containing flashing lights and wailers bounced across the floor, colliding with pews and ricocheting off walls.

Rachel reeled against a pillar and her captor released her, temporarily stunned. There was a click above Nick's head but before the marksman could fire the Coil Shuffler grabbed her and started dragging her back towards them, the knife raised in his hand.

The blood beat in Nick's head. Sweet Jesus! He was going to slaughter her in front of them and the marksman was helpless. He couldn't fire without risking hitting her. Nick acted instinctively. He jumped to his feet and hurled himself at the screen. It buckled and gave way in a shower of stone fragments and he crashed down on to the masked figure below, knocking him to the floor and jerking the knife out of his hand. Both men were momentarily dazed; then, as the Coil Shuffler pulled himself to his knees and scrabbled for the knife and Nick lurched after him, there was another almighty explosion. The damaged window imploded and suddenly the church was full of policemen.

Strong arms reached out for Rachel and she stumbled into them, half-fainting and feeling as if her eardrums were shattered.

'It's all right, Rachel, you're safe now.

We've got him.' Trevor Dickins spoke in her ear and she shuddered and rested her head on his shoulder.

'What's happened?'

'You've been rescued. He's under arrest, he won't do any more damage.'

'How — ?'

'Nick Holroyd jumped him.' There was reluctant respect in Dickins' voice and she opened her eyes and focused on the crowd of men surrounding the Coil Shuffler. He was dragged upright where he swung between two officers, one foot hanging limp, and handcuffs were snapped on his wrists. Nick, who had been helped to his feet and was holding his right shoulder, confronted him.

'Let's see who we've got.' He glanced at Bairstow who nodded and then reached out and pulled the mask off the snarling prisoner.

Rachel watched in bewilderment as the man's face was revealed. To the best of her knowledge she had never set eyes on him before but there was a murmur of recognition from the men gathered round him.

'Holy shit!' exclaimed Nick, backing away. 'It's Damien Winter — the mortuary attendant!'

'Where's Rachel?'

The Coil Shuffler had been cautioned and led from the scene and Nick Holroyd suddenly realised that Rachel was missing.

'She's in the vestry. She wanted to be on her own for a while to recover.' Dickins eyed his rival. 'Christ! Holroyd, I wouldn't like to be in your shoes — you broke just about every rule in the book!'

'I think you'll find my action is covered by section three of the Criminal Law Act. Someone had to so something or he'd have carved her up in front of our very eyes.'

Bairstow came up to them. 'Nick, you need medical attention.'

'Soon, sir, I'm okay.'

'I don't know what the official line will be, but well done.'

'Thanks, sir.'

Nick threw a triumphant look at Dickins and when the superintendent moved away he made for the vestry. Rachel was leaning back in a chair with her eyes closed. She was very pale and there was a streak of dried blood down one side of her neck. She looked up when Nick crossed the threshold and made an effort to smile.

'I'm still bewildered by what happened but

I gather you saved my life — for the second time.'

'All in the day's work. Are you okay? Did he hurt you?'

'Not really. I thought he was going to kill me but you came to the rescue just in time.' She seemed to see him properly for the first time. 'Nick, you're hurt — there's blood all over you and your shoulder . . . '

'Just surface cuts from the masonry and I think I dislocated my shoulder when I hit the ground.'

'I'd offer to put it back for you but you must go to the hospital and get checked out.'

'So must you, the superintendent insists.'

'There's no need.'

'Yes, there is. You've been through a very traumatic experience.'

'Are you going to suggest counselling?'

'It will certainly be on offer.'

'That man — the Coil Shuffler — I thought he must be someone I knew but he wasn't, though he seemed to know all about me . . . '

'Damien Winter. He was never in the frame. We suspected it might be someone connected with the medical profession or even one of us but he was a total surprise. Still, I suppose it figures; he knew all about anatomy — he was used to carving up bodies.' He saw her wince. 'Sorry, Rachel, but it's really bizarre. He killed these people and then helped to cut them up afterwards knowing their deaths were down to him. And working in the mortuary like that he was able to keep tabs on the police investigations, including your connection with Pat Fenton.'

'He's a psychopath. He enjoyed killing and couldn't see that he was doing anything wrong!'

'His defence will probably try and plead insanity, but if you ask me, he was perfectly aware of what he was doing. No one mentally deranged could have planned and carried out those murders as he did. I wonder what motivated him? He must have netted thousands but he seemed to have a very ordinary life style.'

'Stamps.'

'Stamps? What do you mean?'

'He was a stamp collector. He was boasting about his collection and the rare specimens he owned. Now he really was unbalanced about that — completely possessed. They mean far more to him than any human life.'

'How do people become twisted like that? Or was he born like it?'

'He was a cradle Catholic and from what

he said he had had religion rammed down his throat from an early age. He had a love-hate relationship with the Church.'

'The Church has a lot to answer for.'

'Nick, this isn't the time or place to discuss that!'

'No, you're right.' He ran a hand over his face smearing blood and grime in patchwork streaks down his cheeks. 'But did your faith help you back there? Did you trust that your God was going to save you or were you terrified?'

She looked at him steadily.

'I just thought I was going to be reunited with Christopher sooner than I had expected.'

'That's not true!' He gripped her shoulder, his fingers digging in painfully, as the Coil Shuffler's had down earlier. 'You don't want to die, you want to start living again!'

He pulled her into his arms and his face loomed over hers as he sought and found her mouth in a devastating kiss.

The shock was electric. He smelt of sweat and dust and cordite and she tasted the salty tang of blood as every emotion and feeling she had tried to suppress over the last couple of years spiralled out of control and boiled over as if he had lit a fuse inside her. For a few seconds her body betrayed her and she was consumed by sensual passion, excitement and panic chasing each other as every nerve in her body responded to his assault. Then common sense took over and she pulled away and he staggered back against the wall, clutching his shoulder.

'I'm not going to apologise. You wanted that, you've come alive again. You're a woman, Rachel, a passionate woman, not a bloodless automaton.'

He gave her a lopsided grin and slid to the floor in a faint.

* * *

The police began the process of building up a picture of Damien Winter's background. They discovered that he had lived in a block of flats converted from an old maltings which overlooked the river. His apartment was on the top floor and was so sparsely furnished and austere that it was difficult to imagine anyone calling it a home and returning to it each evening to eat and sleep. It was completely anonymous, with no personal touches; no pictures or photos, no ornaments or pot-plants. No effort had been made to provide any domestic comfort and it held no clue to his personality. However, a filing cabinet in the bedroom provided full documentation of his nefarious employment and led the police on to another residence on the north Norfolk coast.

This was a cottage on the outskirts of Brancaster. It was isolated from the rest of the community and from the veranda and picture windows one looked out over vast marram-clad dunes to the distant North Sea. It appeared that besides stamps Winter had also been avidly interested in birds. As well as a large number of bird books he owned expensive optics, a telescope set up on a tripod in one window and several pairs of binoculars including ones for night vision, and he had a collection of stamps from all over the world featuring birds apart from what turned out later to be some of the rarest and most valuable stamps in history.

Damien Winter himself willingly admitted to everything the police threw at him. To Trevor Dickins and his team, who were used to long hours spent in the interview rooms trying to inveigle their suspects into confessing, his outpourings were like verbal diarrhoea.

'He's off his trolley,' said Dickins, reporting to Douglas Bairstow. 'He has no conscience whatever about his killings. Human life means nothing to him, it is totally expendable, whereas he is passionate about his stamps and birds. In my opinion he is barking insane!'

'Yet he was astute enough to plan and carry out all those killings and lead us a fine old dance over the last few years.'

'There's a gap in his mentality, a part of him missing. The part that deals with human feelings and compassion — it's just not there in his make-up. He is like a machine programmed for killing.'

'We've got enough evidence to bring a good case against him but whether we'll get a conviction is another matter. The shrinks are going to have a field day.'

'Quentin Stock's not too happy with the whole business.' Dickins smirked as he remembered the pathologist's initial reaction to the arrest.

'It's understandable. To him Winter appeared a perfectly normal if somewhat zealous employee.'

'I think he's worried that he may have overlooked the fact that Winter could have tampered with pathological evidence when the bodies were in the morgue.'

'I don't think there is any fear of that. Winter was not interested in trying to cover up evidence of murder. He wanted his 'executions' to be known for what they were, hence his visiting card left with each victim.'

The superintendent did not tell Dickins that Stock had admitted to him in private that in theory it was possible for a mortician to alter or cover up pathological and forensic evidence. He also kept from the investigating officer the outcome of his recent interview with Nick Holroyd. Dickins would find out soon enough that changes were afoot with the Brent Hill personnel.

Nick Holroyd had demanded that he be made up. He wanted his old position in CID back and was confident he deserved it.

'God knows you're wasted in uniform,' Bairstow had agreed, 'but you've overstepped the mark once too often, taking things into your own hands in the way you did. Because you were fortunate enough to carry it off and there was a satisfactory outcome I can keep officialdom off your back, but you know as well as I that it could have had a very different ending.'

'I used my initiative to do what had to be done,' Holroyd had said stiffly. 'I was the only one who could do anything and Mrs Morland is alive because I acted.'

'I'm sure she would agree with you but you're finished in this station.'

'What do you mean?' He had blanched

and the numerous tiny scars pocking his face had stood out like gory freckles.

'I mean' — Bairstow had steepled his fingers and looked sternly over them at the younger man — 'that there is no place for you here. You don't fit in, Nick, you're too disruptive, and this time I'm going to insist that you apply for a transfer. Don't get me wrong — I'm going to recommend that you be reinstated as a DI, but not on my patch. Good God, man, there's nothing to keep you here, is there? You've got no family ties and before you start bleating about your mate, Croft, he's making good progress and he doesn't need a nursemaid any longer. Well?'

'Actually, sir, that was what I wanted to bring up with you. I *do* want to move, I'd like to apply for a transfer — as soon as possible.'

Bairstow had hidden his surprise by commenting on Nick's injuries.

'Shoulder all right now?'

'Fine, sir.'

'And those scars on your face — not permanent, are they?'

'I've been assured they'll heal and disappear. They're similar to the cuts you get if you go through a windscreen but stone chippings are not so lethal as glass.'

'Good, good. Well, I'll set things in motion. You're a good policeman, Nick, but you need to make your mark somewhere else.'

* * *

Rachel was trying to come to terms with her experience in her own way. She had refused all offers of counselling, including the ministrations of David Bell, which had dismayed but not entirely surprised him.

'I *haven't* lost my faith, David, but I need to sit back and reassess myself,' she told him when he visited her shortly after she had returned home from hospital. The medical authorities had insisted that she stay in for a couple of days for a thorough check but she was now returned to her flat where an unobtrusive police presence kept the Press at bay. 'We've already talked about my reasons for giving up on the ministry and you know they are not connected with the ordeal I've just been through, but it has tended to refocus my ideas. I need to make a complete break, to get away from here. I've got into a rut — and I'm talking here about my professional work as well as my Church commitments. There is a vacancy coming up for a senior physiotherapist with the Dorset

Health Authority and I am going to apply for it.'

'We shall be sorry to lose you at St Luke's, but perhaps you're doing the right thing. A new environment and different people may help you sort out the wood from the trees. As I've said before the Church needs people of your calibre, be they ordained or laymen, but it is a very important commitment and you have to be absolutely sure.'

David Bell considered the woman sitting on the sofa opposite him. She was still unnaturally pale with dark smudges under her eyes and her movements were brittle as if she were still operating under great strain. He cleared his throat.

'I had thought perhaps you were going to make a commitment to a second marriage?'

'No, David,' she said firmly. 'Mike and I have been — are — good friends but it is a friendship that is going nowhere.'

'I see. Well, don't let old memories cloud your future happiness. It is a mistake to try and live in the past.'

'Believe me, I have learnt that only too well.'

She refused to elaborate on this and he assumed that her ordeal as a hostage had proved a watershed in her life and led her on to look at events in a different light. He did not know how correct he was in this assumption, but after he had gone Rachel pondered their recent conversation and knew that she owed it to Mike to be honest with him. She had spoken the truth to David Bell, her friendship with Mike was going nowhere and it had taken that terrible evening in St Luke's to bring this home to her.

After that she had known that Mike and she had nothing going for them and that she had been deluding herself if she had thought otherwise. It was nothing to do with Nick, she told herself. Nothing to do with that kiss and the way she had reacted but rather the knowledge that all through her ordeal that evening she had not once thought of Mike. She had prayed, she had made conversation with the Coil Shuffler, she had put her hopes in the police presence gathered outside the church but never once had a single thought of Mike crossed her mind and that in itself spoke volumes. She could not let their friendship continue in the same vein, with Mike growing fonder of her and more committed. It wasn't fair on him. He had been very solicitous after the siege but hadn't forced himself on her, seeming to realise that she needed time on her own.

From things he had said she knew that he had also been under terrible strain that evening, forced to experience events at second hand as part of the back-up at the station and unable to play an active part in her rescue. For the first time since she had known him he had been bitter about his disability and being sidelined to a passive role but at least she had no more worries about his physical health. He was improving steadily, his limp becoming less noticeable, and soon he would be able to drive again. He would not need her as a physiotherapist and he must learn to do without her in his private life. She must tell him of the decision she had made and hope that he wouldn't take it too hard.

In the event he wasn't all that surprised. He seemed to have been almost expecting it. She went round to his house one morning when she knew he was off duty and caught him at the bottom of the garden burning rubbish. It was a still, damp day with mist wreathing the treetops and the bonfire belching clouds of blue and plum smoke. She helped him burn the last heap of garden refuse and then he quenched the fire and they went indoors and he made coffee. Whilst he busied himself in the kitchen they chatted and to her over-sensitive ears it sounded trite and banal. He handed her a beaker and she perched on a kitchen stool and cupped it in her hands.

'Mike, I came round to . . . to talk about us.'

He regarded her steadily over the rim of his mug. 'We're not an item.'

She felt relief flood through her.

'No. You've realised it too?'

He considered the question. 'I've been aware for some time that something was missing from our friendship — and I'm not talking about sex. I'm very fond of you, Rachel, I've grown to love you, and I thought we could build on this mutual affection, make a successful partnership, but something was missing . . . '

'The divine spark?'

'I suppose you could call it that. Liking, admiration, respect are all very necessary but you need something more on which to base a lasting relationship.'

'Yes. You're putting my feelings into words. After Christopher's death I thought I should never want or be able to make a commitment to another man but then I met you. I felt comfortable with you. You didn't pressurise me and I felt safe and I began to think that what we had going for us was enough. But that's not true. Love is not about safety and subduing one's feelings; it's about excitement and passion and being touched to life.'

'And that's happened to you.'

'I didn't say that!'

'You don't have to.' He spoke wryly. 'You've been woken up and you're firing on all cylinders again. It's Nick, isn't it?'

'What do you mean?'

'It's you and Nick.'

'No! That isn't true! There's nothing between Nick and me. He dislikes me — surely you know that!'

'Love, hate . . . as they say, there is little between them. I'm not blind, Rachel. I've seen how you react to one another, how you've both fought against it and protested too much.'

'That's not true!'

'It is. You're Beatrice and Benedick all over again.'

'Mike, I can't let you go on like this. There is *nothing* between Nick and me. You surely can't think we've been carrying on behind your back?'

'Of course not. I know you too well for that, and for all his faults, Nick would never two-time a friend. I'm sure you weren't even aware of the attraction between you but now something has happened, hasn't it?'

Rachel fanned out her fingers and pressed them against her cheek-bones. 'Listen, I'll be honest with you. Something *did* happen

384

afterwards in the vestry that evening. It was an isolated incident and it meant absolutely nothing to Nick but it made me realise that nothing would be the same again for me. I knew I couldn't go on kidding myself that I was in love with you — but this has absolutely nothing to do with Nick. He hates my guts and you're not to breathe a word of this conversation to him. He'll be delighted when he learns that I'm leaving the area.'

'Leaving the area? What do you mean?'

She told him about the physiotherapy job in Dorset and how she had heard unofficially that the post was hers and explained that she was putting her Church ministry on hold for the time being. He heard her out in silence and then said shrewdly:

'Are you running away?'

'Whatever do you mean?'

'We've been honest with each other but I don't think you're facing up to your feelings for Nick.'

'You've got it all wrong, Mike. If you don't believe me just talk to him. Now, please leave it.'

'Okay, if you say so. I shall miss you, Rachel.'

'And I you, but I need to get away. I feel as if my life has been . . . contaminated by that man.'

'Damien Winter?'

'Yes. I keep going over the things he said and wondering what turned him into such a monster. Do you know any more of his background?'

'Yes, he's talked about incidents in his childhood. His parents died when he was a baby and his Irish grandmother looked after him. Apparently, when he was four she had a stroke and died and he was locked in the house with a dead body for several days before neighbours discovered him. His obsession with death and bodies dates from this, I guess.'

'How awful. What happened to him after that?'

'He was passed from one Catholic institution to another. I think no one ever got close to him again. He became a real loner, and as far as we have been able to discover he never seems to have shown any interest in the opposite sex. He's admitted that he wanted to become a doctor but didn't make the grade so he gravitated to necrophilia.'

'I still don't understand his tie-in with Pat Fenton.'

'This is where it gets really weird. If we are to believe him there was another killing — the first one he carried out — that we never caught on to. His first victim was a housemaster at Graves School. Winter was working there as a laboratory technician and he poisoned him with a drug overdose. By a strange coincidence Pat Fenton was in the building when the body was discovered, attending the elderly father of the chap's wife. Being a medic she was called to the scene and she must have noticed the Coil Shuffler's card. I reckon by this time she had already helped a couple of people to their deaths and when she saw that card she removed it from the body. It gave her ideas which she later capitalised on.'

'But how does he know this?'

'According to him, he was hanging around the scene keeping an eye on what was happening and he saw her steal his card. Murder wasn't suspected and a verdict of suicide was brought in. Later, he noticed one of her adverts and realised that someone was cashing in on his scheme. He answered this advert and somehow got to meet her and immediately recognised her. The rest is history, as they say. He monitored her movements and got to know about her friendship with you, amongst other things, and when he thought her activities were becoming a danger to his affairs he knocked her off.'

'It's unbelievable.'

'Another case of fact being stranger than fiction. There are so many coincidences in this case, the greatest being, I suppose, that you were the one that was taken hostage, happened to be there at that particular moment.'

'Almost as if it were preordained.'

She gave a little shiver and he reached out and laid his hand over hers.

'I can understand you wanting to cut your ties with that church. Two attempts on your life in the same place — your God was certainly looking after you.'

'Not my God, Mike, but yours as well.'

'Maybe. Who knows, you may have got yourself a convert. With you and Nick both leaving me I shall lose my earthly guidance so perhaps I'd better look into the heavenly sort.' He grinned to show he was being facetious but she didn't rise to the bait.

'Nick is leaving too?'

'Yes, he's applied for a transfer. It's the best thing he could have done — a new start where his past is not common knowledge to every Tom, Dick and Harry.'

'I see. Well, I hope it works out for him.' She tried to speak lightly and gathered up her handbag and gloves. 'I must go, Mike, thank you for being so understanding. I was so worried about hurting you and letting you

388

down. I'm glad we've got it sorted out.'

'You'll keep in touch?'

'Of course. We're still good friends?'

'Good friends it is,' he said gravely, showing her to the door.

15

It was a couple of weeks later and Rachel was making a start on sorting out some of her belongings in the flat prior to her move. She had cleared all the books off the bookshelves and was dividing them into three piles; those she was throwing out for jumble, those she was keeping and taking with her and those she wasn't sure about. This last pile was by far the largest and she was just mentally admonishing herself to be more ruthless or things would get completely out of control when the doorbell rang.

She swept a heap of books to one side and scrambled to her feet, wondering who could be visiting so late on a Sunday evening. When she opened the door Nick Holroyd was standing in the porch. Her first instinct was to slam the door in his face and run back to the security of her sitting-room. Somehow she had managed to avoid any contact with him since that fateful evening in the vestry but now, coming face to face with him so unexpectedly, she felt her knees threatening to give way and could hear her heart thudding away in her chest unnaturally loud. She clung to the door handle for support and slowly registered that he looked as ill at ease and awkward as she felt.

'Nick . . . Is anything wrong?'

'No. Look, I know it's late but can I come in?'

'Yes, I suppose so.' She led the way into the sitting-room and he followed her and stood awkwardly inside the door.

'Is this a social visit?' she asked, very aware of the disorder in the room and the grubby jeans and sweatshirt she was wearing.

'No . . . yes . . . I'm not sure.' He looked round the room. 'When are you going?'

'Not for another month at least but I thought I'd better make a start on packing up some of the stuff I've accumulated. Would you like a drink? Coffee or something stronger?'

She was gabbling to hide her confusion and she took a grip on herself.

'What's the something stronger?'

She opened the sideboard door. 'There's sherry, brandy — I haven't got any whisky I'm afraid — oh, and there's some sloe gin.'

'I haven't had any sloe gin for years, that will do fine.'

She poured some out for him and a smaller measure for herself, indicated that he sit on the sofa and removed herself to another chair across the far side of the room.

'Did you make it?' He swirled the garnet-red liquid round the glass and took an appreciative sip.

'A parishioner gave it to me. What's up, Nick? I'm sure you haven't come here to make small-talk. Is it something to do with Mike?'

'It's always Mike, isn't it, but yes, it's because of him I'm here. He's told me about you.'

'Told you *what*?'

'That you've split up.'

'We haven't had a bust-up. We're still friends.'

'But you're not going out with each other any more?'

'No.' She hesitated and tried to read his expression. 'What else did he tell you?'

'Things that made me realise that I'd read the situation all wrong.' He set the glass down carefully on the coffee table and leaned forward, holding her gaze. 'That night in the vestry when I kissed you . . . I — '

'Listen, Nick.' She interrupted him hurriedly. 'You don't have to say any more. I realise that it didn't mean anything to you, that it was the result of the heat of the moment and the charged atmosphere. I suppose it was a natural reaction.'

'No. You've got it wrong. Christ! — sorry, Rachel, but you must understand — I meant it, all right. Hell! I didn't want to fall for you and I fought against it because you were Mike's woman. I tried to kid myself that you meant nothing to me and that we were completely incompatible, but that evening — I thought you were going to die in front of my very eyes and afterwards when the drama was over I lost control.'

He ran his fingers through his hair and it stuck up above his forehead like a straw fringe. As she made to speak, he shook his head and plunged on.

'For a few seconds I thought you felt the same, then I told myself I was crazy, in shock. You'd always made it quite clear that you disliked me and everything about me and there was Mike to consider. You and I were a complete no-no so I decided to cut loose and get away from both of you.'

She stared at him, speechless, and he shrugged and continued: 'I convinced myself that I was covering up adequately and no one would guess what I was really feeling but Mike saw through me. He realised — had realised for some time, I think — how I really felt about you, and he put me right.'

'Put you right?'

393

'Hinted that you weren't as indifferent to me as you made out and gave me the green light to try my arm. Was he right?'

'I . . . I'm so mixed up, Nick. You did arouse me sexually and I realised that I was cheating by trying to deny that attraction, but . . . but we have so little in common.'

'You're talking about your religion and the way I've always belittled it?'

'I haven't given up on the Church, you know.'

'I don't suppose you have and I respect you for it. I'm just so pig-ignorant about the whole thing — you'll have to take me in hand.'

'But I'm leaving here and you're moving too.'

'We're going to be neighbours.'

'Neighbours? What are you talking about?'

'You're going to Dorset and you're now talking to Detective Inspector Holroyd of Gosport CID. Neighbouring counties — so we won't be far apart.'

'Oh, Nick, I'm so pleased for you. I hope it works out.'

'Us or my police career?' He suddenly grinned. 'Don't look so worried. You've admitted that you're not indifferent to me so that's something to build on. Can we keep in touch and start over?'

He thought at first she was going to refuse. There was a long pause and he could not tell from her expression what she was thinking. Then she picked up the telephone pad and scribbled something on it. She tore the leaf off and handed it to him.

'This is my new address. Perhaps you will look me up some time.'

'Perhaps I shall, Mrs Morland.'

THE END

McLEAN AT THE GOLDEN OWL
George Goodchild

Inspector McLean has resigned from Scotland Yard's CID and has opened an office in Wimpole Street. With the help of his able assistant, Tiny, he solves many crimes, including those of kidnapping, murder and poisoning.

KATE WEATHERBY
Anne Goring

Derbyshire, 1849: The Hunter family are the arrogant, powerful masters of Clough Grange. Their feuds are sparked by a generation of guilt, despair and ill-fortune. But their passions are awakened by the arrival of nineteen-year-old Kate Weatherby.

A VENETIAN RECKONING
Donna Leon

When the body of a prominent international lawyer is found in the carriage of an intercity train, Commissario Guido Brunetti begins to dig deeper into the secret lives of the once great and good.

A TASTE FOR DEATH
Peter O'Donnell

Modesty Blaise and Willie Garvin take on impossible odds in the shape of Simon Delicata, the man with a taste for death, and Swordmaster, Wenczel, in a terrifying duel. Finally, in the Sahara desert, the intrepid pair must summon every killing skill to survive.

SEVEN DAYS FROM MIDNIGHT
Rona Randall

In the Comet Theatre, London, seven people have good reason for wanting beautiful Maxine Culver out of the way. Each one has reason to fear her blackmail. But whose shadow is it that lurks in the wings, waiting to silence her once and for all?

QUEEN OF THE ELEPHANTS
Mark Shand

Mark Shand knows about the ways of elephants, but he is no match for the tiny Parbati Barua, the daughter of India's greatest expert on the Asian elephant, the late Prince of Gauripur, who taught her everything. Shand sought out Parbati to take part in a film about the plight of the wild herds today in north-east India.

THE DARKENING LEAF
Caroline Stickland

On storm-tossed Chesil Bank in 1847, the young lovers, Philobeth and Frederick, prevent wreckers mutilating the apparent corpse of a young woman. Discovering she is still alive, Frederick takes her to his grandmother's home. But the rescue is to have violent and far-reaching effects . . .

A WOMAN'S TOUCH
Emma Stirling

When Fenn went to stay on her uncle's farm in Africa, the lovely Helena Starr seemed to resent her — especially when Dr Jason Kemp agreed to Fenn helping in his bush hospital. Though it seemed Jason saw Fenn as little more than a child, her feelings for him were those of a woman.

A DEAD GIVEAWAY
Various Authors

This book offers the perfect opportunity to sample the skills of five of the finest writers of crime fiction — Clare Curzon, Gillian Linscott, Peter Lovesey, Dorothy Simpson and Margaret Yorke.

DOUBLE INDEMNITY
— MURDER FOR INSURANCE
Jad Adams

This is a collection of true cases of murderers who insured their victims then killed them — or attempted to. Each tense, compelling account tells a story of cold-blooded plotting and elaborate deception.

THE PEARLS OF COROMANDEL
By Keron Bhattacharya

John Sugden, an ambitious young Oxford graduate, joins the Indian Civil Service in the early 1920s and goes to uphold the British Raj. But he falls in love with a young Hindu girl and finds his loyalties tragically divided.

WHITE HARVEST
Louis Charbonneau

Kathy McNeely, a marine biologist, sets out for Alaska to carry out important research. But when she stumbles upon an illegal ivory poaching operation that is threatening the world's walrus population, she soon realises that she will have to survive more than the harsh elements . . .

TO THE GARDEN ALONE
Eve Ebbett
Widow Frances Morley's short, happy marriage was childless, and in a succession of borders she attempts to build a substitute relationship for the husband and family she does not have. Over all hovers the shadow of the man who terrorized her childhood.

CONTRASTS
Rowan Edwards
Julia had her life beautifully planned — she was building a thriving pottery business as well as sharing her home with her friend Pippa, and having fun owning a goat. But the goat's problems brought the new local vet, Sebastian Trent, into their lives.

MY OLD MAN AND THE SEA
David and Daniel Hays
Some fathers and sons go fishing together. David and Daniel Hays decided to sail a tiny boat seventeen thousand miles to the bottom of the world and back. Together, they weave a story of travel, adventure, and difficult, sometimes terrifying, sailing.

SQUEAKY CLEAN
James Pattinson

An important attribute of a prospective candidate for the United States presidency is not to have any dirt in your background which an eager muckraker can dig up. Senator William S. Gallicauder appeared to fit the bill perfectly. But then a skeleton came rattling out of an English cupboard.

NIGHT MOVES
Alan Scholefield

It was the first case that Macrae and Silver had worked on together. Malcolm Underdown had brutally stabbed to death Edward Craig and had attempted to murder Craig's fiancée, Jane Harrison. He swore he would be back for her. Now, four years later, he has simply walked from the mental hospital. Macrae and Silver must get to him — before he gets to Jane.

GREATEST CAT STORIES
Various Authors

Each story in this collection is chosen to show the cat at its best. James Herriot relates a tale about two of his cats. Stella Whitelaw has written a very funny story about a lion. Other stories provide examples of courageous, clever and lucky cats.

THE HAND OF DEATH
Margaret Yorke

The woman had been raped and murdered. As the police pursue their relentless inquiries, decent, gentle George Fortescue, the typical man-next-door, finds himself accused. While the real killer serenely selects his third victim — and then his fourth . . .

VOW OF FIDELITY
Veronica Black

Sister Joan of the Daughters of Compassion is shocked to discover that three of her former fellow art college students have recently died violently. When another death occurs, Sister Joan realizes that she must pit her wits against a cunning and ruthless killer.

MARY'S CHILD
Irene Carr

Penniless and desperate, Chrissie struggles to support herself as the Victorian years give way to the First World War. Her childhood friends, Ted and Frank, fall hopelessly in love with her. But there is only one man Chrissie loves, and fate and one man bent on revenge are determined to prevent the match . . .

THE SWIFTEST EAGLE
Alice Dwyer-Joyce

This book moves from Scotland to Malaya — before British Raj and now — and then to war-torn Vietnam and Cambodia . . . Virginia meets Gareth casually in the Western Isles, with no inkling of the sacrifice he must make for her.

VICTORIA & ALBERT
Richard Hough

Victoria and Albert had nine children and the family became the archetype of the nineteenth century. But the relationship between the Queen and her Prince Consort was passionate and turbulent; thunderous rows threatened to tear them apart, but always reconciliation and love broke through.

BREEZE: WAIF OF THE WILD
Marie Kelly

Bernard and Marie Kelly swapped their lives in London for a remote farmhouse in Cumbria. But they were to undergo an even more drastic upheaval when a two-day-old fragile roe deer fawn arrived on their doorstep. The knowledge of how to care for her was learned through sleepless nights and anxiety-filled days.